The Ascending Ladders Series Book 1

DISCOVERING POWER

Karen Ann Bulluck,

#1 International Best-Selling Author

DISCOVERING POWER
The Ascending Ladders Series Book 1

Inspired Legacy Publishing is a division of (DBA) Inspired Legacy, LLC
PO Box 900816
Sandy UT 84090-0816.

ISBN 979-8-9882276-0-1 (paperback)
ISBN 979-8-9882276-1-8 (hardcover)

Printed in the United States of America.

What People Are Saying

"From the moment I started reading this compelling story, I was hooked and couldn't put it down!!"
-Misti Mazurik, Director of Operations, Your Purpose Driven Practice

"You will be captured in suspense and pulled into the lesson-filled tapestry masterfully woven by Karen."
-Dr. Kasthuri Henry, Ph.D., CTP - Founder, Ennobled for Success Institute

*"**Discovering Power** is a beautifully told story with great dialog and self-reflection."*
-Susan K Younger, Relationship Architect

"Beyond inspired by Karen Ann Bulluck's latest masterpiece, 'Discovering The Power' powerfully tackles what it takes to climb the corporate ladder as a woman…I believe Karen's book is a fabulous contribution at this time to honoring the power & importance of women in leadership."
-Sally Anderson, Leadership Coach to the Influencers

"The material was so inspiring as to how to navigate towards resolution."
-Deborah Wiener, Author, Speaker, Entrepreneur, Healer, Coach

"Discovering Power is a delight to read and a book I'd recommend to both women and men. An absolute page-turner."
-Krista Mollion, Entrepreneur – Business Advisor – Digital Marketer, FROM ZERO 2 SIX ACADEMY

"This thought-provoking novel explores the intersection of career and personal values and asks important questions about responsibility, leadership, and the human experience."
-Tamara Myles, Author, The Secret to Peak Productivity

"Power and Drama in the Boardroom."
-Maureen Ryan Blake, Maureen Ryan Blake Media Production

"I have been inspired by her drive and her determination to not back down and it has helped me see how important it is to do the right thing."
-Brita Bigler Peterson, #1 International Best Selling Author

In loving memory of Cyndie Loven. Her time with us ended way too soon, but her light lives on. I'm forever grateful for her support and guidance as I created this book

Table of Contents

Prologue

November 17

Sheryl Simmons listened to her boss in complete disbelief. Todd Fisher addressed the Board of Directors with his usual charm and charisma, discussing the all-important agenda item that had Sheryl on the edge of her seat. She watched his lean, athletic profile as he moved, the way the other members intently listened to him, almost mesmerized with his grace and striking profile in his finely cut suit.

"And Layla Arch has the aggressive and uncompromising attitude toward profits that we need," he said pointedly. "As Hank and Anthony have pointed out, it's time to take The Diamante from a sleepy boutique investment firm to one of the top players in the industry. Layla is ruthless enough to help us do that," the company president said firmly, clearly catering to the two newest members of the board.

Sheryl's stomach churned. *Why do we need a CFO who is ruthless or aggressive? Those are not qualities I'd ever look for in a candidate.*

"Here, here," Hank Turner chimed in. His leonine gray hair bobbed as he spoke.

Todd flashed him a quick smile, his blue eyes sharp and focused.

Sheryl unconsciously tucked her thumb into her fist. It was her first board meeting ever. *I wonder if it will be my last?*

She forced herself to take a slow, deep breath as she looked around the conference room. Twelve people, ten of them men, were arrayed around the sleek, black table. A large piece of modern art in grays and black hung behind Todd, echoing the somber décor of the room. The only splash of color was a large streak of bright red across the width of the painting. It seemed as jarring to Sheryl as the conversation they were having.

"But Todd," objected Jim Leaders, the head of Client Services, "Layla's pretty young, and she's never worked in an investment firm. Shouldn't we have someone more experienced, like Blake?"

Almost nodding, Sheryl glanced back down at the two sheets in front of her. Blake Jones was the second candidate. He had a great reputation and had worked at a competing financial services firm.

"That's a great point, Jim," Todd said in a conciliatory tone. "But you might want to consider that Blake's been in the industry a bit too long. Is he really going to shake things up and think outside the box?"

Jim nodded his blond head thoughtfully and leaned back in his chair.

Todd looked around the room as if inviting other commentary. Self-consciously, Sheryl tucked her smooth, dark brown, chin-length hair behind one ear. *Should I speak up now? And what should I say? If it was up to me, who would I choose?*

Sheryl didn't know Blake in person, but she knew the man was known in the industry as being decisive and fair, as well as having a great deal of integrity. Reading his CV, she had learned that he had helped transform the accounting department at the other firm, creating better efficiencies and controls while retaining most of the existing staff. Sheryl was also aware that Blake had the reputation of being a great humanitarian and was very active in a large charitable organization that helped troubled youth. Those were all important pluses in her book.

"I don't know, Todd," said Alex Thompson, the Chief Investment Officer, breaking the brief silence. "Blake has been creative in other companies. I'm not sure it's fair to say he wouldn't think outside the box."

"Yes, that could be true," Todd acquiesced lightly, looking squarely at Alex. "But it's been some time since he's done anything *truly* innovative. Unless you know something that's not on his résumé?"

Alex shook his head. "No, but I–"

"For goodness' sake," Hank Turner broke in a bit irritably. He was one of the outside board members, appointed by a group of activist investors a mere six months ago. "Why are we debating this? Layla Arch has the backbone to make the tough decisions. Blake is a good man, but that's the problem. He's too good, too nice for what we need."

"And we do need another female on the board," Anthony Russo, Hank's cohort, pointed out, nodding toward Sheryl. "The optics aren't great with only one." Other heads nodded at that one, but Sheryl cringed. *Is the way things look from the outside, the so-called "optics," the only reason they want another woman on the board?*

Secretly fidgeting with the button of her suit jacket under the table, Sheryl silently conceded that she wouldn't mind having another woman, especially on this board, but not just for the sake of having another woman. *That seems kind of sexist to me,* Sheryl thought, still strongly supporting Blake Jones. *Morale is already so low. Having such a cutthroat like Layla Arch in a leadership role would only make things worse.*

Because Sheryl did know Layla personally, as she worked for the traditional bank The Diamante used. She had met Layla when she had been Sheryl's contact during an integration project the previous year. Layla was relatively young to be in her position, younger than Sheryl's fifty years of age, and Sheryl had to admit that she was aggressive and hardworking. Layla had made some major changes at the bank a few years ago, sweeping out many of her old rivals. Sheryl shuddered imperceptibly. *And I've heard her say more than once that she wanted to get rid of that "dead weight" so that she could bring in younger, "brighter" people.*

Leaning forward, Sheryl started to give her opinion, but she wasn't fast enough.

"Yes," broke in Janine Sanders, the Sr. Vice President of Human Resources, nodding at Anthony's comment. "It would definitely be to our benefit to have another woman on the executive leadership team and the board," Janine glanced at Todd and around the room. The petite woman wasn't on the board, but she had been called in for this portion of the meeting to present the candidates.

At her words, Sheryl suppressed a gasp and immediately leaned back, as she listened to the woman she considered a friend. *I bet Janine's team has no idea she's supporting Layla. I know for a fact that the payroll person hates Layla.*

Her palms began to sweat, and she wiped them inconspicuously on her pencil skirt, out of eyeshot of the others. As the discussion wore on,

Sheryl certainly seemed to be in the minority. Evaluating each person's body language, everyone else seemed to think hiring Layla was a win-win situation: good for the company, good for the external image of the company in getting more women on the board.

Should I speak up? The thought sent a frisson of fear down her spine. *What would happen if I did?*

Sheryl had been so excited for her very first board meeting. Not just attending this meeting. . . *participating* in this meeting was a pinnacle of her fifteen-year career with The Diamante. As much as she wanted to savor it, Sheryl was keenly aware of the intense pressure that came with her new role as the Chief Information Officer—the first and only female board member of their boutique financial-services firm.

Who am I kidding? In the fast-paced world of investment banking, there was rarely time to savor anything. In her twenty-six years in the industry, the drive for more and better was never-ending. Still, she had never experienced it as much as in this board discussion. *Ruthless. Really?*

But Todd was in total command of the room. In the space of twenty minutes, she watched as he skillfully guided the conversation, deflecting the concerns of some of the board members while soothing and cajoling them. She watched him intimidate others with slight body movements and his eyes flashed if they showed an inclination to oppose his point of view.

Sheryl had to keep her own eyes from narrowing. Todd was clearly guiding the board toward Layla Arch, with the blatant approval of two of the outside board members–the two who had been added earlier in the year. She could almost see him preen under their admiring gazes.

Don't trust them, any of them. The words of her mentor, Carl Schmidt, ricocheted through her brain. She fought the urge to shift in her chair. *Was this what he meant?*

Her hazel eyes scanned the room again, looking closely at the faces of her colleagues and the outside board members to see if there was any hint of sympathy toward Blake, anyone who was not succumbing to Todd's domination. *Maybe Alex?* she thought hopefully, seeing a slight crease between his eyes.

"Layla has already given us some great ideas for additional cost-cutting measures," Todd said smoothly. He was about five years younger than Sheryl and had been recruited to The Diamante several years prior as the Chief Investment Officer before Alex. It was no secret that Todd was extremely ambitious, and no one had been surprised when he had been named President less than two years after joining the company. Sheryl thought it was unlikely that would happen with a female employee, no matter how good the "optics" might look.

"Good, good. I'm looking forward to seeing those," Hank boomed, his deep voice carrying easily through the room. "We need to continue to cut costs. Stay on that razor's edge."

Sheryl was comforted to see two of her fellow executives blanch a little at Hank's words. She knew that Layla had taken it upon herself to make similar recommendations in departments that were not her own at the bank, including Information Technology and Client Services. The young shark of a woman had somehow managed to have those changes implemented, though the department heads themselves had objected. That was power. But was it leadership? Was it what The Diamante needed most?

"You will be very impressed, Hank," Todd assured him, a lock of his dark hair falling across his forehead, a lock undiluted by the gray strands scattered throughout the rest of his head.

Hank merely grunted with satisfaction.

Holding back a grimace, Sheryl realized that Todd was very impressed by how Layla had maneuvered the bank's cost-cutting measures—especially in such a short period of time. Sheryl guessed that might be because The Diamante's new board members had been pressing him for financial cuts earlier in the year. *Maybe he figures someone like Layla can take some of the pressure off him*, she thought.

This push for extreme cost reduction was new, only since Hank and Anthony had joined the board, in fact. Having been with the firm for a decade and a half, Sheryl had more seniority than most of the people at the table. She had been hired as a programming manager and risen through the IT ranks fairly quickly, given her strong technical skills, good business instincts, ability to see the big picture, and building such an excellent rapport with her teams. Although her position in the executive ranks was achieved very recently, she had never experienced the pressure to cut back and watch spending as much as she had been feeling now. She knew the economy wasn't great and the competition had grown fiercer, but were these deep cuts really necessary? She couldn't be sure.

"Does anyone have any other questions or concerns?" Todd was asking now as he carefully scanned each face around the table. Now that he was getting what he wanted, he seemed ready to bring the discussion time to a close.

Sheryl could feel her tension winding her tight as a bow. She still hadn't opened her mouth, still hadn't voiced her misgivings and her opposition to the candidate of choice, and perhaps she should, given that Sheryl was likely the only one in this room with direct experience of Layla.

Sheryl took a sip of water from the glass in front of her to keep her cool. She knew the board's characterizations of Layla as "ruthless" were accurate. It wasn't just that Layla was ambitious . . . it was that she was *mean*. While it was obvious the woman had played up to Todd and the other top executives, she was inconsiderate and rude with other associates, especially staff or anyone she didn't deem important. No one that Sheryl knew liked working with her.

Sheryl considered her options. *Would it be worth working with someone I personally dislike so much to keep the peace? To fit in at the board level?* She shuddered inwardly. The very thought made her nauseous. *But how can I rock the boat so early in my first board term? I am the only woman. I don't want to look weak. But, geez, having her on the executive team will be a disaster! Can't they see it?*

No one raised any further issues. Sheryl swallowed hard. *It's now or–*

"Is there a motion to end the discussion?" Todd asked imperiously.

"So moved," came immediately from Hank.

"Second," Jim said.

Sheryl's head dipped. Looking down at her lap, she took a deep breath, pulling herself together. For a moment, she gathered her focus inward, reaching for a place of peace inside herself, trying to calm her nerves and find an answer.

The voting began. Her opportunity to speak up was gone. *Now what?*

Vote one, vote two, vote three, vote four. . . all for Layla.

In fact, everyone seemed as if they would vote for Layla Arch, although she noted some of her colleagues seemed hesitant. *Hesitant apparently means still going with the flow, even if it's against your instincts.*

Finally, it was Sheryl's turn. She knew she was expected to fall in line. She felt the expectant pressure in Todd's gaze. Glancing away from him and around the room, she thought about what it had taken to get here, to have this opportunity to influence the direction of the company she cared about deeply. Isn't this what she had worked a decade and a half for? Her husband Dave would certainly think so.

Since she hadn't said a single thing in the open discussion time, she knew her vote was already counted in Todd's mind. She looked back at him, and then away, her mind spinning.

Do I dare?

Still, she hesitated, stalling. She wanted to say more, but the discussion period had been closed. Everyone was staring at her now, most with impatience on their faces. It was too late to do anything but say yea or nay.

She drew in a deep breath and cast her vote.

Chapter One

Tuesday, September 14 – Two months earlier

Sheryl bent over the large computer screen to more closely scrutinize the prototype Keisha Smith had developed. After a few minutes, her serious face broke out into a large grin.

Sheryl was impressed. The new customer portal design was incredibly innovative. As she examined it, Sheryl was suddenly amazed that no one had created this kind of functionality before. It was simple, elegant, and now that she saw it, an obvious improvement. This update would allow their clients, the people that trusted them to invest their hard-earned money, to access and manage their accounts so much more easily than the portal they had now. The promise of it was exciting.

She hurried out of her office to Keisha's cubicle, which was at the end of the row just down the hall from Sheryl's office.

"Keisha!" she cried, beaming warmly at her associate. "Congratulations. I love, love, love your design. Amazing!"

Keisha's face lit up with the praise. She was a talented designer and programmer, but she lacked confidence and seemed hungry for feed-back. Sheryl often wondered why because, in her mind, Keisha not only brilliant, she was on the fast track for promotions.

"Thank you, Sheryl! I'm so glad you like it. I thought it was good, but . . ."

Sheryl smiled at the younger woman, who was not only gifted but also strikingly beautiful. "Of course, I like it! And it's so innovative. Where did you get the idea for the overview screen?"

Keisha flushed, and Sheryl was a little taken aback to see the telltale sheen of tears in her dark, dark eyes. She hoped they were happy tears.

"I dunno," the younger woman said modestly. "I've been doing quite a bit of research . . . playing around with different things. This one seemed to work."

"It sure did!"

Keisha flashed Sheryl a big smile. It made her exotic beauty sparkle. She had tawny skin and wavy black hair, accented by her flamboyant style and fashionable clothes that showed her tall, willowy figure off to advantage.

"Thanks, boss!" she said gratefully.

Sheryl could tell Keisha was very pleased with her work and doubly pleased that Sheryl noticed. How could she not? All the small nuances and intricacies not only made the portal much more user-friendly but also state-of-the-art. *Keisha,* Sheryl thought silently, *your design could put this little boutique firm on the map . . . as long as we can meet the deadline. Otherwise, we're all sunk.*

The executive, her face portraying only confidence, straightened and with a soft, affirming squeeze to Keisha's shoulder, she turned to leave the cubicle. The cubicles had walls that were a bit under five feet high and matched the general décor: sleek, modern, and mostly gray.

Associates could see over the walls when standing, but there was a little privacy when they sat down. Theoretically, lower walls were supposed to inspire collaboration, but, as in most professional settings throughout New Jersey, the reality was that almost everyone wore headsets when they worked to block out the ambient noise. Most of the programmers listened to music or utilized noise-canceling headsets to help them reach their deadlines. Keisha slipped hers back on as Sheryl started to leave.

She debated taking a quick spin around the floor to see what else was going on. On a nearly daily basis, Sheryl walked through her teams' work areas, believing that it was important to be visible and available. It wasn't unusual for someone to flag her down to show her a new feature or ask a quick question. The community at The Diamante was close-knit and friendly, and her team, less than two hundred people, was small enough that she knew many of them fairly well. Deciding that she had work of her own to complete first, she headed back to her office.

Sheryl was about to cross the threshold when a movement near the stairwell door caught her eye. At five-foot-seven, she could easily see over the cubicle walls, and she noticed a group of security guards in dark blue uniforms enter the wing, each carrying what appeared to be large white folders or envelopes. Sheryl watched, at first puzzled, then alarmed, as they fanned out across the wing. *What are they doing? I haven't been alerted to any security issues.*

One of the guards approached the area where Sheryl was standing, nodded politely, and proceeded to a cubicle down the row, which belonged to Tanya Kinder. The guard, a middle-aged woman who looked quite uncomfortable, put her hand on Tanya's shoulder and bent down to talk to her in low tones Sheryl couldn't hear.

A frisson of dread slid down Sheryl's spine. She felt her hands clench. *This can't be. They wouldn't handle it* this *way. No, I would have been told . . . wouldn't I?*

She saw Tanya as she looked up in shock and started to stand, holding onto her computer mouse. The guard took the mouse out of Tanya's hand and shook her head, continuing to talk in low tones. Tanya opened one of her drawers, clearly flustered, and the guard watched as she took out her purse and walking shoes. When she started to open another drawer, the guard gently shut it and shook her head again, pointing to the exit.

Oh God, Sheryl thought. *Tanya* was *on the list of people on my team to be laid off! Is this what's happening? Now? With guards?*

The guard took Tanya's light jacket that was hanging on the back of her chair and handed it to her . . . and then extended her arm. Even from twenty feet or more away, Sheryl could see Tanya's hand shaking as she unclipped her employee badge and passed it to the guard. The woman carefully guided Tanya out of her cube and toward the door.

Every part of Sheryl's being cringed.

They were partway down the aisle when Tanya turned and looked right at Sheryl, the question clear on her face.

"I'm sorry," Sheryl mouthed, trying to hide the horror she felt. "I'm sorry." It was always wrenching to have to let people go, but Sheryl felt her own panic rising. *I'm not even going to be able to say something kind? Comfort her? Comfort or encourage any of them? Tanya was not the only one on her list due to the enforced budget cuts in every department.*

She watched as Tanya's face crumpled and tears began. Seconds later, however, she saw a shift and Tanya's anger start to rise. Keeping her own as sympathetic as she could, Sheryl met Tanya's incensed and tearful stare. The guard intervened quickly, urging Tanya once again toward the door. Tanya turned and walked out, Sheryl noticed, with as much dignity as she could muster.

Sheryl moved further into the hallway to get a better view. Across the wing, above the cubicles, Sheryl could see other employees being ushered out by guards. She heard the increasing sound of murmuring and rustling as others on the floor began to realize what was happening. The guards were stoic but not unkind; they were firm in their duties. The affected employees were quickly—and as quietly as possible—removed from the floor.

Most of them looked toward Sheryl as they left. She remained standing in the hallway outside her office, feeling more horrified and more saddened by the moment. She tried to return people's looks with sympathy and to express her sadness with her eyes and face, but she knew these people were hurt and angered by the company's betrayal, by *her* betrayal.

Finances had become tight, yes. Layoffs happened sometimes in every company, yes. But this public humiliation with guards? That wasn't something Sheryl had anticipated, and it certainly wasn't something The Diamante had ever done in the past. Her people deserved better.

Sweeping her gaze as far as she could see, Sheryl saw the remaining staff sitting stiffly at their desks, staring at their computer screens, probably praying they wouldn't be next. A few people, however, boldly stood up and watched the proceedings, stark fear and anger on their faces. Even fewer pretended to work.

Sheryl felt equally maddened. She hadn't known that security guards would be brought in. It wasn't just the timing, she hadn't known how inhumane and degrading these layoffs would be.

As a Senior Managing Director, she had been over the headcount and the necessary reductions with Carl, her boss, and Janine, but she had expected to be involved in many, if not all, of the private, professional conversations that would end their employment. She had been in the past, gently breaking the news to the employees and giving them encouragement along with information about their termination packages. *Who had decided to bring in security and just walk people out?*

Looking to her right, Sheryl noticed that Carl's door was closed. He was clearly hiding from what was going on. She wondered how her colleagues in other departments on the other three floors were handling things. This wing, which accommodated nearly seventy people, housed mostly her staff along with a small group of about ten of the people that reported to her colleague, Rick Sutton. *Is this same procedure happening everywhere?* A sudden swell of horror rose in her body. *Dear God, what about the people who are working from home?*

She wanted to contact Janine, or Carl, immediately, but she didn't want to leave the floor, either. She certainly didn't want to hide in her office or miss the chance to offer what sympathy and support she could, even if it was only by her facial expression and visible presence.

Fortunately, it was over pretty quickly. There were enough guards assigned to the floor that only about two or three trips each were needed. Sheryl continued to stand and watch in anguished silence, mentally reviewing the people who had been on her list. *Something seems wrong. It seems like more people are being walked out than I expected.*

She also had staff on the floor below this one. She could only assume the same thing was happening there. *Are those cuts also larger than I anticipated?* Most of the "removals" had been quiet and quick, although a few people argued about collecting more of their possessions, their voices echoing across the floor. The guards were courteous, but implacable, so the arguments didn't last long.

Only toward the end did one of the employees get really upset and vocal. It was Peter, a long-time staff member who Sheryl deeply cared for and knew was fairly close to retirement.

"Damn it," Peter protested loudly, "I'm not leaving. I'm only a few months from retiring. I'm not going to be humiliated and walk out of here like some criminal!"

The guard leaned closer and said something softly that only Peter could hear.

"No, I'm not going to be quiet! This is a crock of shit. I was told in my last review that everything for my retirement was set."

Sheryl started to walk toward Peter, wanting to intervene.

The guard closest to her shook his head and moved to block her path. "Please don't interfere," he said. "We have instructions."

"But he's one of my staff members," Sheryl insisted.

"I'm sorry, ma'am," the guard replied. "You really need to stay out of this."

At that moment, she saw one of the Human Resources staff members hurry toward the guard and Peter. She spoke to them, and all three disappeared into the closest conference room, shutting the door behind them. Sheryl watched the room anxiously but didn't move any closer. Clearly, that wouldn't be allowed.

After about five strangled minutes, the door opened. Peter walked out with the HR representative, his face a mask of fury and resignation. He got his coat and quickly left the floor with her, clutching a large white envelope in his hands. He didn't even glance Sheryl's way. The guard stood nearby and followed a short distance behind, but he didn't talk to Peter again.

Suddenly, Sheryl couldn't take it anymore. She turned abruptly and went back into her office. She debated shutting the door . . . but didn't want people to think she was shutting them out, so she didn't. She sat down and stared at her computer screen but didn't see it. Tears filled her eyes. She didn't know if she was angry, sad, horrified, disgusted or frustrated . . . or really all of that. Worse, she didn't know what to do.

She picked up her phone to call her husband. Maybe he would have some words of wisdom. After nearly twenty-five years of marriage, they had always been able to talk to each other about everything.

Thankfully, he answered after only two rings.

"Sheryl, is something wrong?" he asked, his voice slightly panicked. It was rare that Sheryl called him in the middle of the day.

Sheryl swallowed a sob. "Yes, yes, there's something wrong. They just brought in guards and walked people out of the building like they had done something wrong!" she cried.

"What? Walked who out?"

"The people we had to lay off. They did it all at once!" Sheryl felt the tears sliding down her face.

Dave sighed. "I'm so sorry, honey. It sucks when companies handle layoffs that way. You didn't know?"

"I knew about the layoffs, but no, I certainly didn't know about this new procedure. I didn't sign up for this! This is why I never wanted to go into business," she said frantically, although she tried to keep the volume of her voice down so that the people outside her office couldn't hear her. "I was an Art History major, for goodness' sake. How did I get into this position, anyway?"

Dave murmured soothing words, but she didn't really hear them.

"I've never been all about profits and losses and the bottom line. You know I only became a manager so that I could help people more, *support* them. Not to do this!"

She thought back to her days in school when she had gotten a minor in computer science to appease her father. Sure, she had enjoyed programming and had been damn good at it, but forced layoffs? With guards?

"I never signed up for this kind of craziness!" she repeated to Dave while reaching for another tissue.

"I know, hon, but that's what it takes to be in senior management these days. Making the tough decisions, you know that," Dave said softly.

Sheryl's tears flowed harder. "Yeah, I know that, but still . . . this just sucks!"

"I know," Dave commiserated softly. "Hang in there."

"Thanks, sweetheart," Sheryl breathed, feeling a little calmer now, along with a growing sense of gratitude toward her husband. "I really appreciate you listening."

"Of course," he said, then hesitated for a split second. "You okay? I've got a meeting . . ."

"Yeah, I'll be okay. Go. I know you have work too."

"Great. We'll talk more tonight," he promised.

Setting her cell phone back on the desk, she dropped her head in her hands and took several long deep breaths to calm herself. *I've got to pull myself together.*

After several minutes, she had gathered herself enough to notice that her Instant Messenger icon was blinking. Running her hands through her dark hair, she leaned forward to read the message. It was from her boss, Carl, and it was brief. "Staff meeting at 11:30 a.m.," it read.

She looked at the clock. It was 11:20 a.m. now. *Just ten minutes to some answers,* she thought hopefully. She would need to bite her tongue. Heated emotional displays wouldn't be appropriate at that meeting.

She had just risen from her chair and gathered her notebook when Keisha burst into the room, all but slamming the door closed behind her.

Her face was masked in rage, and her makeup was smudged from what appeared to be tear tracks. She came to a halt in front of Sheryl's desk. Despite being only a few inches taller, her five-foot-ten frame seeming to tower over Sheryl.

"This is bullshit!" Keisha hissed. Her voice was low but incredibly intense.

Sheryl could tell she was trying not to be heard throughout the wing. In spite of this, she took a half step back in shock, feeling a little intimidated.

"This is such bullshit," Keisha repeated. "I can't even believe that you are still in this office. What are you hiding from? Forget that–you should be hiding. *Everyone* in management should be hiding. How could you do this? You ought to be ashamed!"

Sheryl straightened and took a step forward this time. She struggled to remain calm.

"Keisha . . ." she started.

"Don't 'Keisha' me," the younger woman interrupted. "I don't want to hear what you have to say right now. There's nothing you can say that would make any difference whatsoever. I have never been as insulted, degraded, or upset as I am at this very moment. And that's sayin' a lot. I'm outta here. Leaving. Done. Finished. No amount of money is worth what you've put me and all the rest of your staff through today. I don't care how much I've enjoyed my three years here and working for you. It's gone. I'm not going to tolerate being treated with such disrespect, nor should anyone else here."

Still shocked by the outburst, Sheryl looked at her incomprehensibly. *What in the world? Insulted? Degraded? She wasn't let go. What did we do to her personally?*

"I *am* quitting," Keisha stated again emphatically as if Sheryl hadn't gotten the message.

Sheryl winced, although she tried to keep her face calm and sympathetic. She had been in Keisha's cubicle less than forty minutes ago, praising her work. She always treated Keisha very well. In fact, she was high on Sheryl's list for promotions and management roles.

"I'm sorry," was all Sheryl could say. She had no idea how to calm Keisha down.

"You should be," Keisha snapped back. "Did you know all of this was going down today?"

"I knew about the layoffs," Sheryl responded firmly. "But I had *no idea* that the guards were going to be brought in. I was just as shocked and upset as you are. You had to have seen that."

Keisha softened just the slightest bit. "Yeah, you looked upset," she admitted.

"I don't know what to say, Keisha." Sheryl decided to be honest. "We are in a position of having to trim back costs as a company, but I didn't expect the guards, and I did not know that it was going to be today."

"I hate layoffs," Keisha said, but her voice was a bit calmer. "They aren't fair, but the way *this* went down? It was wrong, just wrong."

"Keisha," Sheryl started feeling defensive and a little angry at being attacked like this. "It's not that simple. I agree it's not right, but unfortunately, this seems to be the way companies do layoffs these days," she said, echoing her husband's words. "It's the way things are."

At that comment, Keisha drew herself up to her full height. "Yes, it is that simple. Choices are that simple. You are either right or wrong." Her voice had regained its intensity. "You need to decide what side you are on, Sheryl, and you need to decide now."

With that, Keisha turned dramatically, her dress swirling around her legs. She marched to the door, opened it, and stalked right out. She vanished from Sheryl's view before Sheryl could even voice a response.

Bewildered, Sheryl turned and walked to the window. *What* is *"that simple?"* she wondered as she gazed out onto the parking lot, filled with cars and lined by a neat row of white pines. She guessed almost everyone was feeling the same way Keisha was. The younger woman had just been brave enough, or angry enough, to voice it.

A minute or two later, she watched Keisha stride out of the building and head to her car. Sheryl suddenly felt a presence beside her. Glancing over, she saw that Patrick Kerrigan had joined her. Patrick was Keisha's direct boss. He was a newly promoted director, who was running the high-profile Portal Project for Sheryl. In fact, Keisha was one of the most valuable members of that team. At least . . . she had been.

"Is she okay?" Patrick asked, his normally cheerful face now filled with deep concern. His red eyebrows were drawn together in a frown. Tall and lanky, in his mid-thirties, he had the red hair, blue eyes, and fair, freckled complexion to fit his Irish name. Patrick was very bright and intense about his work, yet he had a comfortable demeanor that usually put people at ease. Sheryl really liked working with Patrick. He generally got things done but with a minimum of fuss and bother.

"What do you think?" Sheryl asked with a sarcasm she didn't usually use in the office.

"Probably not," he acknowledged, giving her a sideways look at the unfamiliar tone. "Is she . . . is she coming back?"

Sheryl looked at him, gauging how much to tell him. Deep inside, she was hoping that Keisha would calm down and change her mind. She probably had grounds to fire her for insubordination and walking out, but Sheryl had already decided she wouldn't go that route. She also didn't want to put herself in the position of being forced to fire Keisha if word of precisely what the younger woman had said to her got out. She trusted Patrick but preferred not to put him in a tough spot either.

"I don't know," she finally said.

"Heaven help us, Sheryl . . . we'll *never* make the deadline if she doesn't," he breathed quietly. Then there was an awkward pause. "We probably won't make it even if she does."

Sheryl spun on her heel to fully face him, dismayed. "What? What does that mean? You know how important that deadline is!"

The Portal Project, as she had come to think of it, had been deemed as mission critical to the organization by Jim Leaders and his Client Services team. The deadline was hard and fast. A cold, cold feeling crept into her toes and started to rise through her. Her job, Patrick's job, the team's jobs were all on the line if they couldn't get it completed on time.

Patrick lowered his eyes. "I know. I thought . . . well, I thought we could pull it off. But I'm not so sure—especially now."

"Not sure or *know?*" Sheryl asked impatiently. This was the last thing she needed to hear.

Patrick paused, clearly embarrassed. "Umm," he stammered, "know."

"How bad?" Sheryl was afraid of the answer.

"Bad. At least three months. Maybe more. If Keisha's gone, definitely more."

Sheryl reined in her bright flash of anger. Lashing out at Patrick right now wouldn't help, although he would make a great scapegoat if she was that kind of person. She took a breath. "Let's talk about this later. I've got enough to deal with right now. You better have some solid reasons . . . and options," Sheryl said tersely, resisting the urge to say more.

He nodded and left quickly as if sensing the level of her anger and frustration.

Sheryl sat back in her chair and tried not to cry yet again. On top of everything, she missed the staff meeting with her boss. As days went, this was one of the worst she had ever experienced. And it was not even noon yet.

Plus, she had missed Carl's meeting, which wouldn't please him—and she had to find out exactly what that had been about. *Is there going to be even more bad news?*

Chapter Two

Sheryl's taut nerves wrenched another notch tighter when she entered Carl's large and spacious office. It was more than twice the size of her office, but she caught sight of him behind a pile of paperwork and computer screens at his desk. His face was grim, his normally generous mouth pulled into a stiff, straight line.

"Hey, I—"

He waved off her apology before she could even get it out of her mouth, something else that was out of character. Sheryl was relieved because she didn't want to tell him about Keisha. It would be easier to protect the young woman if Carl didn't know about her behavior.

Carl peered at her gravely, his light gray eyes strained as she sank into the plush leather chair in front of his desk. "This morning's layoffs went very smoothly," he began in brusque tones. "Todd and Human Resources were very pleased."

Sheryl frowned, but Carl appeared not to notice. He clearly didn't want to get into a discussion. It was typical of Carl, especially when he was uncomfortable.

Her thoughts drifted back to when she had first started working for this man fifteen years ago. Back then, Sheryl had been offended by much of his communication. It had seemed arrogant and demeaning—not at all what she was used to from her superiors. It hadn't taken very long for her to realize that it was neither of those things. Carl was simply so focused on his work, on *the* work, that he often forgot to include the social niceties.

Ninety percent of the time, the man was intense and work-driven, neurologically hard-wired for technology. In the other ten percent, however, when he came up for air, Carl was thoughtful, kind, and astonishingly insightful. Sheryl had often been caught off guard when he made an observation about someone that Sheryl herself had missed.

She considered herself quite intuitive about people, and she was; some-times it even irked her when he saw more than she did. This did not appear to be one of those times.

Refocusing, Sheryl tried to catch up with where Carl was in the meet-ing recap.

"We had a total staff reduction of about fifteen percent, which should reduce—"

"But why the guards, Carl?" Sheryl interrupted with an edge that she couldn't keep out of her voice. Even with her distracted thoughts, she was quite aware that he hadn't mentioned the security team.

"To protect the company and the network," he snapped defensively. "It helps ensure that there is no sabotage or theft. Many companies are using them for large-scale layoffs these days."

"I didn't like it," she said flatly. "It wasn't right."

Carl ignored her and continued. "You should also know that there were a few additions to the layoff list," he went on, avoiding the topic of the guards. "I emailed the additions to you."

"What?" Sheryl asked, shocked. She hadn't seen any emails from him this morning. "When did you send them? And you didn't tell me in advance or ask for my input?" She was gratified to see a flush rise beneath Carl's pale skin. "Were these additions walked out this morning too?"

"Yes, they were also let go this morning. As for letting you know, I didn't want to burden you or your colleagues more. It was difficult enough to make the first list–much less the needed add-ons."

"Needed add-ons? Really, Carl?" Sheryl protested hotly. "These are people on *my* team. I'd rather have been burdened."

Carl simply shook his head. He seemed upset, but Sheryl couldn't get a good read on his feelings.

"One more thing," Carl said and looked at her directly, his eyes stern in his narrow face, his dark, bushy eyebrows coming together. "You are not to have any contact with the people who were laid off today. Please don't reach out to them or answer their phone calls or emails. As you know, it's Human Resources' job to handle all of that." Carl's tone indi-cated that he was very serious about this "request."

"But what if—?"

"No," Carl cut her off. "No ifs, ands, or buts. You know the way this works."

Sheryl nodded and stood up, unable to sit still any longer. She had the sudden urge to shake Carl out of his harsh and stoic demeanor.

She wasn't happy about his pronouncement, but she was also not surprised. In the three, maybe four, times she had participated in layoff discussions with employees in the past, once the employee left the building, Sheryl's contact with the employee stopped. She knew that was to protect both her and the company. Human Resources handled any further correspondence. In this case, that procedure seemed much less palatable since she hadn't had a chance to wish the employees well and express regret at their departure. She was feeling a sense of grief that couldn't be resolved.

She stood there uncertainly, looking at Carl, trying to get a gauge on whether he shared her feelings, but he had turned back to his computer. His mostly bald head was lowered toward the screen, shielding his face from her view. Clearly, the conversation was over.

Stunned that he hadn't asked her if she had any more questions or about her feelings or concerns, she remained standing there. After another moment, her boss still didn't to look up. Having no opening, Sheryl left.

As she walked away, burning, she thought briefly about Keisha's "attack" and wondered what Carl would have done if Sheryl had been as direct and open about her feelings. She sighed inwardly, knowing it wouldn't have gone over very well. She had been highly trained to keep her emotions in check at work, and Carl had been one of her teachers. It just wasn't done to have emotional outbursts and what amounted to temper tantrums in the office, although that's exactly what Keisha had done. As she walked the few steps down the hall, Sheryl had to admit that she secretly admired the girl's bravado, if not her delivery.

Back in her office, Sheryl should have been getting lunch, but she didn't have an appetite and didn't feel up to facing anyone. She sat at her desk, tears suddenly running down her face uncontrolled for the second time that day.

This is NOT how an executive acts, she thought with dismay. She got up, shut her door, and almost slumped to the floor before it. She didn't want anyone to see her like this. To make it worse, she didn't have makeup at the office to "fix her face" and hide the evidence.

Her head swirled with a million conflicting thoughts. Sitting back at her desk, she picked up the phone to call Dave again, but she hesitated. She had already bothered him once. But who else could she talk to? *It has to be someone I really trust.*

Cindy! she thought suddenly as the image of her best friend popped into her head. She dialed.

"Hey, what are you doing calling me during the day?" Cindy's voice sounded concerned. "Is everything all right?"

"No, it's not all right," Sheryl said, without preamble. "Why am I doing this? Why did I go into this business?"

"Doing what? Working?" Cindy asked, sounding perplexed. Sheryl had known Cindy since they were in college together. Cindy knew her as well as anyone, even Dave. "You love your job."

"Not today, I don't." Sheryl sighed, rubbing her throbbing right temple. "We had a bunch of layoffs today. Walked out by *guards* if you can believe it. And *I'm* part of the senior management team. Even though I didn't know, wasn't asked, I'm still, well, *the management,* right?"

"Wow, that sucks," Cindy said, her voice full of sympathy.

"You can say that again. It's not that I didn't know the layoffs were coming, Cindy. I get running a company. I do know that it's necessary sometimes. Frankly, we have had a bit of a rough patch, but did it have to be so, um, so . . . inhumane?"

"Uh, no?"

"Are the title and money worth it, Cindy? I mean, what am I doing with my life? Is this how I want to be spending it?"

"Hey, Sheryl," Cindy said cautiously, "look, it's one day, one event. Yeah, it sucks, but—"

"But it's more than just one thing, Cindy!" Sheryl cried, sitting up straighter. "It is the principle. Companies that value their employees don't *do* things like this!"

"And your company usually doesn't. What's changed?"

"The new board members," Sheryl said bitterly, understanding anew what the core issue was. "Everything started changing when they came on board, backed by those activist investors. I think they want to turn us into yet another hard-nosed, super profitable, cold investment house." Sheryl had presented to The Diamante's board a few times in the last three years, and even from the outside looking in, she could sense a tangible change in the leaders' energy.

Cindy murmured something unintelligible.

"And . . . how am I going to face my management team this afternoon? Carl's words were no comfort to me. I certainly can't repeat them," she gasped. "My denial of knowledge, no matter how honest, isn't going to comfort them any more than it did a woman who quit on me today–if *they* even believe me. My team looks to me for leadership. If I knew nothing about what was going on, what kind of leader does that make me? Ha! A senior managing director and I didn't even know."

"Sheryl, you need to calm down. Of course, your team will believe you. They trust you. You've always been a good leader."

But Sheryl was rocked by another thought. She leaned forward on her elbows. *Am I a good leader? Or am I just a mouthpiece for Carl and Todd and those above me? What authority do I really have here?*

She knew the boundaries of her financial authority and her authority with her staff, for the most part, when something didn't blindside her. But even though she was pretty high up in the organization, what say did she honestly have in the overall scheme of the business?

She hadn't approved the layoffs. She only had authority to implement them. She'd have to be higher up in the company, like Carl, to really have a say in the company policies and strategies.

"Cindy, *am* I really a good leader?" she asked urgently. "I don't feel like much of a leader today, not with being so much in the dark."

"Hey, being a leader is more than just authority in the corporate structure, you know that," Cindy shot back heatedly. "In the last ten years, you've been working your butt off to get to the position you're in.

And you'll get more authority in the future too. You know you will. It's just a matter of time."

"The question now is whether I'd even want that," she replied to her friend. On one hand, she'd like to have a say . . . on the other, well, it was a lot of responsibility, a lot of tough decisions to make, especially when so much of the focus was on pleasing investors.

Abruptly, the shrill of a phone alarm pierced her thoughts.

"Sorry, Sheryl," Cindy interrupted briskly. "I gotta run. Call me tonight?"

"Yeah, I will," Sheryl said, feeling a little calmer just from hearing her friend's voice.

As she disconnected the call, she remembered the other people Carl said had been laid off without her approval. *Where is that email?* She maneuvered the mouse on her desk and looked at the list. She exhaled in audible relief as she leaned back in her chair. *Only three.* They happened to be three she had quietly considered for layoffs but had hoped could be spared, so she had fought for them in the initial meetings. But that battle was over now.

Staring out the window for a moment, she held her chin in her hand. *It could be worse.* They weren't her top performers; they were on teams that had some of the less important projects. She was relieved on one hand, but even so, she felt betrayed by Carl and Janine – Janine, who she thought was her friend. Why hadn't Janine given her a heads-up about the additional layoffs and the awful procedures for carrying them out? It would have required quite a bit of strategy and timing.

Where is Janine, anyway? Sheryl hadn't heard from the Human Resources leader all morning. Sure, she was busy with the whole guard and layoff situation, but it was odd that she hadn't reached out at all. *Guilt? Or am I reading too much into it?* Janine was probably swamped.

Sheryl continued staring out the window, watching the clouds whip by in the brisk fall wind, her pen tapping lightly on her desk. She wondered precisely what she was going to say to her staff when they got back from lunch . . . if they all even decided to come back.

Just over an hour later, all five members of her management team entered the conference room. Everyone except George and Wendy, who had been laid off, showed up on time. Sheryl had managed to pull herself together, washing the residue of her tears off with cold water and smoothing her dark hair back into the polished, chin-length page boy cut that framed her oval face. Then, she'd straightened her linen suit jacket before they walked in.

Her team didn't look quite so composed. Their faces, as they shuffled in, looked somber and possibly a bit angry . . . or was Sheryl imagining that? A few of her team members, Patrick and José in particular, looked at her with accusation in their eyes. She was certain they felt betrayed, just as Sheryl had felt earlier with Carl. Each of the women looked as if they had been crying, and the other man's face was as red as hers had been.

When everyone was seated, Sheryl looked around the room, feeling somehow guilty and very uncomfortable. The tension vibrated in the room, indicating how they all felt—despite the fact that she had warned them about the pending layoffs. She had discussed the changes on their teams with them, and she had even given them a say in who was selected to be laid off. However, like her, they had not expected the guards. *Never the guards. And two of their direct peers are gone. They must feel vulnerable and unsafe right now too.*

Facing them all, she really wasn't sure what to say. No explanation seemed plausible to her. She finally simply looked at them and said, "I'm sorry."

Most of their eyes widened in surprise.

"Really?" José snapped. "What are you sorry for? Not telling us that they were going to call in the army and march people out like crimi- nals?" José was a young, Hispanic man in his early thirties. His dark eyes were always expressive, and now they flashed with hurt and outrage. He had been with the company for fewer than five years. He was assertive— sometimes overly so—and energetic. Still, his teams responded well to him, despite his notorious temper. His angry response wasn't surprising to anyone in the room.

Knowing this, Sheryl kept herself from flinching and met his bellig- erent look. "No, I'm not sorry I didn't tell you—because I didn't know myself. I am sorry that it *happened*, and I'm sorry that you are all upset."

"Well, if you didn't know, what have you got to be sorry about?" José challenged.

Sheryl took a breath. "If you put it that way, you're right, I haven't anything to be sorry about. But . . . that doesn't mean that I don't feel bad about the whole thing. Saying I'm sorry is more of a sympathetic 'I'm sorry' than an apology." She clasped her hands together in front of her. "I know this morning was horrific. It was horrific for all of us."

"It probably wasn't horrific for whoever decided to do it this way," Yvette chimed in. Yvette was a pretty woman in her early forties. Her dark hair was parted in the middle and hung straight down her back. She had brown eyes, but surprisingly fair skin that gave her a striking look. Although thoroughly American, her style of dress harkened back to her French ancestry. She was always sophisticated and chic.

Looking hard at Yvette, Sheryl shook her head. "I'm sure it was horrific for them too," she replied softly, silently hoping her words were true.

Not knowing what more to say, Sheryl pulled up her tablet in front of her. "We have work to do, and we have to inform the people on George and Wendy's teams who their new supervisors are." Inwardly, she cringed at her last comment. *Ugh, now I sound like Carl.* Looking at their faces, it was clear the team thought so too, but she didn't know what else to do. Wallowing in emotion wasn't going to help. Was it?

"Hey, I'm sorry," she softened her tone. "That sounded tough, but unfortunately, it's reality. I'm going to talk to George and Wendy's teams in a few minutes. You already know where they have been reassigned, and you'll want to touch base with them after I do if they are reporting into you." She gave the two appointees a meaningful look. "Do your best to make this as smooth as possible for them. They are likely feeling even worse than you are." She cleared her throat, but she kept her tone soft. "I wanted to check in with you all first. Is there anything I can do to help you? The only thing we can really say to our teams is that there will be no more layoffs for a while."

A sigh of relief passed through the gathering. José still looked angry, and Patrick and Yvette looked not only frustrated but disgusted. Sheryl couldn't help feeling that as their supervisor, they were including her in that disgust.

"What about Keisha?" Yvette asked.

Sheryl looked over sharply. "What about her?"

"Well, everyone is saying that she quit," Yvette said tentatively. "She yelled at you and then stalked out because of the guards."

Sheryl felt her heart skip a beat. If that was the rumor, protecting Keisha was going to be hard. "I think it's best that my conversation with Keisha stays between the two of us. She did leave, but that's all I can say for now," she prevaricated, but the words sounded weak even to her ears.

"What do we say if people ask?" It was Patrick this time.

"Just say that you don't know." Sheryl hoped that Keisha hadn't actually told anyone on the floor her plan before she stalked out.

They all looked uncomfortable but didn't say anything more. If they were like her, they were feeling shellshocked and perhaps a bit panicked at the thought of deadlines and goals with greatly diminished teams. Fortunately, they had all retained the best talent in their groups, though that might not be too comforting in the moment.

"Please, please let me know if you want to talk further, or if you have anyone on your team that I need to speak to. I'm going to try to touch base with as many people as I can over the next day or two, starting with George and Wendy's teams this afternoon, but I want to be here to support you most of all."

"What about the people who were working from home today?" This time it was Norah.

"Damn it, I forgot to find out about that," Sheryl admitted, putting her hand to her forehead momentarily. "Carl didn't say. Let me find out and get back to you ASAP."

"I ask because I've noticed that some people aren't online anymore," Norah added. "It looked like people from The List . . . well, at least from my list." Norah was the quiet one: short, a bit plump and pale, with straight, light brown hair and gray eyes. She ran the support teams, and it was amazing all she was able to accomplish in her quiet, efficient way. Sheryl was beyond glad they hadn't lost her, but now she, like the rest of them, had her hands full.

"Stay here," Sheryl ordered the group. "I'll be right back." With that, Sheryl hurried from the conference room to her office next door and picked up the phone to call Janine.

Janine's administrative assistant answered, sounding overwhelmed and, Sheryl thought, a bit frantic. A quick conversation confirmed that the members of her team working from home today, and on Carl's updated list, had been given notice. To her horror, she learned that guards had been sent to the homes of those who were laid off. They were charged with collecting any company equipment and returning it to the office. Sheryl groaned out loud, pushing her bangs back. It was bad enough to have the guards at the office, but at home, where people's families and neighbors could witness it? In her heart, she realized that could even be perceived by others as indicating criminal behavior–not just a layoff. *Wow. What if that prevents them from getting another job? Or worse? This is truly awful.*

The HR assistant informed her briskly that all of those layoffs were complete. To her relief, she was told that everyone on Sheryl's teams who were still online had kept their jobs and could be informed of that. Sheryl assumed that they all had known the layoffs were going down as they took place; phone calls and instant messages would have taken care of that.

Striding quickly back into the conference room, Sheryl reluctantly gave the team the news. This time, she didn't even bother to hide her own deep disgust from them. The incredulous looks on her staff's faces mirrored hers.

Barely keeping her anger under control, she didn't invite further conversation. She wanted to try to keep herself together for these people–her people. She wanted to be strong. "All right, folks. Let's get in touch with those who are still working from home and let them know that they all have their jobs."

This time, she got urgent nods of agreement, and her team gathered their notebooks, tablets, and cell phones, and hurried out. As she watched them go, Sheryl couldn't help but wonder what other shoe was waiting to drop.

Chapter Three

"I can't believe what is happening at work! And frankly, I'm not sure that I'm handling it all that well," Sheryl complained to Dave that evening, half-reclining into a nest of pillows on the daybed in her home office. In a small bedroom on the upper level of their two-story home, she had lovingly decorated the office in soothing colors and peaceful objects. But even those brought little comfort after the horrors of today's layoffs.

Her husband was traveling again, so they were speaking by phone. She pictured his kind, brown eyes looking at her sympathetically, but she really wished he was home. She could use a long, soothing hug about now because the pillows alone were not cutting it. With Dave's job as a technical sales consultant—something at which he excelled—he tended to travel about sixty percent of the time these days. She was grateful for his success, but at times like these, she craved his nearness, his friendship.

"I can understand that," her husband said. "I've heard of companies bringing in security guards to do layoffs, but I didn't realized it happened all that often. It must be horrifying to experience," he added, with sympathy in his voice. Since Dave worked in consulting with such large organizations, he'd certainly seen his share of layoffs.

"It's beyond what I could even imagine . . . and then, well, Keisha really hit a nerve. She . . . she actually made me question my leadership standards and my morals," Sheryl said as she quickly explained what Keisha had said and done.

"What? That's nuts!" There was a brief pause. "But that doesn't reflect on you," Dave continued reassuringly. "Sheryl, you're a good leader. You know that. You simply don't have control over everything. This will pass. The layoffs should get the company to a better place financially, and then everyone will calm down."

"*Calm down?* Sheryl repeated incredulously, her voice rising. "As in going back to treating people as if they are human? Showing some compassion? I don't know many places that focus on or even consider compassion in the workplace, except when they have to–by law." She was too irritated to want to listen to reason, even from Dave, who was usually her rock. He could soothe her occasional bouts of anger or frustration most of the time . . . but he hadn't been there. He hadn't seen the looks her staff gave her today or felt the pain of seeing long-time staff members, friends, walked out by guards.

"Wow, is this Keisha talking or you?" Dave shot back. "You know things aren't always black and white. Try not to be bitter, honey. That's not going to help anything. And yes, I know, that's easier said than done." Dave's voice betrayed his worry, since cynicism and resentment were very unlike her.

"I know. I know," Sheryl conceded, and she took a breath, rubbing her aching neck with her free hand. "But today it's hard not to be bitter. Look at the examples all around me at work. Even Janine! I can't believe that she didn't tell me about the guards."

"You know she couldn't tell you without taking a big risk," Dave responded. "That's protocol. Have you talked to her since? What does she have to say?"

"I haven't been able to reach her. I'm sure she's crazy busy with all the layoffs. A lot of them must be calling with questions since none of us got answers today. Her assistant said she'll call me when she can, but I thought we were better friends than that. It kind of hurts that she hasn't called."

"I'm sure she will," Dave started to reassure her again, "but what can she really say?"

"Very true," Sheryl said thoughtfully. "What can anyone say?" She paused, locking her gaze on the painting of a hummingbird in flight. "Do you know I even questioned whether I should quit my job today in protest too? Keisha seemed to think I should."

"What?" Dave gasped. "You can't do that. How in the world would that help?"

"Why not? I could," Sheryl said defiantly, jerking into a more upright position. "It would send a message that this corporate culture isn't acceptable. It would let them know that they can't walk all over people. Maybe Keisha *is* doing the right thing. Maybe I should be following her lead rather than plotting to get her back."

"I don't think so," Dave answered, almost too quickly. "Plus, it wouldn't change much, would it? Especially if you were the only one. No one else in a position like yours is going to quit. And where would you go if you did? Keisha's young and at a lower level. There are much bigger consequences for you."

She rolled her eyes and felt her shoulder slump in defeat. "I hate it when you're rational," Sheryl said grudgingly. She and Dave acted as partners in their marriage. They were both closer to the culminations of their careers than starting, and their finances and goals reflected that. She sighed. "I don't want to be rational. Not right now. It's all too much."

"I know, hon, I know you're upset . . ." Dave hesitated and cleared his throat. "What can I do?"

"I don't know," Sheryl paused. "I guess the question is: is this a one-time thing or a permanent change in the way the company works? I've generally been happy there. I've never really felt like my ethics or values were being compromised. Today was different."

"I don't think you can answer that question right now," Dave said. "You'll just have to wait and see. You know I don't want you to do anything to compromise yourself, but don't forget about all our plans. We have that big vacation to New Zealand planned for our twenty-fifth anniversary next year, remember? That's not going to be cheap, not with everything we want to do. You're just going to have to be realistic about how businesses work now."

"That doesn't make it right—or fair," Sheryl snapped, standing up abruptly in her anger. She took a few paces across the small room before she ran into her desk with a thud.

Dave's muffled snort of laughter came from the phone.

The absurdity of her last statement struck her. "And now I sound like a five-year-old," she groaned, leaning on the edge of the desk.

Dave laughed. "A bit," he said. "But it's totally justified today."

That made Sheryl smile. Dave could usually pull her out of a funk.

He was better than most men at not trying to fix things every time she complained. It was one of the many things she loved about him. He let her be herself, and she was stronger for it.

"Thank you," she said gently. She felt a little lighter for having unburdened herself.

"You don't have to thank me," he said. "That's what I'm here for. Feeling better?"

"A little, but it's going to take a while to get through this, I think. For everyone."

"Sure it is," Dave tried to reassure her. "It might be a tough slog for a bit. But I know you can handle it."

"I know I can," she answered slowly, "but I can tell it's not going to be easy."

Changing the subject, she asked about his trip and the clients he had seen. But she couldn't stop thinking about Dave's comment about their travel plans. He was right. They had planned to go first class all the way. Plus, they had other dreams, like that ski cabin in Steamboat Springs they had their eye on, which would be much easier to swing with both incomes and the CIO job that she hoped to get in a few years when Carl retired. Maybe walking away wasn't so simple. *But we can certainly live without the cabin. . . and take a less expensive trip.*

They chatted for a little longer before hanging up. Sheryl felt a little more relaxed, but only slightly, and not for the first time that day, wished that he was home.

She headed to the kitchen to make another cup of tea. As much as she'd like to drown her sorrows with wine, she knew that she and her staff deserved her to be fresh and sharp the next morning, so she wasn't going down that road.

She called Cindy while she waited for the tea to brew. It was nearly 8:30 p.m., so Cindy should be home from work by now, provided she hadn't stopped for dinner. Even after three years of her best friend living in Denver, Sheryl wasn't used to the time difference between New Jersey and Colorado. She had to mentally check herself when she called to make sure it was not some ungodly hour for her.

"Hey, how are you holding up?" Cindy answered the phone almost immediately.

Sheryl sighed. "I'm holding, I guess," she said, idly dunking the chamomile bag in her cup. She filled Cindy in on the details she hadn't had time to relay earlier, as well as her conversation with Dave. She shared *everything* with her friend.

"Wow. I can't believe how tough your day must have been," Cindy commiserated.

"You know it. I feel every bit of my fifty years of age tonight," Sheryl said, sliding on to the kitchen stool.

"Ha! You'd never know you were fifty to look at you," Cindy said. "You don't even have gray hair yet, unlike *moi*."

"Well, you hide it well, my friend," Sheryl shot back, picturing Cindy's curly blonde hair, which was often in wild disarray. "But we have to hide it, don't we?"

"Yup. Young is in. Old is out," Cindy quipped, because they both knew that the IT industry highly favored the young and brilliant. "You can't possibly be tech-savvy if you are over thirty-five!"

Cindy knew. She was an extremely talented programmer, although she had never desired to follow Sheryl into the management ranks. Highly acclaimed and appreciated at her company, Cindy was well-rewarded too.

Sheryl chuckled, although without much humor. "And it's worse for women than men, isn't it?"

"Hey, don't go there," Cindy teased her gently. "Don't go all negative on me."

"I'm afraid, Cindy," Sheryl said baldly.

"About being too old?"

"No, well maybe, but the real issue is that I'm afraid to face everyone at work tomorrow. The whole company was in shock today, but tomorrow, well, they're probably going to be even more upset. Angry, fearful about their own jobs," she sighed, cupping her hands around the mug. "Depressed, too, right? Maybe even grieving the loss of people they care about. I know I am already. It aches like I lost family members in some horrific accident or something—because, of course, I'm never to speak to them again, or it will violate policy. And Carl, he didn't seem to be upset about the way the layoffs were handled at all, although it can be hard to tell with him. I can scarcely believe it. Doesn't he care?"

"Oh, Sheryl," Cindy's voice deepened with sympathy. "I'm sure he does care. He was just putting on the professional face . . . like we're all supposed to do."

"Yeah, well, I'm not liking the professional face much these days," Sheryl said tiredly. "And what about the workload? Everyone knows that they'll have to pick up the slack for the people who were laid off. It's not like we canceled a bunch of projects." She didn't even dare voice what Patrick had said to her today. She couldn't look at that on top of what was already happening. She just couldn't.

Shery rose from the stool and headed into the adjacent great room. Walking around the end of the large leather sofa, she folded her slim frame into one corner, tucking her feet beneath her. She leaned her head on the back of the sofa, her hands still wrapped around her mug for warmth. The room was dark and a bit cold. She hadn't bothered to turn up the thermostat when she got home from work and was now regretting it.

"Did they do it to scare people?" Cindy asked curiously.

"What? Bringing in the guards? You know, maybe." Sheryl considered what she knew about Todd and the board. "I've heard Todd say that fear motivates people, makes them work harder to keep their jobs. Fortunately, he doesn't say it often and only to the top management team."

"Well, he'd be stupid to say it in front of anyone else," Cindy said derisively. "Doesn't he know that kind of management is going the way of the dinosaurs?"

"Ha! You think? It doesn't seem that too many corporate leaders have gotten that particular memo," Sheryl said with disgust. She could see the moon rising over the field through the French doors that led to their back deck. She had a sudden longing to be outside. She got up again and slowly padded the fifteen feet to the doors, peering out into the night.

"Todd's a top-down kind of guy. I don't see that changing," Sheryl continued. "He says all the right things about empowerment, but my sense is that he doesn't really believe or live them."

"Well, fear has been a powerful motivator for a long time," Cindy observed. "And look at how successful it's been. Just think about the dictatorships that thrive on fear. It's all about power."

"It's a sucky way to get power!" Sheryl shot back indignantly.

"Hey," Cindy laughed. "Don't shoot the messenger. I agree with you."

"Sorry," Sheryl chuckled. "I know. I try not to use fear. It's easy to get power that way, but people don't tolerate it well for long. They check out, if they don't quit outright."

"Yeah, you got that right."

"I guess the investors want fear too," Sheryl mused. "They seem to be adding to Todd's fear and anxiety about numbers, as well as the rest of the senior management team. Even Carl seems disturbed by the new board members, who are pushing this cost-cutting agenda – at the behest of the activist investors, I might add. If it weren't for these guys Hank Turner and something-or-other Russo, it feels like none of this would be happening." Her voice rose along with her anger. "They're brutal – only interested in the bottom line, nothing else."

"Whoa there, my friend," Cindy's voice cut through her tirade. "You of all people know it's not that simple. Investments make the world go around."

Sheryl groaned and headed back to the sofa. "You're right. I do know that. I work for an investment firm, for God's sake. And . . . it works wonders for our clients when we're doing it well and right."

Sheryl knew that blaming investors was a popular view right now, and after today's events at The Diamante, it would be all too easy to jump on that bandwagon. But she also knew that her compensation and the compensation of most of the employees at The Diamante (and other publicly traded firms) depended on stock prices and profitability. That was the biggest reality.

"Yup, just like with everything else, the finances of everyone are inter-twined, even if it doesn't seem like it at first glance." Sheryl concluded, sighing, as she plopped back onto the sofa. "We're all so tied together. I wish we could see that more clearly."

"Yeah, and I know that being a part of helping so many people reach their retirement and savings goals is one of the things you love about your job," Cindy reminded her. "Me too."

Sheryl nodded absentmindedly. The Diamante being a boutique firm meant their fees were slightly higher than some of the bigger players, *but that's always been offset by superior and personalized service that I've been really proud of.*

"And that's why the Portal Project is so important," Sheryl murmured aloud, knowing Cindy would somehow pick up the threads. The two women had known each other since college. They could almost always finish each other's sentences.

"Hmm . . ."

"And what I really need to figure out is if this new management style, this pressure, is something I can live with. As you know, I've always been committed to not compromising my integrity, but I was telling Dave that right now I feel like I'm very much on the edge of that right now. He says to wait it out for a while."

"I think Dave's right about that part," Cindy said, surprising her a little. "You're going to have to give that some time. See where things fall out. Now's not a great time to be making any rash decisions."

Sheryl sighed heavily and stifled a yawn. Her tears and emotions today felt like her body had been through a ringer. "Yeah, you're right. What I need most now is a good night's sleep. Maybe things will look better in the morning."

"That sounds like a great plan," Cindy agreed. "But call me if you need me. I love you, my friend."

"I love you too," Sheryl replied, disconnecting the call. She stood for a moment in the dark, hearing only the faint hum of the refrigerator in the kitchen.

It's all well and good for Cindy and Dave to tell me to wait. They're not the ones that will have to deal with the fallout tomorrow.

The real question was what exactly that fallout was going to be.

Chapter Four

Wednesday, September 15

"Keisha didn't show up today," Patrick said flatly, careful to shut the door to her office before making his announcement. It was a little before nine o'clock. Patrick looked terrible, his face pale beneath his freckles. "What do you want me to do?"

Sheryl felt her stomach cramp as a wave of nausea washed over her. She had sincerely hoped a good night's rest would give Keisha some perspective, and she would see the younger woman bright and early that morning. Then, she laughed to herself. *Why would it have?* It hadn't helped Sheryl much. Under her makeup, Sheryl's skin was nearly as white as Patrick's with fatigue.

"Put her in for a sick day," Sheryl ordered. She wasn't ready to give up yet. Yes, Keisha was behaving badly at the moment, but Sheryl didn't believe that this recklessness was the younger woman's true character. She knew the potential Keisha had; in fact, she was counting on it.

Patrick looked surprised. "You sure?" he asked. "Um, Sheryl, she hasn't called or anything."

Sheryl nodded firmly. "Yes, I'm sure. Let's give her a little more time." Inwardly, Sheryl cringed. *How much time can I buy?* She suppressed a gulp. *I could lose my own job if I hold out too long.*

"Time for what? She really did quit yesterday, didn't she?"

"I'm not going to answer that, Patrick. Just put her down for a sick day." Sheryl kept her voice as neutral as possible, but it was full of resolve. *I'm not going to let Keisha derail her career. I'm not.* She thought back to the early days of her own career. Marsha, her very first manager in a corporate space, had saved her when she herself had been young and cocky and thought she knew it all. *If nothing else, I'll pay this forward. I'll never forget how Marsha stuck her neck out for me then too.*

"Got it," Patrick said, understanding dawning on his face. "I really hope Keisha comes back too." He paused, then continued hesitantly. "What about the Project?"

"Is that part of what's bothering Keisha?" Sheryl asked carefully, reluctant to give Patrick more room for doubts.

"Yes," Patrick answered with a touch of anger. "You know how much overtime that team has been working to get the new portal released. She's tired. We're all tired. And now, even I don't know how we're going to meet that deadline with Tanya and Frank gone with the layoffs yesterday." His face flashed with momentary panic, and he added quickly, "Not to be ungrateful, I know we're paid well, but we don't get anything extra for all the overtime we've put in. It's starting to get to everyone."

Sheryl stifled a groan. She knew all about working overtime as an exempt employee. No overtime pay. Just big expectations. She fully accepted that at times it was necessary. Overtime was part of almost any IT job, and she had put in her fair share of extra hours during her career. *But I swore I wouldn't require it all the time, that I would be respectful of people's time. And now look. This damn project.*

"Keisha wanted the deadline to be moved," Patrick continued. "She believed it had to be, that we were being unrealistic, even though she was making great progress on the front end. The back end and some of the reporting pieces have been lagging, and she's spent extra time supporting the team there too." He looked at Sheryl, hesitation splayed across his face. "Is that possible? To move it?"

Sheryl rolled her neck to try to ease the tension. "I honestly don't know, Patrick," she said, giving him an assessing look. "I'd like to say 'yes,' but you know Jim, Carl, and Todd. They don't like deadlines to slide. You need to tell me how you're going to fix this."

"Me?" He looked startled at the question.

"Yes, you. You are the one who promised to meet the deadline." Sheryl wasn't ready to let him off the hook.

"Well . . . can I have more people?" he asked hopefully. He was clearly grasping at straws.

"Patrick, we just had a bunch of layoffs. *Yesterday.* Remember?" Sheryl couldn't help the exasperation that colored her tone.

"Yeah, but that's the only way I could possibly meet the deadline!" he protested, his voice rising.

"And how many people would you need? And would that really help?" Sheryl's intuition was screaming that she needed to push Patrick to be honest and face the situation.

Suddenly, his shoulders slumped. "I don't know how many, and probably not," he answered, his voice thick with emotion now. Patrick looked down. Sheryl waited as he shifted from foot to foot. "Well, the truth is we can't get it done, Sheryl," he admitted bluntly. "And you know I don't want to say that. We were already behind, and look, you know people aren't working very hard or very well right now. Everyone's too upset to work. It's just . . . *bad.*"

Sheryl winced, tucking her hair behind her right ear. "I know, Patrick. I know," she sympathized. *What am I going to do about that? How can I help?*

Patrick looked dejected. His usual can-do attitude was missing. Sheryl cocked her head to the side.

"So, what's really going on?" she demanded, needing to understand all the nuances. "Are we running into problems? Was the Project not scoped properly?"

Patrick's expression turned mulish. "The amount of work was severely underestimated – or rather not estimated at all. If you remember, Carl just kind of picked January 15 as the release date without taking the scope of work, the staff, or the holidays into consideration."

Sheryl visibly cringed. She knew Patrick was right. *Did I negotiate hard enough to get a reasonable date? How can I go back to Carl now? Damn. I'm in as much of a predicament as Patrick on this. How much of a commitment has Carl made to Todd and Jim, not to mention the board?* Carl hated for the IT teams to miss deadlines. He always felt it reflected badly on him, and he prided himself on being on top of things at all times. Usually, he was.

Her stomach clenched, although she tried to keep her face calm. *He's going to have a fit if I ask for an extension. Maybe he'll even fire me.*

Something suddenly struck Sheryl as odd while she considered the situation. Carl was a consummate professional and really talented IT guy. His whole life was IT. Like yesterday's omission in providing details, this lapse in getting a project fully scoped with appropriate timelines was not something Carl usually allowed. *I wonder if something else is going on. I didn't even think to question Carl at the time. I thought the timeline sounded aggressive, but I trusted that Carl knew what he was doing when he picked that date.*

Sheryl became aware of Patrick watching her with more than a little trepidation. *Is he worried that he's been too blunt? Worried about losing his job or more staff?*

I'm pushing too hard. This isn't helping. She sighed.

"Okay. I want you to put together a proposal and justification for a new deadline," she said, much more gently this time. "It needs to be a proposal that the company–all of us–can really live with. Be creative. Maybe we can release some features in phases? That might help Carl, and our team, save face."

She paused, even as Patrick's face began to brighten.

"We need to come up with something—something we have some chance of selling," she continued, noticing Patrick's further relief as she included herself in the problem-solving. "It will be better if we present options, including what we could actually deliver on January 15. There has to be *something* we can offer, even if we don't like it. But Patrick, we can't compromise on quality. We can't afford to put something out there that's half-baked. This Portal is supposed to put us on the map, and it's about service. That's what sets us apart. Let's make sure we live up to that."

Patrick nodded thoughtfully. "But . . . what about Keisha?"

"For now, let's assume that she's here," Sheryl replied quickly. She didn't know if she was being delusional, but as she truly believed in Keisha, she didn't want to concede that battle yet.

"Okay, Sheryl. I'll do it," Patrick said, his voice more optimistic. "I assume you want the proposal today?"

Sheryl shook her head. "No, tomorrow," she responded firmly. "I want you to do a good job, a *thorough* job, not a rush job. You need to get this right."

Patrick nodded soberly. "I will, Sheryl. Promise." He turned and hurried out of her office, clearly anxious to get started.

She watched him go, feeling the knot in her stomach tighten even more. The tension, along with the challenges, continued to escalate. Failure to bring this project home could be career-ending for both of them.

Sheryl was extremely disappointed when Keisha didn't show up again the next day. Still, Sheryl privately instructed Patrick to code the woman's timecard with one more sick day. He raised his eyebrows but didn't argue. Sheryl knew he wanted Keisha back as badly as she did. Unfortunately, every day that went by with her absence only lessened those odds–and any chance of the team meeting that looming deadline. Sheryl had tried to think of the best way to approach the young woman, but so far, she hadn't thought of anything constructive. She was concerned about putting too much pressure on Keisha, but at this point she had to do *something*. Maybe a phone call would help after all.

Sheryl pulled up Keisha's file and found the number for her cell phone. Holding her breath, she dialed. After several rings, the call went to voicemail. Sheryl wasn't surprised, since she knew the company number had likely appeared on the phone's caller ID. She wished she could connect with Keisha directly but settled for leaving a message stating her concern and asking Keisha to call her back.

She was careful *not* to mention work. She kept the message focused solely on her concern for Keisha's personal welfare. It wasn't the whole truth, but Sheryl was legitimately more concerned for Keisha than she was about the job. Projects were projects, but Keisha was someone special. Sheryl recognized that and wanted to support her, even if it meant losing her.

Sheryl had barely hung up the phone when it rang, startling her just a little. It was Janine. *Finally*, she thought, as a sense relief flooded her.

"I've heard rumors that Keisha Smith is MIA, and you are covering for her," Janine said without even bothering to say hello. Her icy tone was anything but supportive.

Sheryl flinched and tightened her grip on the phone. Still, she tried to lighten the tone. "And hello to you, too, Janine," she said with forced cheerfulness. "How are you today?"

"Not funny, Sheryl. What's going on?"

"Keisha's not feeling well so she's been out the last couple of days," Sheryl responded.

"Is it true that she walked out after the layoffs the other day?" From the stern tone in her voice, Sheryl was sure that Janine wasn't buying the evasion.

"She left early that day, yes." Sheryl tried to reframe her answers without lying.

Janine let out a puff of frustration. She had a no-nonsense attitude that often came across as unsympathetic. Sheryl knew better from their long conversations, but she had also experienced Janine's brusqueness. The HR leader wanted the best thing for the employees and the company, but the company always came first. Because of that, Janine could be a stickler about policy, making things black and white to avoid the perception of being biased and rarely straying into the dangerous gray area. Sheryl bit her lip. She was afraid that was where Janine was going now and wanted to avoid it.

"Sheryl, stop playing games," Janine chided.

"I'm not playing games. I'm answering your questions," Sheryl replied calmly. *Playing games? No. Playing for time? Absolutely.*

"Look, Sheryl, it's all over the company that Keisha had a fight with you and walked out. And by 'walked out,' I mean quit. What really happened?"

Sheryl sighed. As much as she hoped to skirt around a direct answer, she wouldn't lie to Janine outright. "Keisha was extremely upset about the guards. *Everyone* was upset about the guards," Sheryl answered. "She came into my office, closed the door, and let me know how distraught she was. I couldn't reason with her. She was beyond that. So, I let her leave."

"And what did she say before she left?" Janine demanded. She seemed determined to drag the whole story out of Sheryl.

"She . . . said she quit," Sheryl admitted reluctantly. "But she was furious, almost hysterical at the treatment of others. She didn't know what she was saying."

"Saying 'I quit' is pretty clear," Janine rebutted wryly.

"I know it is, but I also know my employee. I'm not certain she really meant it, that she really knew what she was doing in the heat of the moment."

"That's even more reason to let her go," Janine stated firmly. "You don't want someone who is that emotional and out of control on your staff. You have even mentioned she could be leadership material."

Sheryl heard a slight tinge of disdain in that last sentence and cringed. She could sense Janine's growing rigidness. Ironically, it was the same mode Keisha had been in before she left. *I can't let Janine fire Keisha,* Sheryl thought a bit frantically. *Keisha is too good, too valuable to lose without a fight. I have a feeling something else is going on with her. I need more time.*

Sheryl braced herself inwardly and dug her heels in.

"Yes, she is leadership material, and for good reason. Even in just a couple of days, the team is struggling without her programming guidance and creativity," Sheryl confirmed calmly but forcefully. "Janine, we all have times when we are emotional. Watching the guards march those people out Tuesday was traumatic. I'm still upset about it myself. I can't blame Keisha for what she was feeling."

"You can blame her for losing control. We can't have people losing control in a professional environment, Sheryl. It's just not acceptable." Janine was adamant. "Even if everyone else is upset, they are here, and they are not yelling at their managers."

"Yes, they are here, but are they working or are they just sitting there talking about how horrible the company leadership is? Or hunkering down for the next blow? This isn't good for business. At least Keisha was honest," Sheryl shot back. She could feel her temper rising dangerously now.

"I don't care whether they're working or not! They are not being insubordinate, and they are not absent without permission," Janine said angrily. "This is a matter of company policy, and Keisha is clearly out of line. You have to fire her."

Sheryl lurched back in her chair, stunned by Janine's vehemence. *What does she mean she doesn't care if they are working?* Sheryl shook her head, not understanding what was happening. *Janine usually cares about people, and she certainly cares if they're hurting or upset. What's wrong with her?*

"If she quit already, I can't fire her," Sheryl retorted tartly, keeping a tight rein on her temper. She chose not to even address Janine's outrageous statement.

"Fine. I'm going to send over the termination papers for you to sign. Write up an account of what happened Tuesday and send it back with the papers," Janine shot back quickly.

Sheryl blinked. *What? Keisha has come so far in the last few months. The woman is brilliant. Her work is unbelievable.* She straightened her shoulders. Her admiration for Keisha, her hurt and anger at Janine, outrage at *everything* that had happened, suddenly crystallized into pure clarity and calm. *The consequences be damned,* she thought defiantly. *Enough is enough.*

"No," Sheryl said firmly.

"No? Did you just say 'no'?" Janine said with disbelief.

"Yes, I said 'no.' I'm not going to sign the papers, and I'm not going to write up a report. I'm going to give the whole situation a little more time." Sheryl was very calm. This wasn't just about Keisha, although she felt strongly about retaining her after seeing how the younger woman had blossomed on this project. *No, if this is the way the company is going to treat one of its star employees, on top of the way the layoffs were handled, well, that makes things very clear.*

Janine was silent, presumably stunned by Sheryl's pronouncement. "You could get fired too," she cautioned.

"So be it," Sheryl said, surprised by her own recklessness but not doubting herself a bit.

There was silence on the other end of the phone. After what seemed like a full minute, Janine finally spoke, and in a much softer tone. "Okay . . . Let's start over. Have you reached out to her?"

Sheryl released the breath she hadn't realized she was holding. "I left her a message right before you called," she replied quickly.

"How long do you plan to give her?"

"I know I can't give her more than another day," Sheryl replied, heavy realism in her tone. "If I don't hear back from her by tomorrow, I know I'll have to do something. I just want to give her a chance. Patrick mentioned to me that there's more to this than just the guards."

"More? What else?" Janine asked.

"Because of inadequate scope, the Project is behind deadline. Patrick and I had a long talk about it this morning," Sheryl admitted reluctantly. "The Project, the entire team really, will be in hot water without Keisha. But you can't share that with anyone yet. I haven't talked to Carl."

"Oh, boy. That's the Portal Project, isn't it?" Sudden understanding lit Janine's voice. Sheryl guessed that Janine was remembering their previous conversations about it.

"Yes, it is."

"Okay. Listen, Sheryl, I'll give you until tomorrow. You'd better hope that Todd doesn't hear about this," Janine said quietly, a note of warning in her voice, but her anger seemed to have dissipated too.

"I am, but I'll take full responsibility if he does. Don't worry."

"You bet you will," Janine said with a little nervous laugh. "I just hope he doesn't hear about it, for your sake."

Chapter Five

"Are you insane?" Dave exploded, his face contorting in anger. "Why would you put your career on the line for one overemotional girl? Janine could have fired you on the spot!"

Sheryl was stunned by her husband's reaction. Her gaze snapped up from the light meal they were sharing at the kitchen island to stare into her husband's shocked, dark eyes. "Hey, I don't need you yelling at me too." She tried to stay calm, but the emotions that had been building all day threatened to boil over. The gratitude she had felt just thirty minutes ago when he greeted her at the door with a glass of wine evaporated. She wanted Dave's support, not this.

"Well, maybe somebody needs to yell at you," Dave said, dropping his open palms on the countertop with a clap. "Do you realize what you're doing? You've already got this huge problem with the project being late, the company in layoff mode, and you want to cover for this irresponsible girl at the same time? Carl will have your head on a platter."

"So, what if he does?" she retorted, her face taut and flushed. "I'm trying to do the right thing here." She put her spoon down and took a long drink of wine, hoping to ease the ever-tightening knot in her belly.

Dave shook his head, disbelief on his face. "The right thing is walking out and not calling? That's called running away, Sheryl. You need to see this exactly for what it is."

He picked up his spoon and started eating again. Sitting next to him, perched on a stool, Sheryl watched with dismay, still stinging from the condescension in his voice as if it were a physical slap. She felt suddenly bereft. *Where is my friend I can talk to? Where is the generous and kind man I love?* She couldn't believe he was acting like this. They had had disagreements about work before, but never like this, never with this kind of heat and . . . contempt.

Suddenly, as much as she had missed him, she wished he hadn't returned from the InsurTech conference in Las Vegas that day. *I'd rather have quiet than this.* She looked away, across the adjacent great room, softly lit by a floor lamp in the far corner. The painting over the fireplace, a wintertime scene of their favorite getaway destination, mocked her, reminding her of the closeness that she and Dave had experienced on that last vacation. *Has it already been over nine months ago?*

"Maybe she is running," she finally ground out, twisting to meet his eyes. "Or maybe she just needs some space. I'd love to avoid the office for a few days myself."

"But you don't have that luxury," Dave goaded. "You have responsibilities and so does she. What kind of message are you sending to all the other employees who are showing up every day?"

Sheryl saw stars. Spinning on the stool, she leaned slightly toward her husband and responded through clenched teeth, "Maybe I'm telling the other employees that it's all right to stand up for themselves, that it's okay to show that you're miserable rather than just sitting numbly in their cubicles and stewing. Because you know that's what they're doing. Even Patrick told me that very little work is getting done. So, what's the difference?"

Dave made a dismissive face. "The difference is appearances, Sheryl." He turned to face her squarely. "The difference is that they are at least making an effort to show that they are part of the team."

"And I'm grateful for every single person that has continued to show up every day, despite the chaos. Sometimes though, the team needs people to show some leadership and step out in front of them," Sheryl shot back.

"Is that what you're doing? Showing leadership by protecting *her* and breaking policies?"

Sheryl looked into his dark brown eyes, trying to understand what was behind these hurtful words. *Leadership is more than a title,* she thought. *Leadership is standing up for what is right.*

"Yes. I. Am," she said strongly, her hazel eyes locked with his. "Keisha's showing a form of leadership, and so am I!" Sheryl wanted to throw something at Dave, even though she'd never done that in her entire life. She could barely stay seated; she was so riled. *How dare he judge me? He has no idea what it's like to lead a large team or have to let some of that team go.* Dave was a very smart man, but he had always been more of an individual contributor, especially since his move into sales.

Dave shook his head again, but this time he remained silent. He stared at her sullenly. She glared back, fierce determination in her eyes. Finally, he looked away. He took a gulp of his Scotch. They both turned to face their food, although neither picked up their spoons.

Sheryl gripped her wine glass with a trembling hand. *What is happening? Dave and I never fight like this. At most, we have stupid, little arguments, although I can't remember the last time we did. And I don't know if I've ever been this angry with him.* She drank some of the wine, feeling the soothing warmth slide down her throat and settle in her belly. She took a deep breath, trying to regain her poise.

When Dave spoke, his deep voice was quieter and calmer, as if he realized he had pushed her too far. "Keisha sounds like a very bold young woman. Do you think she really meant to quit? Maybe she's just trying to get some of the deadlines changed or more money."

"That doesn't sound like the Keisha I know, but I couldn't say for sure, Dave," Sheryl conceded with exasperation. "She hasn't shown up for two days. That's a pretty strong statement."

"Yeah, it is. Which is why I don't have a clue as to why you are covering for her." Irritation slipped back into his voice.

"Can't you give me some support here?" Sheryl asked abruptly, her emotions sliding from anger to frustration and hurt. Dave's accusations were really painful. She didn't even get where he was coming from. *Doesn't he have any compassion for Keisha or for me? This summer, when I was so unsettled by the changes the new board members were advocating, he was so sympathetic and concerned. What's changed?*

"I'm trying to," Dave said defensively. "Sometimes support means telling you what you need to hear even if you don't like it."

"Well, I don't need to hear this," Sheryl snapped. She stood up and took her bowl over to the sink even though she had eaten very little. She grabbed her wine glass and started to leave the kitchen.

"Where are you going?" Dave prodded her. "Are you just going to walk away when things get tough too?"

She whirled on him. "How DARE YOU?" she screamed. "You are acting like an idiot and being an ass, and I don't have to listen to it. When you can be supportive and kind and . . . normal, I'll sit down and talk to you." She stomped out of the room.

Dave didn't follow.

She clomped up the stairs and went straight to her home office. She resisted slamming the door but shut it firmly behind her. She lit a candle, put on a meditation CD, and reclined on the day bed. She was way too upset to actually meditate, but maybe the gentle aroma and calming music would soothe her. She knew the peaceful surroundings–the pale blue walls, the soft white furniture, the cozy throw rug–had worked on her spirits before.

As she tried to relax, she became more aware of her behavior. She had been so shocked by Dave's tone and words that she had reacted much more angrily than normal. *I might have overreacted,* she thought. *But geez, haven't I been through enough today already?* What she couldn't understand was why Dave wasn't supporting her or at least listening without blowing up. *Why is he so angry about what I did?*

She had been so happy to see him when she got home. He had greeted her with wine, which always made her feel special, and he had already defrosted a container of the hearty ham and lentil soup she had made a few weeks ago. Side by side, they made a salad. Neither of them enjoyed cooking much, but they worked with each other to make simple meals, enjoying their time as a couple. It had been nice and comforting, until–.

Sheryl felt her eyes fill with tears, and it wasn't long before she was sobbing in earnest. All the emotions she had been holding onto at work in the last two days just washed over her, and she lay there, letting it all release. She cried for what seemed like a long, long time.

Her tears were just winding down when a gentle knock came at the door. Dave didn't wait for her to answer before poking his head in.

"Are you okay?" he asked quietly.

She shook her head, hoping he could see her motion in the dim light. Her eyes felt swollen, and she was sure they were rimmed with red. Dave walked over and gathered her in his arms.

"I'm sorry," he murmured. "I was an idiot. I shouldn't have yelled at you."

Sheryl didn't answer. She held her body stiffly in his arms, although she didn't push him away.

"Do you want to talk more? I'll just listen and not react," he promised. "I know this is all tough. It's been a crazy couple of days. It's no wonder you're frustrated and distressed."

She nodded again but didn't respond. She relaxed in his arms, absorbing the warmth of his larger frame. She wasn't sure she wanted to talk now. After a while, she spoke softly. "Listen, I'm really questioning my whole job right now," she said, realizing that she couldn't let the idea go.

"I can understand that," Dave said slowly. Sheryl could tell that he was trying to be sympathetic, but his frustration was still there. "But you've been through bad stuff before. Remember when you had been at The Diamante for only about a year, and you had to report the woman that hired you because she was falsifying timesheets? And what about when Carl was out on leave for a couple of months, and you were filling in for him? No one wanted to listen to you, but you got their attention. You'll figure out how to get past this too. It's business. You've always been very objective and rational about your business decisions. It's one of your strengths. You'll get perspective on this once you calm down a little."

Sheryl stiffened. It seemed that Dave was incapable of being supportive tonight, at least in the way she wanted him to be. She had never known him to treat her like a hysterical female before. *I have every right to feel all these deep emotions, don't I? I'm just trying to explain to him how much this is reaching the very core of who I am, who I believe I am.* Dave was usually so good at listening, at having a real two-way conversation. *But even though he promised, he's not listening. At all. He just keeps throwing his perspective at me.*

Sheryl pulled back and looked at him, seeing genuine concern in his dark brown eyes. She couldn't see much in the semi-darkness, but she had his handsome face memorized, his light brown hair graying at the temples, crow's feet prominent around his eyes from squinting in the sun.

Being with him usually made her feel better, loved, and supported, but she wasn't feeling that tonight. He was concerned, but he didn't seem to grasp how distraught she really was.

"It feels more than just an emotional response," she tried to explain. "I don't know how to describe it. I feel like part of me is cracking apart or opening up. It almost feels like this has been building for a while, and everything that is happening now is like the straw that broke the camel's back. The level of disrespect . . . it's tearing at a vital part of me, deep inside, Dave. I'm not sure how to maintain my integrity in this kind of environment."

Dave looked at her with confusion. "I'm not sure I know what you mean," he replied. "I think you are overwrought and tired. You need to unwind and get some rest. I'm sure you'll feel better in the morning."

She really hoped Dave wasn't trying to minimize her feelings again, but it sure felt like it.

"No, I don't think I will feel better in the morning," she said adamantly, suddenly feeling very strongly about that. "I am saddened and emotional, no doubt, but it's more than that. I think this situation is bringing a whole bunch of stuff up for me. Whatever it is, it *has* been building for a while, but I don't think I really realized it until all of this all happened in the last couple of days. And listening to Keisha really got me thinking, although I don't quite have my finger on what it is that's bothering me so much."

"Keisha's an idealistic kid," Dave said dismissively. "She's too young and too inexperienced to know how things work. These kids all think they know everything."

Sheryl wriggled away from him, trying to stem her rising anger. She couldn't believe that he'd brought that up again, and she didn't want to argue about Keisha anymore. It wasn't worth it, and it really wasn't the point, no matter what he said. They had talked enough tonight, and she was afraid they would start fighting again. She didn't need that either.

"Thanks for listening," she said abruptly. "I know there aren't real answers right now, but the hugs helped," she admitted, sliding up into a seated position.

"I'm sorry. I shouldn't have said that about Keisha." He shifted back, giving her more room.

She couldn't bring herself to respond to the apology. All she felt was the emotional distance between them widen. She didn't know what to do about it.

"Do you need anything else right now?" he asked, his tone implying that he hoped not. "I gotta check on a proposal, if that's okay."

She nodded. "I'm okay for now. Go ahead."

He rose, gave her a quick kiss, and disappeared down the hall. Sheryl knew she wouldn't see him for a while, but that was okay. *I need to be on my own right now.* As disgruntled about Dave's reaction tonight as she was about work, she wasn't sure where to turn now.

Suddenly, the song she had heard on the radio on the way home, "You Raise Me Up," popped into her head. Maybe she needed a different kind of support.

Sheryl had always felt the words in that song were about the divine, about being lifted and supported by something bigger and stronger than any human support. *I wonder if there's a message there especially for me tonight.* But she shook her head, chuckling at herself. *Nah.*

Sheryl wasn't religious, at least not in the traditional sense. She and Dave did belong to a local church, and they attended, together or separately, only occasionally. But it wasn't a dominant part of their lives. Sheryl loved the beauty of Easter and Christmas celebrations; she loved the message of love and forgiveness and redemption. She wasn't as crazy about the exclusivity and judgmentalism often found in Christianity. She never felt it belonged there.

Because of Cindy, Sheryl had discovered other forms of spirituality, where there were different means of learning about and connecting to a higher level of consciousness. Sheryl liked to use the term "higher self" to refer to that consciousness or wiser aspect of herself. Cindy was deeply spiritual although firmly anti-religion of any kind. It had been eye-opening to Sheryl what she had gained for herself at a yoga retreat with her friend years ago. Now that she had a regular practice, she was grateful for both a physical release and opening the doors to occasional spiritual experiences.

Thinking about Cindy now, she remembered how her former college roommate had dragged her to a meditation retreat too. Sheryl hadn't loved that as much as yoga, but she did meditate now somewhat regularly, although by no means daily.

All in all, she'd always felt that her spirituality was an underpinning to her life but didn't dominate it. She kept it in its own compartment, separate from work. Cindy was the one who usually tried to pull her out of her compartments. Maybe, amongst all the chaos she was now facing, it would be a good idea for her to make meditation more of a priority.

I wonder what Cindy would say? she thought, pulling her meditation cushion out of the closet. She was just sitting down when her work cell phone buzzed. Startled, she glanced at the screen.

Do u really care about how I am? the text read.

Sheryl almost dropped the phone. *Keisha, thank God!*

Yes, I really do. Sheryl typed frantically.

Silence.

Keisha?

More silence.

Okay. See u tomorrow. Keisha finally responded.

Sheryl sighed with relief, her head and shoulders flopping forward.

Maybe.

Sheryl didn't know what to say to that. Finally, she typed. **Please. I need you there.**

But Keisha didn't respond.

Chapter Six

Friday, September 17

Early on the third morning after the layoffs, Sheryl hurried quickly past the cubicles to her office. Reaching the door, she stopped short.

Keisha was sitting in the chair across from Sheryl's desk. Waiting.

While her shoulders relaxed at the sight of her team member back in the building, she couldn't quite suppress an accompanying jolt of anger. Sheryl's jaw tightened as she began to unwind a bright red scarf from around her neck.

"Good morning," Sheryl said quietly, closing the door behind her and crossing the ten feet or so to her desk. She busied herself with hanging up her coat and getting her laptop settled while she gathered her thoughts. A missed alarm, skipped workout, and poor night's sleep were not conducive to quick thinking.

Glancing at Keisha with eyes that were still a bit red and puffy, she saw a reflection of her own discomfort on the younger woman's face. Sheryl let out her breath in a soft puff, feeling herself soften.

"How are you?" Sheryl asked finally, sinking into the chair next to Keisha rather than facing her across the utilitarian desk. Sheryl noted that Keisha's attire was very subdued: a gray knit top, black pants, and simple jewelry. It was very un-Keisha-like, and, even more noticeably, the young woman wore no makeup.

Keisha gave her a tepid smile. "I might be better than you are," she observed. "You don't look so good."

Sheryl knew she was very pale, with dark bruises smudged under her eyes that her best concealer hadn't been able to cover.

"Ya think?" Sheryl joked halfheartedly, then sobered. "But no, I'm not so good," she admitted. "It's been a rough few days." She directed a serious look toward the younger woman.

Keisha's eyes dropped to her feet. "I'm sure," she murmured quietly. "I'm guessing I didn't help."

Sheryl raised one eyebrow. "No, you didn't help," she said bluntly, but her tone was tempered with kindness.

"I'm sorry," Keisha, meeting Sheryl's eyes, looked contrite. "I didn't mean to cause you more trouble. I just . . ." Her voice trailed off. She looked sadly at Sheryl, her bravado of the other day completely gone, her shoulders hunched.

"You just what?" Sheryl asked gently. "What's going on now?"

"My parents are disappointed in me," Keisha responded, a tinge of pink on her cheeks. "They say that I was immature and irresponsible to walk out like that. They don't want me to quit."

Sheryl nodded, silently thanking the elder Smiths. "And what do you want?" she prompted.

"I don't know!" Keisha cried, but with more bewilderment than heat. "To watch people – my *friends*—get marched out like that . . . it made me crazy. I felt like people were dying or something. I don't ever want to go through something like that again. Even walking in here today, I felt like I was in trouble . . . I hate this whole thing."

"I understand that. I don't want to go through it again either. But can you tell me why it made you act so, um, 'crazy'?" Sheryl asked, half-smiling to take the sting out of the word.

Keisha shifted uncomfortably, but she didn't speak immediately, seeming to consider her answer.

Sheryl felt intuitively that something else was in play. So, she waited patiently, careful to secure an encouraging look on her face.

"That's a good question," Keisha finally whispered. "It just seemed like one indignity too many."

"What other indignities have you faced here?" Sheryl was careful to keep her voice calm.

"Well, I guess they're not indignities, but . . ." She hesitated. "Well, for one thing, there are too many unrealistic expectations of us. It feels like you, uh, all the management think we are robots who can just keep on doing the work no matter what."

Sheryl winced, unable to keep the reaction totally off her face. *I didn't realize that's how I was appearing*, she thought. *And the whole idea of being lumped with 'the management.' Ugh.* She did succeed in suppressing a shudder, barely. "Is this about the Portal Project?" she asked gently.

Keisha nodded emphatically, becoming more animated. "Yes! Exactly. We already have that *ridiculous* deadline, and nobody is paying attention or listening to the fact that it can't be done. Sheryl, for months on end, we're expected to work crazy hours and skip our vacation just to get it done on time–when it won't be good anyway. It's disrespectful!" she cried, her voice pitching a bit higher with each word.

"Like the way the layoffs were handled?" Sheryl returned, feeling vaguely guilty that she had been so unaware of Keisha's feelings.

"Yes and no. While the deadline fiasco is not as obvious as the guards, but it's still . . . *disrespectful.*" Keisha's voice was strong and passionate.

Sheryl hesitated, sensing something else underneath the way Keisha kept repeating the word "disrespectful."

"Is this the only time that you've been treated disrespectfully at work?" she probed carefully.

Keisha inhaled sharply, looking surprised. Sheryl thought she saw tears forming in Keisha's dark eyes. "Noooo." The word was drawn out in a long sigh.

"Do you want to tell me about it?" Sheryl asked, reaching over to touch Keisha's arm lightly. Her eyes filled with worry. *What has happened to her? I hope I haven't missed something major . . .*

"Well, it wasn't here," the younger woman said with resignation, her gaze dropping downward again. "So, I guess it doesn't matter."

"I think it does matter, Keisha. I think it may be why you reacted so strongly the other day. It was an awful day, but I know you don't get *that* upset without a good reason," Sheryl assured her, leaning forward so that she could see her employee's face clearly.

Keisha's breathing quickened and her lips trembled. Her hair was pulled back off her face today, so Sheryl could easily see the varying expressions crossing her features. It was obvious to Sheryl that Keisha was struggling with some very strong emotions. The silence was tangible for a few moments.

Suppressing the urge to embrace her subordinate, Sheryl softly urged her to continue. "Keisha, it's okay. You can talk to me. Whatever you say stays here," she promised.

Keisha nodded and then gulped. "It . . . the layoffs . . . it felt like something that happened at school," she said hesitantly.

"College?"

"Y-y-yes. One of my business professors, he . . . he was very strict. He said he was training us to deal with the real world by treating us very, umm, very 'professionally'? I'm not sure that's the right word for what we experienced. At least what I did."

"What did that feel like to you?" Sheryl asked.

"He didn't let us make excuses or take anything but the assignments into consideration. That was fine, but he told us nothing good—he only criticized everything we did. He informed us that's the way things work in the corporate world."

Keisha paused, looking at Sheryl with wide eyes.

"And what happened?" Sheryl prompted, her stomach beginning to churn.

"We had a group project. It was me and these two frat guys—a couple of real charmers. Our big project was due on a Monday morning and there was some big football game and they wanted to party all weekend. They made excuses not to meet again after ghosting me for weeks while I developed the framework. Then they dumped the whole project on me and went out and got drunk and stuff." She made a disgusted face.

"That doesn't seem fair," Sheryl pointed out, still digging.

"Fair? No, it wasn't fair!" Keisha exclaimed in a fiery tone. "But I didn't want to fail the class. I *needed* the grade to keep my scholarship, and worse still, the guys knew it. Neither of them was on scholarship, just mommy and daddy's budget. So, I did the whole project. I worked all weekend. I barely slept at all." She paused. "And Sheryl, I did a great job . . . it was a good program, especially developing it alone."

Sheryl couldn't help it now. Shaking her head, she reached out and covered Keisha's hands with her own, wanting to alleviate the anguish the young woman was clearly experiencing.

"So, when Monday came," Keisha continued, her voice raspy with emotion, "I got to class early. I had submitted the project at midnight the night before, but I'll admit, I was really mad. Thanks to them, I'd gotten little sleep, plus I had to take off more than one shift at work that I couldn't afford to miss. The guys came into the class. They were joking and laughing about how great their weekend had been–another great party with booze and girls they didn't have to miss. Well, I lost it!" she said, her head whipping back defiantly. "I started yelling at the frat boys right in front of everyone." She looked ruefully at Sheryl, then away. "I guess I shouldn't have done that."

"Well, maybe not in front of everyone, but I can see how angry you must have been," Sheryl replied, empathizing. *I certainly know that type,* she thought angrily. *Some of the guys in my comp sci program were real jackasses too. They made it very clear that they didn't think a 'mere woman' belonged in their courses.*

"Yeah, but instead of listening to what I was saying, the professor got on his high horse. He started yelling at *me,* telling *me* I wasn't being a team player. He said I couldn't blame *my failure* on my partners. My failure!" Keisha gasped, her breathing shallow and fast and her words came in a big rush. "The project was great. Great! High quality–at least an A-."

"I'm sure," Sheryl murmured.

"But he said he was going to fail us all for not doing the project together, despite the fact that I'd done all that work!"

Tears filled Keisha's eyes. She blinked rapidly to hold them back. Sheryl could feel her hand trembling and saw that she was shaking all over. She squeezed her hands gently, nodding encouragingly for Keisha to continue.

"Then he gave a lecture to the class on how you couldn't be emotional in the workplace," Keisha went on, her voice full of disdain, mimicking, Sheryl guessed, the professor's tone. "That people who were overemotional were not executive or C-Suite material. He didn't say it, but from how he'd been treating me and the few other women in the course, I knew he meant women. It was awful."

Tears spilled onto her tawny cheeks. Sheryl felt an answering sting in her own eyes.

"Wow. What a jerk–that *is* awful. What did the guys say? The ones you were supposed to be working with?" Sheryl asked, astounded by the story. She slowly removed her thick, brown wool jacket, suddenly feeling too warm. *This conversation is hitting too close to home again.* She thought back to an older, male boss she had had earlier in her career, one who had acted just like that professor. *Has nothing changed?* She shook herself inwardly. *Not every man in business is like that. Thankfully, Carl isn't.*

"They just laughed it off and acted all cocky, like it was all a big joke. The grade wasn't that important to them," Keisha said resentfully.

"Did you fail the class?" Sheryl asked, shocked and thinking that was unlikely, knowing how bright Keisha was.

"No. I guess one of the guys–the nicer of the two (or the lesser ass)–talked to the professor after the class, and he ended up giving me a B. Still, the professor never said a word to me, neither did either of the guys. I guess I wasn't worth their time," Keisha spat out.

"So, what happened the other day that made you think about all of that?" Sheryl asked, making the connection to Keisha feeling disrespected. "You've been getting kudos from Patrick and other team members about your incredible programming. We had just been discussing your latest developments a few minutes before . . . as you know."

"Kind of, I guess. It's just, well, this wasn't the only time that kind of thing happened, not here, but in school and my previous job. It was so unfair . . . and on our team we've all been feeling so stressed out about the deadline . . ." Keisha's head ducked for a moment. "So you see when the guards started walking people out . . . my friends and teammates and no one was listening to them . . . and I knew the project was going to be late, AND I didn't want to do all the work myself . . . and Patrick wasn't listening to me . . ." She broke down sobbing.

Sheryl pulled her chair closer and thought, *protocol be damned.* She put her arms around Keisha, blinking back her own tears as Keisha shuddered, and finally just quietly wept.

The tears unleashed a torrent of guilt in Sheryl, and she began to silently chastise herself. *Damn it. I obviously haven't been paying enough attention,* she scolded. *I've been so caught up with preparing for the layoffs that I just listened to what Patrick said on the surface. I know better. I should have asked more questions.*

Taking a deep breath, she forced herself to break off the negative thoughts and focus on the current situation. Her arms tightened briefly around Keisha in a gesture of mute apology. It wasn't enough to assuage her guilt. *But I'm not going to let this happen again,* she thought, resolving to pay more attention to her team's feeling. *I'm not.*

After a few minutes, Keisha composed herself, easing from Sheryl's embrace and sitting back in her chair. "I'm sorry," she said, with a rueful look. "I guess I'm still emotional. My parents told me not to do this–lose my shit."

Sheryl smiled. "I'm sure they did, but we can't always control that, can we?"

Keisha shook her head. "I need to be better at it."

Sheryl chuckled softly. "I think I do, too, sometimes. We all have things we can be working on . . . it's a part of growth and self-mastery—inside business and out. Now, are you feeling any better?"

"Yes," Keisha said, now looking a little sheepish. "Thank you for listening. I didn't mean to blubber all over you."

"Eh, you didn't. So, what now? What do you want to do?" Sheryl repeated, looking Kiesha directly in the eyes. She wanted to know what the other woman was really thinking.

"What are my options?" Keisha asked uncertainly. "Can I even come back? I know now what I did the other day was totally wrong," she admitted, lowering her eyes for a moment.

"It was," Sheryl said firmly but with kindness. "I'm not going to lie to you, Keisha, but I think it's recoverable. I'd like for you to come back."

"Does everyone know I quit?" The question was full of trepidation.

"Well, everyone *thinks* you quit," Sheryl responded apologetically. "But I didn't tell anyone, except Janine Sanders, that you actually had."

"Janine? Oh no, she'll never let me back!" Keisha's mirrored her dismay.

"She will. Besides, it's not up to her," Sheryl said confidently. "It's my decision, and I'm not going to let one of my best programmers leave if I can avoid it. I have so much faith in you, Keisha. You have the talent and the potential to go far in this company. Plus, I know we need you on the Portal Project, so I'm a little selfish in wanting you to stay too.

Keisha looked grateful, a slow smile spreading across her face. "Okay." She paused. "Oh, I do want to come back, I think, but the Project is such a mess . . ."

"I know. Patrick and I had a long heart-to-heart about it yesterday. Believe me. We're trying to figure out how to fix that. I don't have answers right now, but I am, no, let me be clear, Patrick and I are, in the process of determining exactly what can be done, including delaying the deadline," Sheryl told her.

"That's good, really good," Keisha said, then paused. "But in the meantime . . . I really made an idiot of myself, didn't I? What will everyone else think?"

"Right now, everyone is making up stories about what happened," Sheryl confessed. "But I haven't said anything, except that you weren't feeling well. I think we can just go with that story and leave it at that. It's probably better, though, if you don't share what really happened. I won't, even with Patrick. That keeps us in control of the narrative, got it?" *To make things as easy as possible for you,* she thought. "If word gets out about what actually occurred," Sheryl warned. "Well, it won't be good for either one of us."

The younger woman nodded vigorously. "Okay. Thank you. I can live with that, especially if you are going to fix the Project," Keisha responded, her face brightening.

"I'm going to do my best, but I can't promise–not yet."

"I understand," Keisha said, then paused. "But I have to tell you that if we can't get the Project fixed, well. . . I might need to find another job."

Sheryl groaned inwardly but managed to keep her face calm. She caught herself tucking her thumb into her fist and consciously relaxed her hand. *Damn, I wish it were that easy for me just to quit and get another job if I wasn't happy with a deadline . . . or anything else.* "I get that," she agreed reluctantly. "But you know that you can't do this again. *This* being the emotional outburst of the other day and leaving without calling in."

"I know *that*," Keisha said, rolling her eyes, then smiling apologetically when she realized what she had done. "But I appreciate you giving me another chance, Sheryl. I am sorry for the way I behaved the other day. I know it wasn't right. I really do, and I won't let you down," she finished sincerely, looking intently at the woman who was her boss's boss.

Sheryl hid a smile. "That's good, because I won't be able to protect you the next time," she managed to say firmly. She hesitated, unsure of the appropriateness of what she wanted to say next. Deciding to say it anyway, Sheryl looked sympathetically at her young staff member. "Look, I can't tell you what to do in your personal life, but you may want to consider seeing someone about some of these issues—if only so they don't get the better of you in the future. You've been through a lot of trauma, and I think you should try to deal with that, heal it. You deserve that."

Keisha nodded, her head tilted thoughtfully. "Yeah, my parents said the same thing. They're going to help me."

"It sounds like you have great parents, Keisha," Sheryl said with admiration and relief. "That's really good. It takes a strong person to know when to ask for help. Don't forget that."

Keisha made a self-deprecating face, but Sheryl saw a glint of tears forming in her dark, brown eyes. *It is too much to hope they are grateful tears?*

"Thank you so much, Sheryl." She gave Sheryl a quick hug, looking a little abashed by her action when she pulled back. "Thank you."

"You're welcome," Sheryl said brusquely, tenuously holding her own emotions in check. "Just remember, I've always told you that you have a lot of promise–that I believe in you. That hasn't stopped. Now," she added gently, "I suggest that you go rinse your face, then get back to your desk. I need to meet with Patrick and figure out what we're going to do with this Project. If you have any ideas, let us know." Sheryl smiled as she stood up, gratitude filling her heart. Keisha was back, and maybe, just maybe, she had helped her protégé get on a better path.

"Got it," Keisha said. Pulling herself to her full height, she nodded another thank you before striding to the closed wooden door. She glanced back at Sheryl as she opened it, then, squaring her shoulders, stepped out into the corridor.

Sheryl took a deep breath. One crisis solved, for now, but revising the timeline for the Portal Project was getting more urgent by the minute.

Her desk phone rang, startling her. The caller ID said "Carl Schmidt."

"Yes, Carl," she answered crisply.

"I need to see you. Now," came the abrupt reply.

Chapter Seven

Carl was waiting behind his massive desk when Sheryl rushed into his office, a frown on his face.

"What's wrong?" she demanded. "You just hung up!"

Her boss waved her into the plush burgundy chair in front of his desk. "I understand you have a personnel issue that you haven't discussed with me," he said roughly, his gray eyes glowering at her from beneath bushy eyebrows.

Sheryl's heart sank, but she met his gaze determinedly. "What issue is that?" she asked.

Carl hmphed. "You know what issue," he said brusquely. "That young woman who walked out. Keisha."

Damn. Did Janine rat me out?

"There's no issue," Sheryl returned calmly. "Keisha took a couple of sick days, but she's back in the office now."

"I heard otherwise."

"From whom, may I ask?" Sheryl responded boldly, her queasy stomach belying her outer calm.

"From Harriet, if you must know," came the grudging reply.

Ah, Carl's administrative assistant. I should have known. That woman misses nothing. Sheryl was surprised that Carl actually admitted it.

"Well, Keisha is here and is back to work. I just finished talking to her in my office before you called," Sheryl replied.

"And did she really quit?" he shot back.

"Well–"

"Never mind," Carl interrupted. "I'm sure I don't want to know. I trust that you'll deal with it appropriately," he said with a stern look.

"Yes, I will. In fact, I just did," Sheryl quickly affirmed. "But, Carl . . .?"

"Is there another problem?" he asked, raising both eyebrows as he gave her a sharp look, peering over the rims of his reading glasses.

Sheryl hesitated. She had a great relationship with Carl, but he was at least fifteen years older than her, about seven or eight inches taller, and very lean. On top of that, he had a formal, somewhat old-fashioned demeanor accentuated by the dark suits and white shirts that he habitually wore. Even his ties were dark and unimaginative, and he always wore one, even after the company had gone business casual. Sheryl couldn't remember a time when he didn't have one on, except perhaps at the company picnic.

She hated to admit it, but even after fifteen years, he still intimidated her a little. She looked up to him . . . and hated to let him down in any way.

Sighing, she decided to bite the bullet. She wasn't ready, but . . . "Well, I guess I do need to give you a heads-up about something, about the Portal Project."

He pulled off his glasses and looked at her expectantly. "Good news?"

"Of course, it is," she said drily. "That's why I rushed in here to tell you."

"Okay then, tell me," he said, his voice very serious.

Sheryl eyed him closely before she continued. *Should I mention his role in picking this ridiculous deadline?* she wondered. *And how would he react to that?*

Carl had been one of the big reasons she had joined The Diamante. Even back then, he had a reputation in the industry of being incredibly smart and innovative. He had not been the CIO yet, but he was high up in the organization and on the brink of that bigger role. He'd spoken selectively at industry events, and Sheryl had heard him at a technical association meeting where he was one of the officers. She had been so impressed by his deep grasp of software development that when an opportunity came to join The Diamante, she had jumped at it. And she hadn't been disappointed; she had learned an incredible amount from Carl over the years. He was a good mentor and supporter, and he knew IT inside and out–every aspect of it—and stayed up on trends better than anyone she knew.

Swallowing hard, Sheryl plunged in. "I know you don't want to hear this, but it doesn't look like we're going to make the deadline for the Portal Project."

She watched as a scarlet hue suffused Carl's normally pale cheeks. *Uh oh.*

"I'm sorry," she went on quickly. "I didn't know until I talked to Patrick yesterday. He's been trying to hold it together and make it work, but it's just too big. The, um, scope wasn't really defined that well before we set a deadline," she added deferentially, deciding not to blame her boss, at least not outright.

Carl took a long time in replying. He looked like he was trying to control his temper, or perhaps another strong emotion. "You know how important that Project is," he growled softly.

Sheryl nodded, feeling her chest tighten.

"Then how could it be that this Project is so far off track? I personally guaranteed . . ." His voice trailed off, and she saw a flash of anger in his eyes. She could almost hear him silently curse, but he quickly composed his expression. "How far off?"

"At least three months, maybe more. I really don't know yet." Sheryl didn't see any reason to hold back now that the proverbial cat was out of the bag.

He visibly cringed, the white fabric of his dress shirt wrinkling around his shoulders. "Do you have a plan?"

"We're working on one. I was going to wait until I had more before–" She stopped abruptly when Carl shot her a warning look, which she took to mean that she'd better not hold anything back. She continued in a measured tone. "I'm meeting with Patrick later today. We'll have something–with options–as soon as I can. Maybe Monday. Possibly Tuesday. I want to be sure that we've thought it all through."

"Make it good," he barked, the top of his balding head now suffused with red as well.

"I will," she promised quickly. "It's part of the reason that Keisha was so concerned." Carl needed to know this part too.

"She's on the Project?" Carl didn't wait for an answer; he knew. "What's the problem?"

"The guards, the deadline, the hours, the lack of respect."

Carl grimaced. "Lack of respect?"

"Yes, and she has some valid points. However, if we can be reasonable about the deadline, we might be able to keep her. She's not threatening to quit directly, but she might, and Carl, she's the *lynchpin* to the whole Project. I'll be frank. I've been told we can't finish it without her," Sheryl told him bluntly.

"Well, we can't promise no more guards," he said flatly. "I know no one liked that, but you know we can't risk a security breach or sabotage. We *have* promised that there will be no more layoffs for the foreseeable future."

Sheryl nodded unhappily. She searched her mentor's face. "I didn't like the guards, Carl."

"I didn't like them either, Sheryl," he said, his tone chiding.

"Oh." Sheryl didn't know how to respond to that.

"You have no idea what pressure I'm under right now," he suddenly snapped, his voice sharp and angry in a rare display of emotion. Sheryl reared back a little. "Since Hank Turner and Anthony Russo got on the board," he seethed, "things have changed. They are holding Todd's feet to the fire, and he's determined to appease them. He has his eye on bigger fish, and he can't afford to fail here. Hank has enough clout in the industry to make or break Todd, or any of us, for that matter."

Sheryl paled at his admission. Carl had alluded to pressure before, but he hadn't been quite that open about it. *Maybe that's why he seems less focused, more tired, and more abrupt.*

"I'm sorry," she said, apologetically. "Janine has discretely shared some similar things. I'll do everything I can to help. I promise."

"I know you will, and I appreciate it," he said gruffly. "But I need to see a *great* alternative plan for the Portal Project. You've only got one shot. Better make it damn good!"

"Will you help?" she asked, alarmed by his reference only to her. Sheryl understood that there wouldn't be any second chances on moving the deadline . . . if they even got this one. She and Patrick had their work cut out for them, but she'd ultimately need Carl's help. He had to support them and had to believe in the plan.

"Yes, yes, of course," he answered. "But you're closer to it than I am.

You've got to do the heavy lifting." His shoulders were still bent, and he wore a slight air of defeat that Sheryl had never seen before.

"I will, Carl. I, uh, thanks for listening. I'm sorry about, well, the board and all. Let me know if there's anything I can do to help." Sheryl didn't like seeing Carl like this. Something just *wasn't right,* and it felt like more than this one project.

But Carl had turned back to his computer, a scowl of concentration on his face. She gave him one more probing look–with no further acknowledgement from him–before walking quietly across the large office to the door. She had been summarily dismissed, another behavior rather unlike her mentor. Looking back over her shoulder as she opened the door, she saw that he hadn't moved. Heart heavy with worry for him, she let herself out and hurried down the hallway.

Once back in her office, she lifted the phone to call Patrick. She desperately needed to know where he was with the new project plan. She glanced at her watch. *Nearly eleven. I'd better wait until after lunch.* She still needed to check her email and check in with the rest of her staff. Putting the phone down, she scheduled the meeting through Outlook, then focused on other tasks. *Plus, it will give Patrick a little more time to get his new plan together, I hope. At least by now he will know Keisha is back on the team and that ought to give him some relief and a touch more confidence.*

At exactly one-thirty, Patrick hurried into her office, a sheaf of paper and his laptop in his hands. His face was flushed, and she saw the beading of perspiration on his upper lip. Her stomach clenched.

She gestured toward one of the two gray chairs next to the small table squeezed into the corner. There was barely room for all the paper he had brought, but he spread it out as best as he could.

Sheryl saw immediately that it was a timeline, printed out from Microsoft Project, that stretched far beyond the original deadline, which was still visible on the beginning pages. Far beyond. *Dear God. No wonder Patrick is sweating.*

"Patrick," she exclaimed with exasperation. "I had no idea things were this bad!"

The younger man's flush deepened. "Well, I, uh, I didn't know how to tell you. You just kept insisting that we had to meet the deadline," he stammered. "To make the upgrades everyone insisted on, *and* with the quality you demanded and Carl had promised. I really wanted to make it work."

"Like this?" Sheryl retorted, anger coloring her tone.

Patrick's face took on a stubborn expression, and he crossed his arms across his chest.

"Okay, okay," she sighed, conceding that she had in fact said that. *Just like Carl has been saying to me.* She took a deep breath. "Let's go over this, one step at a time," she said, pausing to study him. "Do we need Keisha here too?"

Looking chagrined, he nodded. "Yeah, honestly, it would help," he admitted. "She knows more of the details on the interface part."

Giving him a sharp look, she took three rapid steps back to her desk and called Keisha, who answered immediately. A glance at Patrick told her that the programmer had been warned to expect the call. The fact that Keisha answered with a quick, "I'll be right there," confirmed her suspicion.

Sheryl had just dragged another gray chair up to the small table when Keisha slipped into the room, closing the door behind her. The three bent over the Project plan.

It quickly became obvious to Sheryl that Patrick had been more than fudging dates in order to impress her. Now that he was being brutally honest, she could see why Keisha had been so irate.

Three months? she thought, remembering what she had just told Carl. She suppressed a groan as she reviewed Patrick's proposed timeline. *We'll be lucky if we get this done in a year!*

She shook her head, bringing her focus back to the Project. Keeping her voice calm, she encouraged Patrick and Keisha to share their ideas. Within minutes, the three of them were embroiled in a lively discussion about how to restructure the Project. Freed from the concept of adhering to the rigid deadline, she was pleasantly surprised to hear innovative and creative ideas from *both* Patrick and Keisha. With Sheryl providing guidance based on her deep experience, they began to formulate a workable plan.

Over two hours later, Patrick leaned back in the chair and eyed Sheryl optimistically. The pages in front of them were now covered with comments, arrows, and a few sticky notes, although nothing had been entered into the official Project plan yet. "What do you think, Sheryl? Will this work? Can you sell it to Carl . . . and the others?"

She noticed Keisha leaning forward with anticipation too.

"Yeah, boss? Can you?" she chimed in.

Sheryl rolled her shoulders and gave them a tired smile. "Maybe," she said frankly. "I think what we've laid out here is good, but," she warned, "it's still a far cry from January 15. Jim Leaders is not going to be happy. Neither is Carl, nor Todd."

Their faces fell.

"Hey, I didn't say 'no,'" she reminded them. "But we have to be realistic. I think we've given them pizzazz with the promise of extra features that could appease them." Sheryl had been thrilled by the added features Keisha had suggested. They would create an amazing customer experience that would far exceed the competition. *The key is the backend work that supports Keisha's interface. If the other team members can get the deeper development done in parallel, we could roll the Portal out in phases.* Unfortunately, the realistic projection for the first phase was still three months past the initial deadline, but . . . *the rewards for that extra time are extraordinary.* And the rest of the plan was just incredible. Still, she fought to keep her shoulders from sagging; if the board decided to be sticklers, she had no control over that.

"Look, let's all sleep on this. We're tired," she suggested. "Carl's not expecting anything until Monday. We have time to let this all sink in and review it again first thing Monday morning."

They both nodded, clearly disappointed that she wasn't as enthusiastic as they were at this stage.

"Hey, don't look so down. You guys did a great job!" she exclaimed. "This is just so important that it won't hurt to take another run through it. Maybe you'll have even more great ideas over the weekend, especially time-saving ones."

They smiled at that, nodding their agreement.

"Now, let's go finish up whatever else is on our plates today so we can get out of here. Sound good?"

They all stood up, smiles back in place.

"Yes, boss," Keisha said. "Sounds good." She pushed her chair back in front of Sheryl's desk. Sheryl noticed it was the same chair where Keisha had sat sobbing uncontrollably that morning. Now, she was relaxed and smiling. *What a difference a few hours can make.*

Patrick gathered up his papers, marked up with all their new ideas. "I'll make these changes in Microsoft Project this weekend," he volunteered. "It will be easier to review them that way on Monday."

"Good idea," Sheryl said. "But that's going to take a lot of work." She knew firsthand how challenging it was to get the project documentation correct in that particular software.

"I know," he acknowledged, "but I'll have it done by Monday." He gave her a confident, reassuring look.

Sheryl stared at him thoughtfully, half-tempted to tell him not to work over the weekend, but all she said was 'thank you.' He needed to atone for allowing the Project to get so out of control, for his sake as much as anything else. This was definitely a teaching moment and softening the blows wouldn't help him or his career in the long run. After all, she was learning that rapidly too.

She watched the two younger people walk more comfortably to the door, both pausing to give her a quick wave as they left.

Relieved that they had made such good progress on a workable plan, Sheryl paused to consider Patrick's role. He had come through this afternoon with some good ideas and *seemed* to have a solid understanding of the Project scope, but she was still unsure about how far to trust him. *It's such an important Project,* she thought. *And he doesn't have a lot of experience with something this big.*

She made a sardonic face, thinking that she had known this before she had assigned it to him. Patrick was her least seasoned Director, which is why he only had the one team. *It would probably just make things worse to make a change right now, as much as I'm tempted. Unless Carl makes me.* She wasn't sure she could totally shield Patrick from the impact of his "optimism," but the important thing for everyone was to get the Project back on track. She hoped these new, more realistic deadlines would make the cut.

Taking a moment to breathe deeply and consider the plan they had just made, Sheryl decided that she needed to revisit the staff allocations of the two teams that had been displaced with the layoffs. It only made sense to provide Patrick with more resources on the Portal Project, even if it might put lesser projects behind.

She pulled up her organizational charts, reviewing the recent reassignments carefully. *Who are the best people to put on the Portal Project? I'll make Patrick happy and empowered.* She sighed. *And piss someone else off.*

She'd have to talk to her other Directors and Janine too. Increasing the size of a team after a layoff could be tricky from a legal standpoint, she knew from experience. She didn't want to open the door to wrongful dismissal lawsuits from the team members who had been laid off because it appeared that they really had been needed.

She was mentally running through her options when a loud bang came at her office door. Startled, she looked up, seeing a tall, blond man standing in the doorframe. Her heart sank.

"I understand you have some problems with your staff who are assigned to *my* Project," Jim Leaders stated baldly. "I want to know what you're doing about it, because if you think you're going to use it as an excuse to miss that deadline, you are very, very mistaken."

Chapter Eight

Sheryl froze and felt her jaw drop as she stared at the menacing look on Jim Leaders' face. His typical smarmy expression was completely gone. "Jim!" she exclaimed. "What . . . what are you talking about?"

"The Portal Project," he answered smugly, advancing to the front of her desk in two long strides. "You know, the one that is due in *January*."

Sheryl blanched, feeling cowed by both his words and the tall, athletic frame looming over her. She stood up, stretching herself to her full height, which was still five inches shorter than the Client Services executive. "Yes, I'm familiar with the Project, Jim," she said, keeping her voice firm and calm, all the while feeling like a schoolgirl being taken to task by the principal. She had no doubt that was exactly what Jim wanted.

"A little bird told me that a key programmer on the team quit," he announced, almost gleefully. "But I'm not going to let you off the hook. This Portal upgrade is too important. You'll just have to figure out how to get it *all* done in time."

"No one quit, Jim," Sheryl prevaricated. She refused to confess that the Project was going to be late quite yet . . . *especially after this*. Besides, Jim was Carl's peer, not hers. Carl should be and would be the one to tell him.

"No? Then where is Keisha Smith?" His eyes narrowed as he spoke.

Sheryl smiled. "At her desk, Jim." She glanced at her phone, suddenly realizing that it was after five. *Where had the afternoon gone?* "Or perhaps she's gone for the day by now since it's Friday."

"She hasn't been in the office since she left after the layoffs the other day," Jim sneered.

"You're wrong, Jim. She was working all day today," Sheryl stated baldly, "much of it in my office, on the Portal Project."

He quirked one blond, perfectly groomed eyebrow, wrinkling his forehead for an instant. Unlike Carl, Jim didn't wear suits to the office, unless he was going to a client meeting. He preferred bright golf shirts and khakis, even in the winter. Sheryl privately thought he chose his attire to show off his golfer's tan and large Rolex watch. *He reminds me of the kind of frat boys that Keisha was talking about.*

Resisting the temptation to repeat her statement, Sheryl met his bright blue eyes directly, watching him tilt his head to the right in a quizzical gesture. He didn't say anything, just stood there looking at her as if he expected her to crumble.

Not this time, Sheryl thought, remembering how she had ceded to him about three months ago, in the early days of the Portal Project. He had pressured her about not integrating the customer relationship management system (CRM) with the Portal. She had backed down to the dismay of her team, especially Keisha, and had learned a valuable lesson.

All too aware of his classic blond good looks, Jim was alternately charming or intimidating. As he had been unable to charm her–or Carl, for that matter–he usually resorted to intimidation with them. But Carl had learned to hold his own with Jim, and she would too. *I'll be damned if I let someone else push my buttons this week.*

"That's good," Jim said slowly, leaning slightly forward. Then, he tapped a long finger on her desktop as he added condescendingly, "Then there should be no problem with the Project."

Sheryl stiffened and met his gaze head on, but inwardly she squirmed. *How do I respond to that?* she thought a bit frantically. *I need more information. Plus, Carl would kill me and rightfully so.*

Jim stared back, eyes glinting with suspicion, as the silence stretched between them. Sheryl forced herself to stay quiet, even though it felt as if every cell in her body wanted to blurt out a full confession.

"Hmph. Not saying much today, huh, Sheryl?" Jim said finally, a note of disgust coloring his tone. "Well, I'll have to have a talk with good old Carl next week."

Sheryl nodded curtly but still said nothing. The musky smell of his cologne in the small space was beginning to nauseate her. *Or is that just the man himself?* In the silence, Sheryl felt her tautly held control begin to slip.

Jim gave her one last, hard look. "I'll let you get back to it, for now," he mocked, an edge of warning threading through his voice. "And, oh, have a good weekend," he finished with a smirk, a vestige of his pretentious charm back in place.

"Um, you t-too, Jim," Sheryl stammered. She watched, her heart in her throat, as he pivoted and strolled casually to the door. He gave a flippant wave when he reached it, an ironic reminder of the friendly waves she had received hours earlier from Patrick and Keisha. Then, he disappeared down the hallway.

She remained standing until she was certain he was gone, then collapsed back in her chair. *Good Lord, what am I going to do now?* She picked up the phone and called Carl's office, but he didn't answer. She grimaced. Carl rarely left before six. *I guess I'm going to have to get here early on Monday, so that I can get to Carl before Jim does.*

She briefly considered calling Carl on his cell since the man expected everyone to be on call 24/7, but in the end, she decided not to. She settled for a quick text warning him of Jim's potential visit, then she turned back to her computer. *I'll answer a few more emails, then I'm getting out of here myself. God knows I need the rest, and it's been a helluva week.*

The next morning, Sheryl woke up in a foul mood. It was already after seven, late for her, even on the weekend. She still felt tired and had no interest in doing *anything.* After trying to go back to sleep for a few minutes, she reluctantly conceded that she did actually have to get out of bed.

Rising, she pulled a worn, pink flannel robe over her pajamas and slid her feet into cozy, matching pink slippers. She went directly to the kitchen, grabbed her favorite mug, and poured herself a cup of coffee. As she breathed in the smell of it, she thought, *Thank goodness Dave got up before me.*

She padded over to the small table that was tucked in an alcove between the kitchen and the great room, where she flopped down in one of the wooden chairs. Her personal laptop was lying there but opening it didn't appeal either. Sighing, she brushed her dark bangs back from her eyes, then gazed out the window.

Sheryl usually loved this bright space because it looked out over their backyard, but today, even the view didn't help. Rain pouring from low gray clouds lashed the windows, driven by a gusting wind that whipped the trees along the back property line into an erratic dance. *Those poor trees look like I feel right now,* she thought, wrapping her hands around her mug as she watched as a few remaining fall leaves careened across the backyard.

Dave wandered in from the basement fifteen minutes later. Looking up, Sheryl saw that he was dressed in jeans and a Phillies sweatshirt. His short brown hair was neatly combed, although Sheryl knew he hadn't showered yet because the water running in the bathroom always woke her up. She was still at the table, sipping her cooling coffee and staring outside.

Taking one look at her bathrobe, rumpled hair, and puffy eyes, Dave made a soft sound of sympathy. "Uh oh. Rough night?"

Sheryl rolled her eyes. "What do you think?" she quipped. She still felt uneasy about talking to Dave following their argument. He had been conciliatory the next day, but still to this minute, he had not apologized. Not wanting to start more conflict, Sheryl hadn't brought it up either. It remained an open wound, untended and sore. Mentioning anything about Jim's verbal attack yesterday just felt like pouring salt all over it.

"I'm sorry," Dave murmured. "It sucks when you don't sleep." Bypassing her, he refilled his own coffee mug.

"Yeah, it does," Sheryl agreed grumpily.

Dave walked over and dropped a quick kiss on the top of her head. "I love you, and I'm here if you want to talk."

Sheryl looked up with a trace of wariness in her hazel eyes. "Thanks, but no. I'll let you know if I do."

He nodded and strode quickly off to his office, she assumed, as if he too were relieved not to be drawn into another uncomfortable discussion. His sneakers made a slight squeaking sound on the kitchen floor as he left. In her current mood, even that bit of noise grated on Sheryl's nerves.

Her thoughts turned back to work, her mind roiling. As she gazed back out the window at the gathering storm, Sheryl had a sudden insight. She was upset at herself for letting Patrick down. She really tried to be a manager people could talk to, but Patrick obviously hadn't felt comfortable discussing the situation honestly with her. And she had wanted to blame him for it.

He said it was because he knew my hands were tied, but was that it? Or did I just not listen? She frowned. *Or do I just make myself unapproachable when I know—or think—that I can't change anything, when I feel trapped myself?* She suspected it was more of the latter than the former, but she wasn't sure. Either way, she was disappointed in herself on top of all the *other* disappointments at the office this week.

Shaking away her self-judgment, Sheryl got up, poured herself a small bowl of healthy cereal, and sliced a banana on top. Wanting to center herself, she tried to be mindful about what she was doing. Those yoga teachers and those meditations Cindy was always sending her constantly mentioned being "in the moment." She noticed her bowl, white and simple, the warm, honeyed wood tones of her cabinets, and the granite countertops marbled in shades of browns and tan she and Dave had picked out together because they were stylish and soothing. She forced herself to breathe in a steady, even rhythm.

As she turned to the refrigerator, Sheryl observed the composite floor that was slightly darker than the cabinets. She chuckled to herself, remembering when they had built the house eight years before. The kitchen designer they had hired had wanted light, almost white, floors, but Sheryl had insisted on floors that wouldn't show the dirt that easily. For one thing, she and Dave tended to make a mess on the rare occasions that they cooked, and neither had the time for OCD-mentality daily sweeping and mopping. Plus, having a warm, cozy feel to the kitchen, despite its large size, was very important to her. The darker floors accomplished both objectives *and* looked great. For a moment, she let the corner of her mouth curl up at the memory that even the designer had loved the total effect when the kitchen was complete.

Settling back at the coordinating maple table, Sheryl let her attention slide back to her whirling thoughts and a desire for greater peace again. She picked up her spoon and thoughtfully took a bit of cereal. Somehow, this crisis had awakened—or perhaps reawakened—her sense of herself as a spiritual person. *I guess that's what happens to people in these kinds of situations.* Life crises made one think about one's life and the meaning it held.

While she wasn't facing death or serious illness, this felt like an existential crisis within her. *My work is such a huge part of my life. Is this how I want to be spending my life and my energy?* She rolled her eyes. *Ugh. Now that's an impossible question.*

Sheryl had always prided herself on being a good person. She gave to charity, both in time and money, although realistically, she hadn't had as much time to give in recent years. She sought to be loyal and loving to her friends and family members. She honored her wedding vows. Now, taking a final bite, she gripped her spoon and thought, *I know I'm making a contribution at work, and I've always felt I conduct myself with integrity, despite my mistakes.* Overall, she felt that the good outweighed the bad.

Suddenly, that didn't seem to be enough.

She slapped her spoon back onto the table with enough force that the clatter startled her. *You can't just sit here wallowing in self-pity,* she reprimanded herself. Resolutely, she got up from the table and put her dishes in the dishwasher. *There are plenty of productive things you can be doing. You need to just get to it.*

She marched up to her office with a full cup of coffee, determined to at least check on the household finances and pay the bills. Sitting down at the off-white corner desk, she started her desktop computer and yanked open the desk drawer where she kept the unpaid bills and checkbook. But it was her journal, sitting on top of the pile of envelopes, that caught her attention. She paused.

Groaning, she finally reached for it. *When was the last time I wrote in this?* She flipped through the pages, finding the last entry was dated several weeks ago. *Argh.* She took a breath. *Maybe I should write in here first?* Abruptly, she pictured Cindy's curly head nodding emphatically and smiled. It was Cindy's fault that she had this journal at all!

Sheryl glanced at her computer screen, surprised to see that it was already nine o'clock. *Still too early for her,* she thought, clutching the soft leather cover in her hands, *although I'd really love to talk to her.* As her college roommate, Cindy was the one who had introduced Sheryl to journaling during their freshman year at the University of Pennsylvania. Now, she and Cindy sent each other new journals for Christmas every year. It made it special. It made it important.

She picked up a pen. *Maybe . . .*

Her work cell phone rang, making her jump.

"Patrick? What's wrong?" she asked, straightening in her chair, alarmed by this unprecedented weekend call.

"Sheryl, I'm sorry to bother you, but you said . . ."

"No, it's fine. I did say to call me. What's up? What do you need?" Her voice was brusquer than she would have liked.

"Well, I've been going over our notes from yesterday, updating the MS Project file, and, um, Sheryl, we missed . . . well, maybe not missed . . . we forgot?" Patrick sounded like he was scared to death.

"Patrick, stop. Take a breath and spit it out," Sheryl said gently even while tapping her pen on the desk.

"Well, we put a couple of the big programming segments in the same block. The final Project, based on our projections, really won't be ready until August or–"

"September?" Sheryl gasped, dropping her head onto her free hand. "How can that be? Our plan now says that everything will be ready in June, July at the absolute latest, already seven months past the due date, Patrick!"

"Yes, but that's because we have parts of Phase Two and Phase Three in overlapping time periods. Those are both three-month sprints," Patrick explained.

"How did we do that?" Sheryl asked sharply. "I thought we went over everything carefully."

"I think I wrote it down wrong," Patrick admitted glumly. "I'm sorry."

"Can we adjust anything? Are the whole phases overlapped?" Sheryl shot back, then paused, scanning Friday's session in her mind. "No, they can't be. We would have noticed that."

"No, you're right. It's not *all* overlapped. Some of it is just, um, jumbled up, I guess," Patrick answered. "I'm trying to untangle it now, but, well, you told me to let you know if I needed help . . . and, well, I need help," he finished with a voice full of apology. "We can't run a single bit of any of the phases concurrently as you know because the final piece of each phase must be in place to accurately begin the new. It's just impossible. I'm so sorry."

Sheryl bit back a groan, slumping forward in her chair.

Didn't I just say that I wanted him to feel comfortable asking?

"Yes, I did say that, and I meant it, Patrick," she assured him, straightening in resolve. "What exactly do you need?"

"I've been at it for hours already, and I think I need help sorting all this out again," he replied, his voice still anxious. "I was going to ask Keisha, but . . ."

"No, don't ask Keisha," Sheryl spoke as his voice trailed off, her mind already racing ahead. "I'll help you. We'll only ask her if we need to. I don't want to freak her out again, although we'll have to fill her in on Monday. I assume you want to meet at the office? Today?"

She heard him release his breath in a whoosh. "Yeah, that would be great," he replied gratefully. "It's hard to do this on a laptop anyway. My bigger screen at the office will help."

"Okay, I can be there at . . ." She paused. "How about we meet right after lunch, say one o'clock?"

"Yup, I can do that."

"Okay, see you then," Sheryl said, clicking end. She pushed her bangs back from her face. *Damn it. How did we miss that?*

Sighing, she put the journal back and closed the desk drawer. There was no way she wanted to write down *these* thoughts. They weren't fit for human consumption. Nor was she interested in paying the bills. She turned away from the desk. *Do I have time to get a workout in?* she thought, calculating the time. *I'm going to need to burn off some of this energy before I get together with Patrick. Otherwise, I might just kill him,* she thought ruefully. *But at least he asked. That's something.*

She decided she definitely had time for a good, hard workout. Changing quickly into tights and a singlet, she jogged down the steps toward their partially finished basement, which housed their workout equipment. She stopped at Dave's first floor office on the way, filling him in, briefly, on her conversation with Patrick.

"No problem," he said cheerfully, when she informed him she had to leave for the office. "I have work to do too." He glanced out the front window. "But be careful out there. It's really getting nasty."

"Yeah, I will," she said gloomily, not looking forward to the drive.

"Okay then. You're working out before you go?" Dave guessed, eyeing her attire.

"I need to burn off some of my nervous energy," she admitted uncomfortably, aware that Dave often took that as an excuse for them to be intimate, which was *not* what she needed right now.

But he just nodded and said, "I'm sure," in an agreeable tone, with no sign of interest in anything else. "Enjoy then. I'm going to get back to this proposal," he added in a tone that was almost too casual.

Sheryl watched dumbfounded as he swiveled to face his computer, effectively shutting her out. She didn't know whether to be relieved or outraged. Pondering that, she turned slowly and started down the hall toward the basement door. The state of her relationship was starting to worry her.

She was just reaching for the doorknob when she heard Dave's voice behind her:

"Hey," he said softly. "I'm so glad you called."

Chapter Nine

Monday, September 20

Sheryl followed Carl into his office on Monday morning without waiting for an invitation to enter. She had arrived a full half hour before he did, shortly after seven, and had been nervously watching for him to arrive.

"Sheryl, is this about the text you sent Friday?" Carl asked, a deep frown creasing his forehead. "Can I at least take my coat off?"

"Yes, yes," Sheryl acquiesced but still stood across from his desk. "Of course. I just wanted to see you before Jim gets here."

"So your text said." Carl shrugged out of his long black coat and hung it in the small closet in the corner of his office.

"Jim was asking about the Portal Project on Friday. I guess you had already left," Sheryl said breathlessly, her short pearl necklace feeling like a choker against her throat. "He implied we were going to miss the deadline. I guess he heard about Keisha, and–"

Carl held up a hand. Gesturing to a chair at his mahogany conference table, he walked back to the door and murmured something to Harriet, his assistant, then firmly closed the door behind him.

"Okay, now we can talk. Harriet will hold Jim off if he arrives in the meantime." He strode to the head of the table.

Sheryl nodded, feeling her shoulders lower a notch. "Thank you."

"Now, tell me what happened," he said, sliding into a chair and steepling his hands. Sheryl observed idly that her dark green suit was a perfect complement to his deep navy one. They were both in their "Mondays mean business" mode.

Sheryl launched into an account of Jim's visit and did not hold back on the man's intimidation tactics.

"You said *nothing?*" Carl chuckled. "That must have driven him mad."

Sheryl smiled weakly. "Maybe. I was too busy trying not to panic to notice much."

"You'd better get used to dealing with Jim," Carl warned. "He's not going away. He's too close to Todd."

"I know," Sheryl acknowledged, grimacing. She tucked the cuff of her cream silk blouse back under her jacket sleeve. "I'm working on it, but I'm glad I have you as a buffer."

"I won't always be here," Carl cautioned.

"Why? What?" Sheryl asked, confused. "What do you mean you won't be here?"

"I just meant that I'm out of the office at times," Carl said impatiently, almost belying the warning tone in his previous statement. "You know, you can't count on me to be here every second."

Sheryl gave him a puzzled look. "Yeah, I know that, but still . . . I'm just glad I have you to back me up. Jim, well, he's a tough one."

Carl grunted in what Sheryl assumed was agreement. "Where are you with the new schedule?" he questioned her. "I'll need to be prepared when Jim does get here."

Sheryl sighed. "I spent all afternoon Saturday with Patrick," she began.

"Friday *and* Saturday?"

"Yes, Saturday. It had to be done. But I think we have a good plan now, a doable one, although it won't be easy. We didn't put much slack in there for things to go wrong," she admitted. "At all."

"When?"

"Mid-August?" Sheryl responded with an apologetic frown.

"That's a full seven months late!" Carl snapped, flattening his palms on the table.

"Yes, but we can do it in two phases," Sheryl answered quickly, looking to appease him. She and Patrick had condensed the phases over the weekend, hoping to strengthen their position. "We could potentially release Phase One in March, early March, maybe late February, and with some attractive, cosmetic features that have been requested by our customers."

"Why not add the features later?" Carl challenged her.

"Because it's the backend that's going to take so long," she responded firmly. "We would add the features for Phase One on the old infrastructure, while we work on the new infrastructure. And the really awesome new features are better than we originally promised. Carl, Keisha's interface design is a marvel."

Her boss frowned.

"Of course, we might be able to get the whole Project done by late June or early July, if we skip the interim release," she said frankly, echoing Carl's earlier question.

She and Patrick had scoped out this Phase One concept on Saturday to appease Jim and the others, but she didn't think it would meet the customers' real needs. Sheryl knew that the current Portal was a bit cumbersome and somewhat outdated, but what really perplexed her was that *she* had never heard any significant complaints from clients. Jim had made such a big deal that they had lost important customers solely because of the client interface. *Is there any evidence of that, or was it just Jim being difficult?*

"Will it answer the concerns of the customers who left?" Carl demanded, as if hearing her thoughts. "Phase One?"

"You know, I don't really know," she said frankly. "I was just thinking that I honestly haven't seen many complaints in the support database, and I reviewed all the call logs after this Project was assigned to me. All of them. There were a lot of people who suggested that the Portal could be streamlined, which we all agree with, but complaints? Not that many."

"What?" the older man's frown deepened. "Then what was Jim talking about?"

"I don't know. Some people don't complain, they just walk. I get that. But it seems odd that there were no complaints or even many support calls from any of the three big customers Jim specifically mentioned. Maybe the financial advisors heard them and didn't notify support?"

Carl rubbed his hand across his bald head. "They should have logged support calls *for* the customers if the complaints went to them."

"Agreed, but you know that rarely happens."

"Jim just keeps hounding me about when we are going to be done," her boss said, pulling at the knot of his dark blue tie. "He says he's afraid of losing more clients because of us."

Sheryl put her elbow on the table, cupping her chin in her right hand. Something just didn't feel right. "Carl, has Jim given *you* any documentation about the complaints?"

He shook his head. "No, I haven't seen anything. Only what Jim said."

"Then, is there something else going on here?" she asked curiously. "Is Jim making a bigger deal out of the Portal complaints than he should be?"

Carl shrugged, looking very ill at ease. *Why wouldn't Carl know that for sure?* Watching him, Sheryl wondered again whether something was wrong with the older man. Rumors about Carl that had been circulating in the last few months suddenly popped into her mind. Whispers had started shortly after a security breach that had occurred six months ago.

The breach had been a significant one, although not catastrophic, and the head of security at the time and one of his subordinates had been fired. The problem had been, in part, a failure to update some critical software, and consequently, one of the rumors was that Carl was getting too old to stay on top of things. Sheryl had discounted it at the time, but now she wondered if Carl had heard the rumor and whether it was getting to him. After all, being in charge of all The Diamant's IT resources—internal and outsourced—was a huge job.

"I don't know." Carl paused, then shrugged. "It's a good question, but unfortunately, at this stage, it doesn't matter."

Sheryl nodded. *The complaints are accepted fact now, real or not.*

"You know that we couldn't afford to lose those clients. Why do you think we had so many layoffs last week?" Carl stated suddenly, almost to himself.

"And they really left just because of the Portal?" Sheryl was doubtful. She wasn't a financial advisor, but she couldn't help it.

"That's what Jim said. That's what he told Todd and me. He was really worked up about it. He told us it had to be fixed immediately, but I told you that already. *Months ago.*" Carl was impatient now. He never liked going over the same material twice.

"Yes, you did. And, *that's* why the tight deadline was set," Sheryl said matter-of-factly.

Carl made a face. "Yes, yes. We've been over this already too. So, what are your options? I still don't know how we're going to sell this change to Jim and Todd."

Sheryl laid out copies of the two Project plans that she and Patrick had finished on Saturday without errors. Sheryl was as happy with the primary plan as was possible to be. They had tried to scope the work in a way that was efficient but still had enough improvements to make a real difference to their clients. But she also had a second plan, the quick and dirty Phase One plan, that they could use if Carl, Jim, or Todd really balked at missing the deadline.

She breathed a silent sigh of relief as Carl responded positively to the new design and functionality they were proposing. Keisha had a great concept and mockup, and he quickly grasped that it would take a lot of work behind the scenes to make the functionality that simple. He also expressed concern that Jim and Todd might think it was a lot easier to implement than it looked, which often happened with non-technical people. That was the problem with elegant design. It looked simple, but it usually wasn't easy to program.

Sheryl was glad to see Carl review the plan in detail, asking pointed questions, nodding at her definitive answers and occasionally making suggestions on where the timeline could be tightened up or a feature might be enhanced. The conversation, once started, flowed easily, with the kind of back-and-forth brainstorming that Sheryl appreciated with Carl.

After a full hour-and-a-half of discussion, though, they were still at the same place timewise. She could see acceptance and perhaps growing resignation in Carl's eyes. As she acknowledged this, Sheryl could also sense that her boss was becoming very, very uncomfortable . . . and rattled at the reality of the situation.

Carl sat back in his chair, then looked over at Sheryl thoughtfully. "We should have had this conversation two months ago," he said. He held up his hand when she started to protest. "But we didn't. You won't be making this mistake again either, will you?"

"No, it was a rookie mistake," she admitted, but she had to bite her tongue as she wanted to tell Carl it was more his mistake than hers. "I didn't ask enough questions, of you or my team," she did add pointedly, then admitted, "I put too much pressure on and too much trust in Patrick. After that, we didn't follow protocol because we all felt that there were no other options. I should have spoken up then, but–"

"You didn't think I would listen." Carl finished the sentence for her. He sighed. "And I might not have. I felt under pressure, and I didn't think it would be this much work, although I guess we could go with this simpler option."

They both looked again at the quick-and-dirty option Sheryl and Patrick had concocted on Saturday. The bulk of the changes that the current backend could support could be ready by early February, but the features wouldn't be even close to what was really needed for the Portal to *shine*. It would also end up slowing the whole process down if they eventually did want to get it right.

"It's not great, but it comes close to satisfying the timeline if Todd and Jim insist on it," Sheryl said, scrunching her face in disdain. "It won't make anyone very happy, I'm afraid, and will still require a good deal of overtime for the next four to five months, right through the holiday season."

Carl's face matched her own. "Yeah, not great."

"I'm not happy about the overtime and holidays part of this option. That's not going to go over well, especially with Keisha . . . and a few others," Sheryl added quickly. She was fairly certain that Keisha would leave if this plan was selected, although she couldn't help but hope that her protégé would begin to understand the complexities of the situation and stay.

"Neither am I, but we may not have a choice," Carl admitted. Despite his own single-minded focus, Carl wasn't entirely unconscious that other people wanted more in their lives than work. And the reality was that the quick-and-dirty solution really wouldn't bring that much value to the clients or the company. The shortcut wasn't going to solve Jim's problems, whatever they really were. And it really wouldn't serve the clients or the company in the long term. They could both see that.

Carl stared at the plans, rubbing his hand repeated over his head.

"Let me think about this overnight," he finally said. "I take it you're recommending doing this right and pushing the delivery date off until next July? Sheryl, you do understand that's almost a year away?"

"Yes, but look how awesome it will be!" Sheryl replied passionately. "It will put us way ahead of our competitors if we take the time to do this right and really integrate all the backend systems, not just the two we have there now. We could really make it *full service,* and so fast and easy. We'd blow the competition away!"

"Is it worth it? Can we win the clients back with this?" He asked the questions more to himself than to her.

"I don't know, Carl," Sheryl answered honestly. "But I think we have a good shot. As far as I know, there's nothing like it out there. It's truly state-of-the-art."

Carl nodded and gathered up his set of the papers. "Let's touch base tomorrow morning." He glanced at his phone calendar. "Send me an email by eight a.m."

Sheryl nodded. "Thanks–"

The sound of shouting came from outside the office door, cutting off Sheryl's gratitude. Both she and Carl shifted their attention toward the entrance.

"I'm tired of waiting! I've been waiting for over an hour already–now get out of my way!"

The door burst open. There was Jim Leaders, pushing his way past poor Harriet, his face red with fury.

"I should have known you would get to him first," he growled, spotting Sheryl at the table.

"Jim, stop," Carl said firmly, standing up. Sheryl couldn't help but notice that at his full height, he was a few inches taller than his colleague. "She told me you wanted to see me, but *I* decided to have this meeting with her first."

"Yeah, so she could butter you up before I got here to give you the bad news," Jim sneered, waving his arm dismissively at Sheryl.

Carl turned to her, his expression composed. "Sheryl, thank you. I've got it from here," he said.

Sheryl stood up. "Of course, Carl." She nodded coolly to Jim as she slipped by him. He didn't acknowledge her but kept his focus solely on Carl.

Sheryl closed the door as she left, exchanging an exasperated look with Harriet. "Thank you," she said quietly. The older woman was barely five foot two. Sheryl marveled at how she had kept Jim out of the office for so long.

Feeling a bit guilty for leaving Carl alone with Jim, she turned and headed down the corridor to her office on the far wall, skirting the edge of the cubicles on her way. She spotted Keisha at her desk as she neared her door and quietly gestured for her to follow. She stuck her head into Patrick's nearby office and waved him along as well. *I might as well fill them both in at the same time.*

They both followed her eagerly into the office, clearly aware that she had been with Carl.

"Well, did he like it? What did he say?" Patrick burst out, his eyes almost bulging with curiosity.

Keisha stood in silence, an expression of rapt anticipation on her face.

Sheryl handed Patrick her copies of the plans. "Here. We made a few changes. Carl had some good ideas. You'll need to update the MS Project files. Both of them."

Patrick's face fell. "Both?"

Keisha gave them a sharp look. "Both? We only had one plan."

"Yes, both," Sheryl answered. "Patrick and I came up with a backup plan, in case . . ."

"In case they don't give us the extra time," Keisha concluded. "Smart."

"Exactly." Sheryl felt secretly relieved that her protégé seemed to be grasping the enormity of the situation and was now in on the solution instead of being mired in her reaction.

"But when did you do that?" Keisha asked.

"Saturday," Patrick admitted. "I got confused when I was entering stuff in MS Project and messed it up. I had to ask Sheryl for help because I couldn't fix it, and I knew it needed to be perfect."

"Hmph. Project can be tough," Keisha commiserated with her supervisor.

"Let's focus. Carl wants to review both plans again, just to make sure there's nothing that was missed. He'll let us know in the morning," she added, although she wondered what might change because of what was happening right now with Carl and Jim.

"Hey, these changes look good," Patrick interjected, ruffling through the pages.

"Great, then let's get the files updated and copies back to me and Carl STAT," Sheryl said briskly.

"Got it, boss." Patrick saluted her. "On it."

Keisha rolled her eyes but smiled at his antics as they both walked out, nearly bumping into the doorframe in their eagerness to review the changes.

Despite her worries, Sheryl smiled too.

But she couldn't get her mind off Carl, and how completely ruffled he had seemed by the end of their meeting, even before Jim's dramatic appearance. *He isn't himself. Does he know about the rumors?* She flashed to the stories and shivered. *They* were *pretty vicious. Or is something else bothering him?*

Sheryl wished she knew. She was certain that the security breach had upset him tremendously. It had her and everyone else in IT management. And now this.

She glanced at her watch, wondering if Jim was still in with Carl and what was being said. *Should I call?* she wondered, but then she shook her head. *Best to get back to work. Surely Carl can handle Jim.*

But . . . what if he couldn't?

Chapter Ten

Tuesday, September 21

An eerie silence hung over the building as Sheryl made her way to her office on Tuesday. It was early, only 7:30 a.m., but the hum of computers and conversation would normally have begun even at this hour thanks to all the hardworking salaried employees like herself. She stopped and looked around carefully, her head cocked a little to the side in confusion.

Where is everyone? There was not a single head to be seen above the low gray cubicle walls.

Sheryl's low-heeled pumps made a muffled thud on the mottled industrial carpet that covered the floors as she strode quickly down the corridor. The sound contrasted dramatically in the big, empty space, and it echoed loudly in her ears. She increased her pace, uncomfortable being so alone.

Shrugging out of her coat, she hung it on the back of the door and slid her laptop out of her briefcase. She rolled her shoulders, feeling the tension in them deepen.

But what can I do? she thought, as she powered up her laptop while keeping an alert ear for the sounds of arriving employees. Still nothing. Even the Portal Project team were not yet at their desks, when two weeks ago they easily all would have been. *How in the world can I help them . . .* she thought morosely, *especially when I haven't been able to climb out of my own funk?*

Sighing deeply, she pulled up her email and began to concentrate on clearing her inbox. Glancing quickly through it, she zeroed in on the items of greatest importance, which were inquiries from members of her leadership team that needed immediate attention. *I've been neglecting everyone else because of this damn Portal Project.* In total, after the layoffs, she still had over 170 people in her organization. The Portal Project team was less than 20 percent of that total. Frowning, she brushed her bangs back from her face and opened an email from Jose, who had marked it urgent. Fortunately, all he needed was clarification about the scope of one of his team's projects that she could handle easily.

She moved to the next email, her forehead creased with concentration and worry, especially when she saw it was from Layla Arch. Emails from Layla, a key contact at The Diamante's bank, were rarely good. And this one wasn't. Layla was complaining about delay instigated by Yvette's team, which Sheryl already knew had been caused by Layla's unit. She groaned inwardly. *When is this woman going to stop?* She typed a tactfully worded response that put the ball back in Layla's court, for now. Sheryl's experience was that it wouldn't stay there for long.

By the time Sheryl came up for air and was ready for more coffee, it was close to nine o'clock. Leaning back, she was happy to see that she had answered most of the emails in her inbox and sent messages to all of her direct reports and several other managers on her team. *I need to make sure that I'm giving everyone attention,* she reminded herself, especially this week. *They all need support.*

Walking out onto the floor, she was relieved to see that the majority of her team on this floor had arrived and were settled into their work-day, and she assumed it was the same on the floor below. Heads were bent over the computer screens, some adorned with headsets. But still, it was too quiet. Eerily quiet.

She also noticed that only a few people looked up and nodded as she passed their cubes. She was suddenly struck with the stark realization that most people kept their heads down – the friendly smiles and interaction that she was used to were noticeably absent. Sheryl felt her stomach tighten. She couldn't help but take it personally. *These people are angry with me! And I know it's not only the layoffs.* The increased pressure to perform in the last six months on top of it was also taking a toll.

Threading her way through the cubicles on the floor, she smiled and warmly greeted anyone who did make eye contact. She tried not to notice the empty seats of the recently released workers. But her smile felt stiff even to her, and it was rarely returned. In fact, some of the looks she received were downright furious.

Swallowing hard, she forced herself to walk through the aisles and make eye contact with whoever would look her way. She plodded down the stairs and repeated the process on the floor below her, before slipping into the breakroom to get more coffee. Thankfully, it was empty.

Filling her mug, Sheryl pondered the situation. She realized that while she had met with her management team, she really hadn't addressed her entire department since the brutal layoffs a week ago today. She knew why. She hadn't wanted to. *I haven't known what the hell to say, for one thing.* But if she was honest with herself, she certainly didn't want to face the open hostility that she was likely to encounter.

Sheryl found herself in a position that she had rarely experienced in her decades at The Diamante, namely having to represent the company's management when she didn't agree with their actions. And, now that she was being uncompromisingly truthful with herself, she also felt that she couldn't openly condemn what had occurred without risking her own position, her own career. Part of the upper management team, she simply couldn't throw her peers under the bus, so to speak.

But something has to be done, she thought unhappily, trudging back to her office without pausing to make eye contact this time. *Clearly morale is down.* People were unhappy and not working very hard. Sure, that would probably change over time as people forgot or moved on. Her heart raced as she thought about several important projects on her plate and the people she cared for deeply. *Just what will be lost in the meantime . . . and who?* She'd already lost people she'd known and enjoyed working with for years.

Realistically, more people could also be let go – this time for what was in her opinion, a more legitimate cause, for not meeting goals! Her managers and project leads, like Patrick, would also be at risk. She cleared her throat. Not to mention her own job. Things could get really ugly if they were left to fester.

Sheryl sat down in her chair, leaning her elbows on her desk as her mind raced.

Good heavens! I've been so caught up in my own feelings, in the situation with Carl and Patrick and Keisha, that I lost sight of the bigger picture and everyone else on my team. She sighed. *I need to address all of them, but when? And more importantly, what in the world do I say?* She was not used to feeling helpless and powerless, and she didn't like it at all.

Her personal phone vibrated with an incoming email. She was surprised to see that it was from Cindy and took a welcomed breath. Opening it, she quickly scanned the contents.

Sheryl, Saw this article this morning and thought of you and what you are going through. I thought it might help with how you are feeling. Sending lots of love, Cindy. xoxo

There was a link at the bottom of the email that Sheryl clicked. The *Huff Post* article that opened was one about loss and grieving and how under-appreciated that process was in contemporary life. Sheryl drank it in, noting that most of the article was about personal loss, including job loss, but there was a paragraph at the bottom that mentioned the loss, grief, and tangible pain that coworkers felt when people left the workplace, especially if the exit had not been voluntary. Perking up, she read that the communal need to mourn was often ignored in the rush to continue business as usual and avoid the blame and shame that often accompanied those losses.

The ending sentence of the article surprisingly left her choked up: "The result can be detrimental to individuals, teams, and even entire companies that might not ever recover."

The message felt like an arrow through her heart. Sheryl put her hand on her chest and rubbed gently as she absorbed the emotional impact of the words on the screen. *Wow! This is exactly what I'm feeling . . . and what I'm witnessing most everyone else in the company is feeling.*

Shaking her head, Sheryl wondered how Cindy's sixth sense had been so accurate once again. Leaning back in her chair, she read the article again quickly, noting that the rituals and ceremonies that had accompanied loss in earlier civilizations had been largely relegated only to death in today's Western societies. *That's so true,* she thought. *Only to death, while there is so much to grieve* here . . . *when the loss is so real.*

She let her mind go back in time to the various losses she had faced, even her most difficult loss, when her father had died. She remembered, despite the funeral services, how quickly she had been urged to keep moving forward either by her friends and peers or by her own sense of not wanting to lose ground. How many other losses had gone completely unmourned in her life?

An idea started to form. *Is there a way to allow people, at least on my teams, to grieve or acknowledge the loss, without it turning into a gripe session about the company?* She knew she didn't really want to face the accusations or have to defend the company's position. *But maybe there's another way to approach this.* Mind whirling with possibilities, she turned back to her email.

Sheryl made it through the rest of the day with no drama. She didn't hear from Carl about the meeting with Todd and Jim regarding the Portal Project deadline, but she and Patrick made progress on the potential presentation and managed to trim a little time from the overall schedule by streamlining some of the work. They also finalized the three people on Sheryl's other teams who could help with the Project without needing too much time to get up to speed. She didn't reassign them yet, wanting Carl's approval first, but she was happy to have more specifics in the proposal. Specifics made her more comfortable and would play well with Todd, if she had a chance to present them. Unlike many top execs, he was prone to dig into the details.

Still, the thought of her staff and their feelings kept running through her mind, disrupting her concentration. After lunch, Sheryl took the time to reach out to *all* members of her leadership team, in person when she could. Up and back from her desk multiple times, each conversation only weighed on her further, and strengthened her conviction that *something* needed to be done, despite her discomfort with the idea of standing up in front of the staff. She knew she had to project a strong and confident image, and she wasn't at all certain that she was capable of that, yet.

By the time she slid onto the soft leather seats of her Lexus at the end of the day, the seed of an idea that had started forming when she read Cindy's article was sprouting into a full-blown plan. Guiding the car onto the highway, she used the voice recognition system to call her friend, hoping that she wasn't in a late-day meeting. Sheryl was grateful when Cindy picked up.

"Got a minute?" Sheryl asked, hoping the answer was yes.

"Sure, but only a minute," Cindy replied briskly. "I have a meeting in ten that I can't miss."

"Got it," Sheryl said. "I have a crazy idea I want to run by you."

"I doubt that," Cindy said with a laugh. "You rarely do crazy."

"Okay," Sheryl chuckled. "Maybe not crazy, but definitely out of the box. It's about that article you sent this morning, the one about loss acknowledgement."

"Excellent. I'm glad you got it."

"Yes, thank you for sending it. I needed to see it, but I'm not the only one. Sooo, what if I create some kind of recognition ceremony for those people who were laid off? I'd create a way for the remaining folks to acknowledge their contribution and energetically wish them well in their future?" Sheryl realized she sounded both skeptical and excited about the idea.

"A ceremony?" Cindy asked. "That sounds pretty formal."

"No, no. I don't mean it to be terribly formal. Maybe ceremony isn't the right word, but you know what I mean. Some kind of gathering where people can acknowledge and express their feelings."

"That could get dangerous," Cindy warned. "I mean it, Sheryl. What if they all turn their anger and frustration on you? After what you told me, I'm sure there are plenty of daggers directed at you right now . . . and the rest of the management team."

"They could," Sheryl acknowledged. "That's honestly what I'm afraid of. I'm realizing I'd have to structure it to minimize that likelihood. It would not be about me or the company. It would be about the loss of their coworkers and the ability to gain some sort of closure."

"They probably think the loss was unfair and undeserved," Cindy cautioned, echoing Sheryl's own trepidations.

"True, and as you're aware, anger is part of the grieving process. I'd have to honor it while establishing ground rules about that," Sheryl responded thoughtfully.

There was a long pause before Sheryl heard Cindy clear her throat. "Uh, Sheryl?" she said hesitantly. "You know I love you, and I love what you are trying to do with this, but I sent you that article to help *you*, not to start you on a crusade with your team."

"But they're so unhappy!" Sheryl cried, her voice echoing in the confines of the car. "When I left just now, there was no one on my floor or on the level below mine. *No one.* I often leave late, but I'm rarely the very last to leave. To be honest, I'm not sure how much people are working even when they're there. I want to *do something*!"

"I understand," Cindy tried to commiserate. "But that will fade over time as people forget. The wounds will heal by themselves."

"Really?" Sheryl shot back bitterly, her face awash in surprise. "Do you hear yourself? I can't believe *you* said that. You know that many wounds just get buried, but they never heal. That's exactly what the article was talking about! Not having a chance to process and being expected to simply move on. That's what we're doing – expecting people to move on." She punctuated her statement by slapping the steering wheel with her gloved palm.

A long exhale came from the other end of the call. "You're right," Cindy said, her tone regretful. "I'm sorry I said that. I know firsthand how wounds don't heal by themselves, not deep ones, anyway."

Sheryl wanted to feel momentarily triumphant, but she couldn't, knowing that her comment had hit home, knowing Cindy was referring to her traumatic divorce and move out west. Her dear friend was still struggling to heal, even after nearly ten years.

"Look," Cindy acknowledged, "I need to think about your idea more. All I can do at the moment is react. I have this meeting I'm rushing to. Let me ponder it and call you back later or tomorrow."

"Okay," Sheryl breathed, disappointed by Cindy's lack of enthusiasm. "I know it's kind of crazy. I said that, right?" Her shoulders slumped. *Maybe this isn't the great idea I thought it was.*

Cindy laughed. "You did. I guess you were right after all. I gotta run. You okay?"

"Yeah, I'm okay. Love you."

"Love you too. I'll call you back soon. Bye."

"Bye." Sheryl hit the button to hang up on the steering wheel of her car. *I guess I'll have to think this through more. Maybe do a bit more research. I could also talk to Dave.* She laughed out loud at that thought. *He'll also probably think I've lost my mind.*

"Are you insane?" Dave burst out, when she reached him by phone nearly four hours later. Despite the additional research Sheryl had done on the topic, she now had an unhappy feeling of déjà vu. Dave was in Nashville tonight, another trade show. It was late, and his voice was tired and tight after a long day on the exhibition floor. "Sheryl, you know you can't do something like that!"

Sheryl sighed deeply, tucking the bed covers more tightly around her chest. He hadn't even let her finish her explanation. Now, it seemed like they were going to have a repeat of their argument from last week.

"No, I'm not," she replied tartly. "Maybe misguided, but not insane. This stuff is real and important."

"Look, Sheryl. You are their manager and boss, not their therapist or their minister. If they need help processing, they should be going to HR or using the Employee Assistance Program to find a therapist. You should *not be doing therapy*." Dave's voice was higher than normal and very animated despite it being nearly eleven. She had definitely riled him up.

"Dave, I'm not trying to do therapy," Sheryl argued hotly, her own anger rising. Although she still had her own doubts about a ceremony or ritual being the right way to go, somehow, she couldn't bear her husband criticizing yet another one of her ideas.

"Well, it sounds like that to me," he snapped, his voice hard. "You can't do stuff like that. What would Janine say?"

"She'd probably have a fit," Sheryl admitted quietly, tucking her hair behind her ear. She gazed at the large wedding picture that hung opposite the bed, idly wondering where that smiling, ecstatic couple was now. "The thing is, Janine doesn't want us to talk about the layoffs at all, but that's just leaving the very large, pink elephant sitting square in the middle of the room."

"Well, the elephant will eventually get up and walk away," Dave said dismissively. "You need to worry about the Portal Project and getting your job done before *you* are one of the people who are laid off or let go."

Sheryl felt her eyes sting with burgeoning tears. Lying in the large king bed, she felt the vastness of the empty covers beside her. It was so far past her normal bedtime, but she hadn't been able to reach Dave earlier. She swallowed a sad and irritated sigh. *I almost wish I hadn't reached him.* The room was dark, illuminated only by a single aromatic candle on the bedside table, which Sheryl had lit in a vain attempt to relax. She had been meditating while waiting for Dave to call back. *I wanted support, not criticism, although I should have known better, I guess.* She didn't know what to say to him now, so she remained silent.

Silence stretched across the connection. She could hear Dave's uneven breathing and guessed he was struggling with his own anger. *I can't believe he's acting like this again. My idea is not THAT crazy. Is it?* She wriggled into a more upright position and picked up her mug. The phone was still connected, but she half-wished it wasn't. Of course, they had never addressed their disagreement from last week, although he had offered that one weak apology. Deep down, Sheryl felt they had not resolved their differences or mended the rift that argument had caused.

The tears spilled over onto her cheeks. *Is it too much to ask for a little support and understanding, even if he doesn't agree?* Frustrated, she swiped at her cheeks with the back of her hand. *And why is he so angry? It isn't his job on the line.*

It felt like a full minute before she heard Dave swear under his breath. "Sheryl? Are you still there?"

"I'm here," she answered, keeping her voice cool and controlled. Cradling the phone between her head and shoulder, she wrapped her hands around her lukewarm cup of peppermint tea.

"Sweetheart, you know I love you. I'm not trying to upset you." Dave could probably tell she was upset and near tears. He knew her well. "Talk to me."

"I can't." She was sniffling now, the tears coming harder. "I just can't."

"Oh, honey, don't cry," Dave begged gently. "I'm sorry. Don't cry."

"I can't help it," she murmured, stifling a sob. "I'm just trying to do the right thing, trying to help my staff, and all you can do is criticize me."

"I'm not criticizing," Dave argued. "I'm just trying to help you see another perspective. You can't fix everything, and you know you would be putting your own job on the line if you did something like that."

"Why would I be risking *my* job?" Sheryl challenged him, sitting up straighter as her tears gave way to anger. "All I see right now is more people getting laid off or fired if things continue on their current path!"

Dave paused, taken aback by her vehemence. "Well . . ." he said cautiously, "yes, to some extent. The question is, how far does that go?"

"This is an emotional trauma the company has caused," she retorted hotly, clenching the comforter in her free hand as she leaned forward. "We have an obligation to try to heal it! *I* have an obligation to help heal it. I may not be their therapist, but it *is* my job to be their mentor."

"Hey, don't shoot the messenger," Dave quipped, clearly trying to lighten the mood. He paused. "But, really Sheryl, I can't imagine that Todd or Carl or Janine would be on board with this."

Sheryl snorted softly. "They should be. They should be equally as concerned about morale as I am; it's part of all our jobs!"

"Well, sure, but why can't you simply encourage people by being upbeat and positive?" he suggested, exasperation thick in his voice.

Sheryl's whole body stiffened. "Are you serious? I don't think some rah-rah speech is going to cut it right now," she answered sarcastically.

She heard a big sigh. "Probably not," Dave conceded.

Sheryl let his words hang in the air. She took a deep breath and leaned back against the pillows but found she was trembling. She took a sip of tea, inhaling the soothing mint scent.

After a long pause, Dave tried to defuse the argument. "Look, sweetie, I know you are trying to do the right thing, and I admire you for that. Let's both think about this some more and talk about it again when it's not so late and we're not so tired."

Sheryl sensed that he wanted to say more but was holding his tongue for once. *Smart man.*

"That's a good idea," she replied with resignation. "I hope I can get some sleep tonight."

"I hope so too." He sounded relieved that she allowed the change of topic.

"Good night, then," she said quickly, now more than anxious to get off the phone. "Thank you for listening. I'm sorry I'm being so emotional about this." The minute she said it, she made a face. *Why am I apologizing for my feelings again?*

"It's understandable. But try to put it out of your mind so that you can sleep. I'm sure things will be clearer in the morning, for both of us," Dave's assurance was a little too hearty. "I love you, Sheryl," he added, and it seemed like it was almost an afterthought.

She sighed, blinking back another rush of tears. "I love you too," she said halfheartedly. "You get some sleep too. I know you have another long day in front of you."

"I do at that . . . and so do you. Good night."

"Night," she said, pressing the end icon. She took a final swallow of her tea. She sat for a few more minutes in the candlelit room, deepening her breathing and bringing herself into a more relaxed state. She didn't want to think about Dave any more than she wanted to think about work. She'd never sleep if she did. With the tea gone, she blew out the candle and snuggled all the way under the covers.

I'm going to do this for my people . . . my career be damned, was the last thought that crossed her mind as she drifted off to sleep.

Chapter Eleven

Friday, September 24

What the hell? I need answers! Sheryl hung up her office phone more roughly than she had intended and pushed her bangs back from her face. Carl hadn't answered again, and it was already ten o'clock.

As if on cue, Patrick and Keisha peeked into her office. *They want answers too.* Sighing, she waved them in. They approached her desk cautiously.

"So, what do we do, boss?" Patrick spoke first.

"We need to know how to move forward with the new plan," Keisha quickly added.

Sheryl hesitated.

"What did Carl say?" Patrick burst out.

Grinding her teeth in frustration, Sheryl glanced down, unable to meet Patrick's and Keisha's expectant faces. She picked up her office phone yet again, dialing her boss' line for what seemed like the thousandth time in the last four days. Again, he didn't answer. *It's like he's downright refusing my calls!*

She stood up resolutely. *Enough is enough. My team deserves to know how to proceed.* Straightening her gray suit jacket, she marched out of her office, leaving Patrick and Keisha gaping in her wake.

She didn't notice the startled looks that followed her as she strode quickly down the corridor, her face a mask of determination. She didn't know if she was more frustrated with Carl or herself. He hadn't hosted his normal staff meeting, and neither she nor any of his other direct reports had had any contact with him. And, she thought in disgust, *I haven't taken any action on my idea for the 'memorial' service.*

Shaking her head to clear it, she reached Carl's office and was confronted with a closed door. She stopped in front of Harriet's desk. The older woman looked at her with surprise.

"Sheryl?"

"Harriet, where is he?" she demanded. "I've been trying all week to get in touch with him. My team and I are waiting for a response or we can't move forward."

Harriet flinched slightly at her tone, and Sheryl felt a twinge of regret. *None of this is Harriet's fault.* "Please, Harriet," she said more softly. "It's important."

Sheryl liked Harriet, who was a long-time employee of The Diamante. She had worked for Carl since he'd gotten his first managerial assignment, growing in her role as Carl had ascended the corporate ladder. Sheryl had often found it amusing when the older woman took a motherly approach to Carl and to most of his direct reports.

Not known for her reticence, Sheryl was taken aback that Harriet simply harrumphed.

Sheryl, still feeling determined, pushed harder, but Harriet refused to budge. She insisted that Carl wasn't seeing anyone. Sheryl's unease grew the longer the older woman stonewalled her.

Stumped, Sheryl finally headed back toward her own office. It wasn't like Carl to just refuse to see anyone without an explanation, and Harriet was clearly upset, although she was doing her best to hide it. *What to do now?* Keisha and Patrick had disappeared, but she knew she had to get back to them. *When I have news,* she thought. *They'll realize that.*

Figuratively throwing up her hands, she sat back at her desk and opened a report she was preparing about the database upgrade Jose's team was doing for the fund managers. *Someone needs to work, and it might as well be me.* Drawing on years of self-discipline, she dove back into the tasks at hand–at least what she could tackle without Carl's approval.

It was nearly four o'clock when Sheryl returned to her desk after yet another afternoon meeting. She had just settled in her chair when her phone rang. Recognizing the name and number of her colleague, Lauren Peters, Sheryl picked up the receiver quickly. *Maybe Lauren has news.*

"Lauren! What's up?"

"Hello, Sheryl," came Lauren's formal response. Sheryl rolled her eyes. Her team always complained about Lauren being uptight.

Younger than Sheryl, with less tenure at The Diamante, Lauren was one of Sheryl's peers who also reported to Carl. "Do you see all the people who are leaving early today? It's not even four o'clock!" she cried indignantly.

Sheryl groaned inwardly. Lauren was such a stickler to policies and procedures that there was never any gray in her world. Sheryl supposed that's what made Lauren most unpopular with her teams.

Glancing out her office window, Sheryl observed a small stream of people filing into the parking lot. "Hmm, I do now," she replied, noticing that the lights were just coming on to counter the darkening sky.

"What are you doing about it?" Lauren demanded.

"Actually, I'm not doing anything," Sheryl replied.

"Why not? I'm going to talk to their managers! They have to make the time up next week or be docked."

Sheryl pulled the receiver away from her head and looked at it incredulously. Shaking her head, she returned it to her ear. "Really, Lauren? They are salaried employees. We don't dock them for leaving early. You know that," Sheryl reminded her, disbelief coloring her voice.

"Well, it has to be stopped. People aren't working." Lauren was clearly up in arms.

"You noticed that too?" Sheryl asked her, while consciously keeping her voice calm. "It's been very quiet this week. Honestly, I have been trying to figure out what to do."

"I'm going to have a meeting on Monday and tell people to knock it off!" Lauren stated angrily. "This sulking has gone on long enough."

Wow. That's going to be helpful. Sheryl was shocked by Lauren's insensitivity. "Come on, Lauren. Sulking?" she said impatiently. "Don't you think they are entitled to be a little upset?"

"Why? We're running a business, not a charity. Carl was very clear that we are not to discuss the layoffs further. It's done. It's all done. We have to move on." Lauren sounded a bit defensive.

"Are *you* moving on?" Sheryl's question was soft.

"Me? Of course, I am. I'm a professional. I'm worried about getting the job done, which is what everyone else needs to do," Lauren snapped.

"Does being a professional mean that you don't have feelings?" Sheryl was genuinely curious now.

"Of course not," Lauren responded with exasperation. "But it does mean you manage your feelings. You don't let them dominate you, and you continue to work no matter what you are feeling. That's what we're all being paid for. You'd think they'd have more sense than to act like children."

Sheryl felt a stab of anger at her colleague. "That's pretty insensitive, Lauren. I'm surprised at you," she retorted.

Lauren paused. "I'm not insensitive. That's not fair," she finally said with a hurt tone.

"Maybe," Sheryl conceded, watching more people head to their cars. "But don't you think our teams need us to have a bit more compassion?"

Sniffing, Lauren said. "Can we afford to do that?"

"Can we afford not to?" Sheryl countered. There was a silent pause.

"I don't know," Lauren answered, more thoughtful now. "But you know, people aren't working very hard."

"Yeah, I know," Sheryl agreed, still with that tight feeling in her stomach that hadn't gone away. "But I don't think threatening them is the right answer."

"Well, I don't know what else to do," her colleague said petulantly.

"I know. I'm not sure either," Sheryl admitted. "It's Friday." She paused. "Maybe we should just leave early too," she suggested.

Lauren gasped and then laughed nervously. "If you can't beat them, join them?"

Sheryl chuckled. "Something like that. At least for now. Maybe we'll have some brilliant ideas over the weekend." She wanted to add more but wasn't ready to share her idea with yet another potential naysayer.

"Yeah, maybe," Lauren agreed. "Have a good weekend, I guess."

"You too," Sheryl replied, ending the call.

She stared at the phone, wishing Carl would call her. She couldn't shake the feeling that she had to find a way to reach her boss and soon! Harriet continued to stall, giving Sheryl the same information that she had earlier. An earlier walk by had confirmed that Carl's door was still closed, and he had not answered the phone. She glanced out the window. Sheryl knew Carl was still in the building. His car was still in the parking lot. *I have to get to him before the weekend.*

After another thirty minutes of sporadic attention to her work, Sheryl headed to Carl's office again, determined not to accept any more excuses. Thankfully, Harriet was away from her desk. Sheryl took a deep breath and knocked on the door. No response, although she heard a faint rustling on the other side. She knocked again, waited another moment, and then swung open the door. She stuck her head in the opening and began apologizing before she could even see into the room.

"I'm sorry, Carl, about barging in . . ." Her voice trailed off. She couldn't see her boss, but the room was in complete disarray. Confusion filled her as she saw boxes and files everywhere. "Carl?"

Carl stood up from behind his conference table, where he had been bent over a box of something that looked like books. He appeared disheveled, something Sheryl had never seen and something twisted up inside of her at the sight. His eyes were dull and bloodshot. The dark blue suit jacket he always wore was slung carelessly across his desk chair, along with his tie. His pants were creased, his shirt unbuttoned at the neck, and his sleeves were rolled up.

Sheryl's eyes widened in shock.

"If you're going to come in, get in here and shut the door!" he barked roughly, startling her. At least he hadn't told her to leave.

Sheryl quickly jumped into the room and shut the door behind her. Then she turned and gazed around the room in disbelief. "I'm sorry, but I really needed to talk to you," she said. "But what's going on?" The twisting up inside her doubled. "Or shouldn't I ask?"

"You shouldn't ask. You shouldn't be in here," Carl stated flatly. "Whatever it is, you'll just have to make the decision yourself. I can't help you anymore."

"You can't help?" Sheryl was struggling to make sense of the fact that Carl seemed to be packing up his office. "Are you leaving?"

Carl shot her a hard look. "What does it look like?" he asked sarcastically.

Sheryl recoiled at his hard tone.

Then his voice softened. "Yes, I'm leaving, but you can't tell any of your colleagues or friends or *anyone* yet. An announcement will be made later, but I need to be out of here first."

Sheryl sank into one of the chairs near the conference table, struggling to take it all in. She could feel the defeat, the hurt radiating from him.

"I take it that this wasn't your idea?" she asked tentatively.

Carl sighed. "Not entirely, although it was a mutual decision."

"Really? Why?" Sheryl gasped as she struggled for air.

"Why? Because I got myself into a mess and I can't fix it," he said angrily.

Sheryl was shocked. "Carl, what mess?" Her heart dropped. "Oh my gosh, this isn't about the Portal is it? Is Todd that upset? Did you talk to him?"

Carl grimaced. "Yes, I talked to Todd. No, it's not entirely about the Portal, although I shouldn't have made that promise." He shook his head. "It was a dumb thing to do," he admitted. "You knew that, but you've been gracious in not saying it. Others haven't been so gracious." Carl sat down in the chair next to her. He looked at her intently. "But it's not just that. There are other factors. But you are okay," he assured her. "You don't have to worry about your job."

"But Carl, this makes no sense," Sheryl argued. "It's *one thing*. It's ridiculous to lose you over just one project."

Carl looked away. "No. If you remember, there was the security breach, and a couple of other things that you aren't aware of."

Sheryl could only nod, and a silence fell between them. "But you've done so many other great things!" she finally blurted. "Look at all the projects we have completed on time AND on budget. We've pulled off some real miracles. What about the new accounting system last year? Or the operating system upgrade? It's only a couple of misses out of dozens of successes!"

"Thank you for reminding me of all of that," Carl said gravely, "but it doesn't matter. I don't feel good about things either. Maybe the rumors about me are true."

Her face fell. "Oh dear God. You've heard them?" Sheryl asked, dismayed. "My team told me about them, the ones about you being old." She cringed at her own words. "You know they're not true!" she finished passionately.

"Maybe, maybe not." Carl sounded beaten. "Look, I don't want to get into all of this, and I really just want to get out of here. I had a long talk with Todd, and I simply don't belong here anymore."

"But that's crazy!" Sheryl cried. "And why do you have to leave right away?" She was angry on Carl's behalf. Carl had been with the company for more than twenty years. He lived and breathed the company and technology. He was always on top of the latest tech and always working toward keeping The Diamante on the leading edge. *How can this be happening?*

"Because I don't want to drag this out, and I don't want scenes like this one," Carl growled pointedly.

Sheryl didn't respond, staring at her boss with a face full of anguish.

"Don't look at me like that. Life will go on . . . I guess." Carl's shoulders sagged. "I don't know what that's going to look like. Todd and Jim think that I'm over the hill and can't keep up with technology because of my age. I'm no longer young and hip enough. It's time for me to retire," he said bitterly, giving credence to his earlier words about his leaving being a mutual decision.

Sheryl stiffened. "Todd didn't really say that! That's age discrimination!" Sheryl exclaimed indignantly.

"Of course, he didn't say it exactly like that, but I can read between the lines. Everyone thinks technology is a young person's game. Not for people over fifty, and certainly not for people in their sixties. Even as bright as you are, you'll have to be more careful as *your* years progress."

"But you're barely in your sixties," Sheryl protested. "And you're more on top of tech than anyone I know, including the young guys in their twenties and thirties. We all come to you for the latest and greatest."

"Thank you for that, but it's not good enough," Carl retorted resentfully. "Nothing is good enough." Suddenly, his face crumpled. "Sheryl, what am I going to do? You know that this job and technology is my whole life. It's all I do!" He sighed deeply. "I don't have any hobbies. Technology is my hobby. I'm only sixty-one. I don't want to retire, but I don't love this job the way I used to. The stress and the aggravation *are* getting to me. I have to admit to that. My health has even started to suffer. When Todd *suggested* that I retire, well, suddenly it didn't seem all bad."

Despite his words, Sheryl could see that Carl was devastated. His face was pale, and she thought she saw tears in his eyes before he rose and turned away. *I'll bet he's making it sound better for my sake.*

"You need to leave now," he said quietly.

"Carl, what do you need?" she asked, her heart breaking. "How can I help you?"

"Sheryl, you can't help. You can just keep this to yourself. I never meant to say this much to you . . . to anyone . . ." His voice broke, and Sheryl could tell that he was battling his emotions. "You can help me most by helping me maintain my dignity."

"Of course," she replied promptly, her aching heart going out to him. "I won't say a word. I promise. But how can I help you? What can I do to support you? This is so terribly unfair. What is Todd thinking?" she cried, feeling helpless and irate. "It has to be his decision. And what about HR?"

"Sheryl, I know this is upsetting for you, but HR can't do anything. I've agreed that it's best that I move on. It's not that I'm not being taken care of financially. And Todd? Well, Todd is in a tough spot. The new board members are increasing the pressure on him. You need to know that. You're going to feel it more yourself. You already do, but it's going to get worse."

Her boss looked grim as he turned to face Sheryl again. She saw that he spoke with greater urgency as he added, "I shouldn't even tell you this, but I like and respect you. You've done a great job for so long, although you should have pushed back on me sooner about the Portal." He held up his hand to stop her protest. "I'm not blaming you. I'm telling you to be more forthright more quickly. This *truly* has nothing to do with you. I'm really just warning you to be careful with Todd and with Jim. They are both driven and ambitious and won't hesitate to use scapegoats when anything goes wrong." He looked at her pointedly. "They both want more than The Diamante; they are out to make names for themselves."

Sheryl nodded, finding she was unable to speak because she'd become too choked up. Never in a million years would she have expected Carl–strong, indomitable Carl–to be treated like this. She didn't buy for a minute that this was his choice. He was extremely dedicated, and he put so much effort into his job. She knew he was right. He didn't really have a life outside of The Diamante, except for his work with the technology association, which was where she had first seen him speak. And now it had all been taken away. Sheryl was shaken. She couldn't imagine how he felt.

Carl approached her and took her by the shoulders. He looked straight into her eyes. "Don't trust them, Sheryl, especially Todd, Hank Turner, and Anthony Russo."

She inhaled sharply as she recognized the names of the new board members, whom she had never met.

"I know you are a naturally trusting person and that you like to believe the best about people," Caryl continued gravely. "That's a good quality but not this time. That's all I can say. I've probably said too much already, and you can never, *never* repeat what I said. I just want to help you in this last way that I can." He pointed to the door. "You need to go. Try to make sure that no one sees you leave my office, and don't let them know I'm here if you are seen." He shuddered. "I can't bear to talk to anyone else. I'll call you when I . . . well, when I can."

Sheryl didn't leave yet. Instead, she reached out and pulled Carl into a hug. No, it wasn't politically correct, but hell, he'd been her boss for a long time. Giving him a hug was the least she could do. "Thank you," she whispered as she kept her tight hold. "Thank you for everything you have done for me, for all of us. You've been terrific. Please be in touch. I'll reach out in a bit if I haven't heard from you . . ."

She felt Carl nod and then she turned quickly to the door and peered out carefully before she slipped out. In relief, she noticed that Harriet was still away from her desk and the aisle was empty. She walked quickly to her own office and closed the door. Sinking into her chair, she felt tears threaten, but somehow, they didn't spill.

God, I'm so tired of crying.

But she found she was too shocked to cry now. Her emotions were a mass of confusion: anger, sadness, confusion, frustration, and more, all following each other in quick succession. She would miss Carl. She didn't know what her whole world would be looking like now. She felt it spinning out of control.

Then another thought struck her. In light of the situation with Carl, should she still be considering her department meeting? *Am I asking for even more trouble?*

Chapter Twelve

"I'm not going to make it home tonight," Dave had said in a conversational tone, when he called Sheryl early Friday afternoon. It was a conversation Sheryl had replayed in her mind several times in the last few days.

"You're – what?" Sheryl had blinked, struggling to switch gears after her conversation with Carl. "It's Friday. Aren't you already supposed to be on the plane? Did you miss your flight?"

"Um." There had been a short silence. "Um. No, I didn't miss my flight. I decided to stay over so that I could play golf today."

"Golf? You don't even have your clubs with you."

"I got invited to play at Pebble Beach this afternoon," Dave had said, his voice full of excitement. "Isn't that cool? I've never played there before."

Sheryl had cringed. She had never been interested in golf, but Dave had recently become obsessed with the sport. "Yeah, I know Pebble Beach is a big deal," she had agreed reluctantly, picturing the beautiful vistas she had seen in television coverage of pro golf events.

"So, we have a tee time in just a few minutes," Dave had hurried on. "I've gotta run. I'll text you when I know what return flight I'll take tomorrow."

Except that return flight hadn't happened. The Friday afternoon tee time had turned into another one on Saturday, and then an important client meeting on Monday morning in San Jose had made the trip home impractical. At least that's what Dave had told her. Not that Sheryl doubted him. In the twenty-nine years she'd known Dave, he'd never lied to her.

Or not that I know of.

To make it worse, she hadn't even had a chance to really talk with him, to tell him about Carl, or what she had finally decided to do about the grief ceremony.

Sheryl instead spent the weekend doing more research on the topic, which had only strengthened her conviction. She was especially fascinated by the work of Nicholas Janni who had written a book called *Leader as Healer*. Sheryl had not had time to read the book, but she had read a few articles that the man had written. He embraced the exact same concept as the article Cindy had sent. Something about his words resonated with how she had been feeling, and the knowledge had given Sheryl an even stronger sense of purpose and confidence in her idea.

To her delight, Cindy had even started coming around to her way of thinking when they talked Sunday afternoon. "That's pretty interesting, Sheryl," Cindy had told her with a chuckle. "I guess you're not as crazy as I thought."

Now, about ten minutes after ten on Monday morning, Sheryl was standing in front of the six stunned faces of her direct reports, clinging tenaciously to that confidence. She had just announced her intention of holding the grief ceremony to them, and she could see that they were struggling to take it in.

Finally, Norah raised her hand.

"Norah, we're not in school. You have a question?" Sheryl tried to lighten the atmosphere with her grin.

"Can you please repeat what you said? I'm a little confused?" Norah's voice rose more at the end of the sentence than needed for a simple question.

"Sure," Sheryl replied, keeping her tone even and calm. "I'm going to hold a meeting tomorrow to honor those people who were let go in the layoffs fourteen days ago. I realize it's a bit delayed, but think of it as kind of a memorial service. After talking with all of you, it has felt to me that we all, collectively, deserve-maybe even need-to have space to honor those people, grieve, and let go."

"Hmmm . . . Yeah, grieve?" Norah shifted uncomfortably in her chair, doubt clouding her pretty face. "Isn't grieving for when people die? I mean, nobody *died*."

Sheryl smiled gently and looked around the table. They sat in the same sterile conference room where they usually met, the one closest to Sheryl's office. The curtains on the long row of windows were open, revealing a gray winter sky and treetops swaying in the brisk wind.

From their faces, she gathered that Norah was articulating many of their thoughts. "Yes, we do associate grieving with death in our society, but in reality, we grieve for *any* loss–whether we fully recognize or acknowledge it or not," she explained. "Grief is not for death only. We lose things, people, parts of our lives in many ways. Some are more impactful than others, but all involve a grieving process. Unfortunately, we've lost the art of acknowledging and ritualizing those losses, and I think we all suffer because of it."

"Um, Sheryl," Jose's rich slightly accented voice filled the room. "You sound more like a shrink than a manager. What makes you qualified to diagnose our feelings?"

Sheryl took a deep breath. "I'm not a psychologist, Jose. You're correct, but it doesn't take a psychologist to recognize feelings of loss and grief in others. Any manager, any good manager, needs to be aware of the feelings of his or her team. You know that. I've watched you embody that many times."

Jose nodded cautiously.

"In fact, you're actually a good example," Sheryl went on. She paused when he looked surprised. Jose was a strong programmer and good manager. He also was very intuitive, but she noticed he often hid his sensitivity beneath a veneer of machismo. Expressing feelings other than anger was not his normal style, although under Sheryl's tutelage he was learning to bend a bit.

"I am?" he asked, his deep voice thick with skepticism.

"Yes, you are. Think back to how you responded on the day of the layoffs. How did you feel? What did you say?"

Jose hesitated. "I was angry," he admitted, his shoulders rising in a guilty little shrug. "I think I kind of yelled at you."

Sheryl smiled warmly. "Yes, you were angry. There's nothing wrong with being angry, but it's also one of the stages of grief."

"Yeah, I've heard that," Jose mumbled, shifting his gaze toward the table.

"What are you feeling now?" Sheryl asked gently, trying not to embarrass him. She noticed a few sidelong glances of support from his colleagues.

"Now? I'm still pissed off," he shot back defiantly, his eyes darting around the room in disgust. "I'm still trying to figure out how to get everything done, and my team isn't working up to their potential. I'm frustrated, but I don't want to push them. They're upset enough."

Suddenly, he looked up, understanding dawning on his face.

"Thank you, Jose," Sheryl said, acknowledging that realization by meeting his stunned eyes before shifting her focus to Yvette. "What about you, Yvette? You didn't say much at the first meeting, but you looked disgusted and frustrated. Is that what you felt?"

Yvette's fair skin flushed. "Well, I was disgusted and upset. I guess angry, but also sad. It just seemed unfair. I mean, I know the layoffs had to happen, but how it happened . . . well, I didn't like it." She paused, looking around the room, and her face crumpled for a moment as she admitted, "And, I miss them, you know, the people who aren't here." She tilted her chin up as if challenging anyone to contradict or criticize her. And Sheryl understood; clearly, it wasn't normal for her to express such honest feelings in the workplace.

"Yvette, I think we all miss them. Honestly, that's kind of the point," Sheryl confirmed gently.

"Oh, yeah," Yvette said thoughtfully. "I think I get what you're saying now. I guess it does make sense that we're grieving."

"But I've never heard of anyone talking about grief at work . . . or at least not that kind of grief," Norah interjected. "Are we, um, *allowed* to do that?"

Sheryl could see that question on all their faces.

"Norah, I really don't know if we're 'allowed' to do that," Sheryl responded, using air quotes with her fingers. "But I'm not going to ask permission. I know it's not something that's normally done, but it really should be. As a leader, I feel that I have the right, no, I have an obligation to try to help you as my colleagues acknowledge feelings and honor the people they miss. It seems silly to ignore that, even though that's what we usually do in corporate culture. In my opinion, we're seeing the high price in our teams being paid by simply ignoring and expecting everyone to get back to a high level of productivity."

Sheryl saw more heads nodded, including Jose's, and took a hopeful breath. Since each of them had been struggling to meet deadlines with their teams, her words were hitting home. "Look, I don't want to make people cry or upset them further," she continued firmly, "but I do feel we can provide a little closure and emotional release. These are people whom we all worked side by side with every day, and now they're gone . . . a *bunch* of them are gone. Losing one or two people is hard enough. The fact is, we're usually happy for people when they move on, when they are leaving of their own free will. We say good-bye; we celebrate them. We didn't get a chance to do any of that with this group of people, who were abruptly dismissed through no fault of their own."

"Mostly," Patrick said, making a goofy face as he acknowledged that a few people had been on thin ice with their employment prior to the layoffs.

Everyone chuckled as the smiles broadened. A few nodded ruefully, but most kept their eyes locked on Sheryl.

"So, any more questions?" Sheryl looked around the room, sensing a growing excitement amongst the group. She felt a shiver go through her, the good kind.

"I'm in," said Yvette, already sitting straighter in her chair.

"Me too!" came from Patrick.

"I'm in," Norah said softly, but she had a big smile on her face.

Sheryl felt her heart swell as the others nodded in agreement. *Wow, this is really happening. They* want *to do this!* Any lingering doubts about her actions vanished in the enthusiastic responses of these, her trusted leadership team. She felt her body thrumming with energy.

"So . . ." Yvette leaned forward, her eyes gleaming, "you want us each to write a paragraph about the things we 'honor' about the people who left?" Her hands were raised in air quotes, her dark hair swinging with the motion.

"Yes, please," Sheryl replied, grinning widely now. "Just a few lines. It doesn't have to be long or dramatic. Just a way to give everyone a sense of who they are, even if they didn't work closely with them. Got it?"

"Before we leave today?" Jose grumbled. "I don't write that well, man."

"You're not writing a masterpiece," Sheryl chided, her lips turning up. "I can clean it up. Just give me the essentials. It can even be bullet points."

Jose looked skeptical again but nodded as did the others. Sheryl could see Patrick and Norah already writing notes. She smiled happily. *So far, this has gone much better than I thought.*

"Okay?" she asked.

"Okay," they answered in unison. Somehow, they all stood up together, and Sheryl noticed some genuine smiles for the first time since the layoffs. *Wow, it looks like even discussing the idea is already helping.* Sheryl was now even more excited about the bigger meeting tomorrow. *Maybe I really am doing a good thing.*

Sheryl ended up leaving the office later than she intended that evening. She had been so energized by her staff meeting that she spent some extra time preparing for what she had simply called a "Mandatory Team Meeting" with the full department. She hadn't wanted to give anyone an opportunity to object before it even got started.

As promised, her managers had quickly sent her material about each of the laid-off employees. She added a few insights of her own and polished up the comments about the two managers who had been laid off. She reviewed and updated her opening comments again, adapting based on the response from her management team. It was nearly six before she felt she was ready.

Walking out, she passed by the closed door of Carl's office, and her stomach clenched. She knew Carl had not been in the office that day, underscoring the tragic conversation they had had on Friday. *I wonder why no announcement has been made.* She frowned. *Is it possible that they've changed their minds?* But she shook the thought away, certain that Carl would have called her if plans had changed.

She paused, considering going back to her office and calling Janine. *I haven't heard from her either.* Sighing, Sheryl continued toward the main staircase and the parking lot, saying a silent prayer for Carl . . . and herself.

Sitting in heavier than normal traffic, Sheryl wondered again who would take Carl's place. None of her peers seemed ready for the job to her. *Todd will probably bring another colleague in from the outside, someone he knows and trusts–and one perhaps that he can more easily manipulate.* Sheryl shuddered. *God, I hope not, but that might be another reason why no announcement has been made yet.*

By the time she took the highway exit for home, it was after seven. Sheryl had called ahead to order Thai food from her car and stopped to pick it up. She and Dave were lucky to have a good variety of local restaurants, and the Thai restaurant was good and fast. Tonight she felt good she had chosen a relatively healthy option. At least it had vegetables. The aroma tantalized her senses on the last leg home, and she laughed as her stomach growled, exposing her hunger. Looking forward to the meal with a glass of wine and the television for company, Sheryl had gotten so used to being alone on weeknights to the point she'd even come to value the time to unwind and settle her mind.

But after being alone all weekend already, this evening felt different, lonelier. The Thai food didn't taste as good as normal, and the house seemed much quieter and darker in its shadows. Sitting on the plush leather sofa, she pushed her food around her plate, forcing herself to take a bite or two. Then she flipped through channels on the TV; nothing appealed, and she eventually shut it off in disgust.

No matter what she did all evening, it was hard to turn her thoughts off. Sheryl was alternately excited about her meeting with her team, upset about Carl, and unnerved by the silence from Todd and Janine.

And then there was Dave. He had always been so good about keeping their Friday night dates, despite his increasing travel schedule. She realized he was traveling more than ever, and the trips lasted more and more into Friday. Before, he had typically been gone mostly from Tuesday to Thursday. And now, he hadn't come home all weekend.

She was happy that he had been able to do something special from his bucket list, but that just didn't sit right with her tonight.

Sheryl poured a rare second glass of wine. *I need to calm down,* she chastised herself. *I must be getting paranoid because of all the craziness at work. Dave is just busy, and after close to twenty-five years of marriage, it's only one weekend that weather wasn't the reason for his absence.*

Deciding that she was overreacting, she pulled her yoga mat out of the hall closet and spread it on the carpet in front of the smart TV. Sheryl found a relaxing stretch routine on Yoga Download and let the gentle flow of movement and long, slow breaths pull her into a more centered place. When she was finished, she felt more connected to her higher self again.

It wasn't until she was drifting off to sleep that night that she realized that Dave had never called or even sent a text! Her eyes flew open, and she grabbed her phone.

But there was no answer to her call and no response to her good-night text. It took a long time for her to fall into a restless sleep. With no news about a return flight after his San Jose meeting that day, Sheryl had no idea when her husband was actually coming home.

Chapter Thirteen

Tuesday, September 28

Lauren practically ran Sheryl down as she entered her office at five after eight. The normally rigid, younger woman was flushed and out of breath, clearly upset. Her straight blonde hair was in an unusual disarray.

"What happened? What do you know? Did you see the email?" She fired questions at Sheryl one after the other in a rush, barely pausing between them.

"Whoa, slow down," Sheryl answered, confused. "What email are you talking about?"

"Carl," Lauren breathed. "It says . . . well, it says that he's leaving. Retiring. Friday was his last day! Did you know this?"

Sheryl's eyes widened, and she tensed under her colleague's intense stare. She quickly pulled out her laptop. *No email about Carl was in my inbox when I left home.* She knew. She had been distractedly checking her email, voicemail, and texts, looking for some kind of communication from Dave. There had been none.

"What? I didn't know about the email," Sheryl ground out, wrenching her thoughts away from her missing husband. "What else does it say?"

A male voice answered. "It said he was retiring and thanked him for his service. It said that he didn't want any fanfare, so he decided to leave before the announcement was made. Only that doesn't make any sense," Rick Sutton recounted hotly, pushing into the office and practically slamming the door behind him. "And everybody got it–not just us!"

Lauren's draw dropped and her face crumpled. "*Everyone* got it? Oh crap, I didn't look. I thought, well, I thought it was just his direct reports."

"So, now what? What happens to us?" Rick asked the obvious question, gesturing to himself and Lauren. Carl had been their boss too. "Who do we report to now?"

Sheryl shook her head. "I don't know," Sheryl responded honestly. "Don't you know, Rick?"

Rick raised his hands. "No, I don't know," he said, shooting Sheryl a suspicious look. "But I thought I saw you near Carl's office Friday afternoon, Sheryl. Did you see him? Did he say anything to you?"

Sheryl grimaced. She didn't want to lie, but she had to respect Carl's confidence. "He didn't say much more than what is apparently in that email," she said ruefully. "He didn't want to talk."

"Was he upset?" Lauren prompted her.

Sheryl rolled her eyes. "What do you think?"

Lauren frowned, sinking down in one of the chairs in front of Sheryl's. "Of course, he was. He never talked about retiring before."

Rick took a couple of steps further into the office and sat next to Lauren. He ran a hand across his balding scalp, and Sheryl saw that his striped shirt looked more rumpled than usual as he added, "What the hell?"

Sheryl didn't reply. Logging into her laptop, she opened her email and clicked on the message. It was, indeed, very short and didn't say a thing about what would happen next, only that more organizational announcements would be forthcoming. Her heart dropped, hoping those would all be positive, but she certainly wasn't sure of that. Todd had signed the email, but from the language used, it seemed to Sheryl that it was Janine's writing. *No surprise there, but good grief, why hasn't she called?* Worse still, it was apparent that not one of Carl's direct reports had been notified in advance of this email.

What does that mean? This is just one more major shift in company practices. And Lauren is right, we should have been told first. Period.

The door cracked open, catching her attention. She saw Patrick poke his head into her office, but he retreated quickly when he saw her colleagues there. Sheryl's jaw tightened. *Is Patrick here about the grief meeting? Oh boy,* she thought, running her fingers through her hair, *that just got a lot more complicated.* The department assistant Tina had scheduled her meeting for 10:00 a.m. that morning. *It's going to be a real doozy now, especially when I don't have answers to anyone's questions, including my own.*

The desk phone rang loudly, startling all of them. The caller ID said it was Janine. Sheryl picked it up. "What the heck?" she asked, not bothering with a greeting.

"Good morning," Janine replied cheerfully.

Sheryl flinched at her tone.

"You need to be in Todd's office at 9:30 a.m. We'll talk then."

"But I have a full department meeting scheduled for ten," Sheryl protested. "I can't be there."

"You need to postpone your meeting, Sheryl," Janine advised firmly. "Todd and I have to see you at 9:30 a.m. It's not optional."

Sheryl's eyes widened. Seeing Lauren and Rick's riveted interest, Sheryl asked cautiously, "Just me?"

"Yeah, just you. The others will have their own time slots. I'm calling them in next." Janine paused. "Um, Sheryl, who is with you right now?"

"Lauren and Rick."

Sheryl heard a muffled groan. "Tell them to go back to their desks. I'll be in touch with them shortly," Janine said, her tone suddenly crisp.

"That's really all you're going to say?" Sheryl asked.

"Yup. See you at 9:30 a.m." Janine hung up.

Sheryl looked at the now silent receiver in her hand, then at Lauren and Rick.

"Janine's calling you next," she told them. "It sounds like you better get back to your desks."

They looked at her curiously, then they both shrugged and left. Sheryl wasn't sure what they had overheard, but she could tell that they were puzzled about why she had been called first. Sheryl looked quizzically at the phone on her desk. *Hell, so am I!*

Sheryl picked up her receiver and punched in the extension for Tina. "Hey, I'm sorry to do this, but can you push the department meeting to this afternoon? Maybe 2:30 p.m. or 3:00 p.m.?"

"Sure," Tina said. "I assume this has something to do with the announcement about Carl?"

Sheryl swallowed dryly. Apparently everyone really did know. "Yes," she said. "It does. Please tell everyone I'm sorry."

"Okay, but I think they'll know it's not your fault."

"Thanks, Tina, I appreciate that."

"On it . . . and good luck." Tina was always upbeat. Sheryl smiled as she pictured her assistant's bright smile and shining blue eyes. Tina was a blessing for whom Sheryl was very grateful this morning.

After hanging up, Sheryl rose and closed the door. She didn't want any other visitors asking questions before she met with Todd and Janine. She looked quickly at the time. *What am I going to do for forty-five minutes?* She suddenly felt lost and ungrounded. *Is there something I need to do to prepare?*

Taking a deep breath, she knew that one thing she needed to do was calm down. Again. The little peace that she had barely managed to achieve during her morning commute had eroded with all the commotion. She had managed to put her concern about Carl somewhat out of her mind too, but now it was front and center. *And what about me? Are they calling me in to fire me too?* After all, she was the one whose team hadn't delivered on the Portal Project.

Sheryl pulled her long sweater more closely around her, feeling chilled. She had intentionally worn a long-sleeve dress along with the tan knit topper today, so she would appear less formal and more approachable during the department gathering. Sheryl shivered again as Dave's ominous words about her career echoed loudly in her head. Her stomach now in knots, she tried to look at her email but couldn't stem her rising panic. *I know I said I was okay losing my job, but wow, when I'm really faced with it . . .*

She forced herself to take a long, deep breath. *No, I'm not going to let this get to me.* She quickly put her desk and cell phones on 'Do Not Disturb' and spun her chair around so that her back was to the door. She closed her eyes and deliberately regulated her breathing into a slow, even rhythm. She brought the words and music of Jordan Smith's "Stand in the Light" to the forefront of her mind, imagining herself enveloped in white light, allowing herself to be soothed and then strengthened and finally invigorated. She let the image still her worries and thoughts about what could happen next.

At 9:25 a.m., Sheryl picked up her file on the Portal Project as well as her meeting notebook and headed toward Todd's office. The floor was abuzz, in sharp contrast to the quiet of last week. She guessed that everyone was talking about Carl and his so-called retirement.

Todd's office, the largest in the building, was on the top floor of the four-story building and overlooked the grassy area between the various buildings in the complex. It wasn't much of a view but was certainly an upgrade to the parking lot.

There was an area for Todd's administrative assistant outside the black double doors that led into his office, and the boardroom was just down the hall. Sheryl remembered, with a twist in her stomach, that Jim Leader's office was in the same area, with the sales and support teams who reported to Jim in the wing off to the north. Picturing Jim's craggy face, which had been so sneering during their last encounter, Sheryl said a quick prayer that Jim would not be part of *this* meeting.

Janine, already in the reception area, greeted her warmly. Sheryl gave the older woman a halfhearted smile in return.

"Don't be nervous," Janine reassured her. "You're not in trouble."

Sheryl pursed her lips. "I didn't think I was in trouble," she said, "but I don't know what to expect after Carl . . ." Her voice trailed off.

"After Carl retired unexpectedly?" Janine finished her sentence, her petite frame tightening as if expecting a blow.

"Yeah, it was very unexpected." Sheryl couldn't keep the sarcasm out of her voice.

Janine didn't respond.

"I guess you're not going to fill me in," Sheryl pushed.

Looking away, Janine nodded to Todd's assistant who waved them through the closed doors. "Let's go in," she said, opening the doors and moving confidently into the office.

Trailing behind, Sheryl looked around at the simple yet very elegant décor in the large room as she followed Janine toward the long conference table stretched along the inner wall. While much of the building was quite modern in design, Todd had gone with a more traditional look, choosing dark wood furniture and more conventional artwork. The man himself sat behind a large desk with simple lines; a matching credenza stretched behind his chair under a wide picture window. Even with that, Todd was the gravitational pull in the room, and he knew it.

Her big boss, buttoning his black suit jacket, stood up and interrupted their progress, gesturing toward a grouping of four large, comfortable chairs upholstered in burgundy leather with a round, glass coffee table in the middle. "Good morning, ladies. Why don't we sit where we'll be more comfortable?" he said more than asked.

Sheryl blinked in surprise and veered left to join Todd there. *I wish I had worn a suit today,* she thought, taking in Todd and Janine's very formal attire.

"Todd," Janine greeted her boss calmly and took a seat to his right.

"Hello, Todd," Sheryl said with what she hoped was a pleasant smile. For a nanosecond she debated sitting next to Todd or opposite him, quickly deciding to sit across. *It will be easier to watch his face and body language with a direct view.*

But before she could sit down, Todd stepped toward her and shook her hand, a warm smile on his face. Sheryl couldn't suppress a tiny huff of surprise. Tugging at the knot of his bright blue tie, he gestured her into the seat next to him. She followed his lead but sat stiffly on the edge of the soft chair rather than leaning back as he did. She kept her back straight and feet planted on the floor, not ready to let down her guard. *Why is Todd being so friendly?* His behavior was not at all what she had been expecting.

Once they were all seated, Todd nodded to Janine, who in turn looked at Sheryl.

"I'm sure you have a lot of questions and concerns about Carl," Janine began, pushing her square, wire-rim glasses up further on her nose. "And I'm equally sure that you know we aren't going to comment. All we can say is that Todd and Carl came to an agreement."

Sheryl nodded. She wanted to say more, but the look in Janine's eyes cut her off. It was definitely a keep-your-mouth-shut look. Trusting her erstwhile friend's guidance, at least for the moment, Sheryl remained silent.

"What we *do* want to talk to you about is what happens next," Janine continued. "Carl has been here a long time, and it won't be easy to fill his shoes. The board, Todd, and I have debated the best way to proceed."

Sheryl raised her eyebrows at that. The fact that that board had already been consulted was very surprising. *Carl's retirement must have been in the works for longer than it appeared.*

"We seriously considered bringing someone in from the outside, although you know that is not the company's preference most of the time," Janine continued. "We finally decided that it would be the least disruptive and most efficient to promote from within. Carl generally did a very good job, and we didn't feel that a *major* change in direction was needed for IT at this time. Obviously, we expect some change, particularly with project management and deadlines for key projects, but nothing that an internal candidate couldn't handle."

Janine paused as if to gauge the younger woman's reaction. Sheryl was also aware of Todd's intense scrutiny. She forced herself to remain still as she ticked off the candidates from which Janine and Todd and the board then would have selected. *Rick. It will probably be Rick.*

"I agree that the department is running pretty smoothly," Sheryl said cautiously. "Although I know that the deadlines around the Portal Project have been, well, problematic."

To her surprise, Janine smiled and sat back in her chair. Todd leaned forward and picked up the conversation, his blue eyes sharp and focused.

"Sheryl, we asked to see you first because we'd like you to consider taking the position," he said.

Sheryl sat up straighter and drew in a quick breath. *What?*

"Your track record has been good, the Portal Project notwithstanding," Todd went on confidently. "You've shown good leadership, and Carl has clearly relied heavily on you. You have an astounding grasp of IT, given your background. In fact, it was Carl who recommended you for the job."

Blinking rapidly, Sheryl stared between Todd and Janine to see if they were serious. *They are!* Her breath left her in a whoosh.

Wow, I wanted this job eventually, but . . . God, not with Carl leaving like this. She forced her back to stay straight, but inwardly she slumped. *I'm not ready. I need more time with Carl. Yes, I have a good track record, but I've worked almost exclusively on the software side of things.*

Sheryl was well aware that hardware, networking, and security were not her strong suits, although she had a more than decent working knowledge of them. *I need more time to get up to speed on those things.*

Feeling their gazes, Sheryl became aware that Todd and Janine were still watching her closely. Todd had a knowing look, full of amusement even, on his face as if he sensed her thoughts. Janine simply smiled encouragingly.

"I'm surprised," Sheryl finally managed to say. "I thought . . . well, I thought I'd have more time to learn the security aspect. Carl had mentioned . . ."

"Oh, you can learn the security aspect. Carl was quite confident of that," Todd assured her, clearly anticipating that objection.

Sheryl stirred slightly in her chair at a realization. *Carl went to bat for me.*

"Yes, Sheryl," Janine chimed in. "I'm sure Rick will help you get up to speed, and we'll support you in getting additional training if you find that necessary. While it would have been nice if you had had more time with Carl before he left–" She broke off as Todd gave her a dark look, "you've had the experience and demonstrated leadership that Rick and others in the department haven't," Janine continued. She beamed. "You've always picked things up quickly, and we have no doubt that you will do the same now."

Sheryl's knuckles whitened as she clutched her unopened notebook. "Okay . . . I guess you want an answer now?" she demurred.

"Yes, that would be ideal," Todd said smoothly. "The less time with uncertainty in the leadership role the better. I'm sure you understand."

Sheryl's mind whirled. *I'm not ready to make this decision now!* But she could feel Todd's unspoken pressure to say 'yes' right then and there. She brushed her bangs back, suddenly realizing that she should be demonstrating her confidence in herself. *A man in my position wouldn't be hesitating, would he?*

"I, um, I," she sputtered, in spite of herself.

"I know this is sudden for you," Janine interrupted gently, a look of understanding in her gray eyes. "But like Todd said, it's important to give everyone the confidence that the role has been filled by someone they know and are comfortable with. You know that people are a little on edge with all the recent changes."

Sheryl's spine stiffened even further as she gave Janine a sardonic look. "Really?" she murmured under her breath. Fortunately, Todd didn't seem to notice.

"Yes, Sheryl," Todd barged right in. "Can we count on you to step up? Of course, there will be a salary increase along with other benefits. Janine can go over all of those details with you. And, you realize that this role comes with a board seat." He paused dramatically. "You will be the first woman on The Diamante board—ever. Think how exciting that is!" He finished with a flourish of his hand. He looked at Sheryl expectantly. Clearly, he thought this promotion was a no-brainer.

Sheryl couldn't help the thrill of excitement that coursed through her. *A board seat!* Feeling both trapped and excited, Sheryl nodded slowly. "If that's what you need . . . Of course, I'll do it," she said, her voice gaining strength with each word. "I'm honored that you've chosen me, Todd, Janine." She nodded at both. "It's a big responsibility, but I'll certainly do my best."

Todd's shoulders relaxed almost imperceptibly. "Excellent," he said, standing up. "We appreciate you stepping in with so little notice, but I'm confident that you'll be great in the role."

He held out his hand to shake hers again. She stood up and took it firmly.

"Thank you, Todd." She was pleased that her voice didn't shake because her insides certainly were.

"Great, great." Todd's tone now held a hint of smugness. "Janine will fill you in on the details. We'll want to make an announcement later today. Janine will go over that with you too. I'll give you a little time to get settled, and we'll meet tomorrow. My admin will set up the meeting time." Todd nodded to Janine, then turned, and strode assertively to his desk. Clearly, they had been dismissed.

Janine took Sheryl's elbow and guided her out of the office. "Come on," she said. "We'll finish up in my office. You did reschedule your morning meeting, didn't you?"

My meeting! Sheryl thought with dismay. *Oh no, how is* this *news going to make everyone feel?*

Chapter Fourteen

"This is so great!" Janine enthused, as the two women settled in her office. It was clear that her associate could barely contain her excitement. "The first woman on the board, on the executive committee! Sheryl, this really is historic! And you are going to be so good. No one deserves it more. It will be wonderful to finally have a female voice there. I know we haven't been seeing eye-to-eye recently, but I *am* really happy that it's you. You are perfect to handle all of the guys after all your years in IT."

Sheryl's adrenaline was still through the roof, but she sighed. "Janine, I know, but it's hard to get excited since this is coming at the expense of Carl. In my opinion, he didn't deserve to be pushed out." She shot a pointed look at Janine across the little conference table in the older woman's office. *Stop with the crap, my friend.*

Janine had the grace to look a little guilty. "Look, he *retired*. He talked about it with Todd." Clearly, Janine was going to stick with the party line.

"Really? That's all you can say? Come on, Janine, it's *me*." Sheryl was becoming more than a little frustrated. She realized this had been building up since Friday.

"I know it's you, but there's really not much to say. Honestly, I was told after they talked," Janine said simply. She paused and cocked her head. "Sheryl . . . aren't you at least a little excited?"

"You've obviously had more time to think about this than I have," Sheryl replied, laying her open palms on the table. "My head is still spinning. Todd didn't even give me twenty-four hours to think about it."

"What's there to think about?" Janine asked, looking genuinely surprised. "I thought this is what you've always wanted! First of all, your annual reviews clearly indicate a willingness to expand your leadership role *and* the performance to back it up. You've consistently met or exceeded your objectives with very few exceptions for years. Plus, isn't this *exactly* the dream we've talked about during all the empowerment lunches we've organized for women in STEM *and* at The Diamante? Frankly, I'm puzzled by your hesitation."

"I don't know. It just seems so sudden, and I feel so unprepared," Sheryl hesitated, her mind locking in on one of her fears. "I haven't had time to process it. And oh gosh, Janine, the hours! I don't want to put in the hours that Carl did. In fact, I'm not going to."

Janine laughed lightly. "Good for you! Carl was a workaholic. No one would ever work the kind of hours that he did. I don't think Todd expects that of you," she assured her. "Obviously you *will* have to put in more hours, at least until you're up to speed."

"And how long will that take?" Sheryl asked with a trace of bitterness.

Janine looked surprised. "You really don't want this?" she asked.

Sheryl paused for a moment, tucking her hair behind her ear. "It's not that. I do want it. I've thought about it for a long time. It will be nice to have a bigger voice, and you're right; it's what I've been working toward. Janine, it's the circumstances surrounding it. I wasn't prepared." She pressed her friend's arm lightly. "I'll be okay. I just need some time."

Janine nodded. "I know the circumstances are tough," she acknowledged, "and I am sorry about that. But you shine when working through obstacles. You always have. Trust me when I tell you, you will be great." The last was said with a big smile on her face.

Sheryl smiled back, though she knew it didn't make it to her eyes.

"Okay, here's a letter with your compensation and all the details." Janine's tone became very business-like. "You will need to review and sign it for your official acceptance. There's also a contract with your new role and a contract for your board service. You'll want to review and sign those. You can have a lawyer look at them, and Dave, of course, but otherwise they are confidential." She handed Sheryl a thick envelope.

"When do you need these?" Sheryl asked, feeling the weight of the envelope in her hands. *This is a lot of paper.*

"I need the letter as soon as possible. Now, really, the contracts can wait until the end of the week." She eyed Sheryl's hands gripping the envelope, her knuckles showing stark white against the manilla color. "There are duplicates in there. Don't panic at how thick it is."

"But what if I don't like the contracts? Doesn't this letter commit me to them?"

Janine made a face. "I guess it kind of does, technically. But everyone's signed the contracts. There's nothing unusual in them, promise."

"Janine, I'm sorry. I made a verbal commitment to you and Todd, but I want some time to review all of this." She waved the envelope. "It's only reasonable."

"Okay, you're right. I know Todd wanted to make the announcement today."

"Today? Can't it wait till tomorrow at least?"

"I guess, but I need to talk to Rick and Lauren and . . ."

"I know, I know," Sheryl interrupted her. "At least give me an *hour* to read them?"

"Sure, take two!" Janine laughed. "I'll stall everything for a bit."

"Thank you," Sheryl replied seriously. "This isn't a bit funny to me."

Janine seemed to finally appreciate just how upset Sheryl was. She regarded her with a sympathetic look. "I'm sorry, Sheryl, I shouldn't have joked. I know this is very serious and very important. I know you would be more excited under very different circumstances–and not feeling so rushed. Please, go take a couple of hours to review everything. We can touch base at one o'clock? Will that work?"

Sheryl dropped her head for a moment, then looked up. "Sure, I'll come back at one. I'll let you know if I have any questions in the meantime, okay? I wish this didn't have to be so rushed."

"Yes, please. Call if you have any questions. I'm sorry it's so rushed. It's just that . . ." Janine's voice trailed off.

Sheryl stood up, picking up her notebook, folder, and the envelope. "Yes, it's just that . . ." She echoed Janine.

Janine stood and came around the table. She surprised Sheryl by pulling her into a hug. "It's okay, my friend. It will all be okay," she whispered. When she pulled back, Sheryl was surprised to see a glint of tears in her eyes. *Maybe Janine is more affected by all of this than I suspected.*

That thought was comforting. *Although I wonder what she'll think when she finds out about my meeting. If she finds out.*

"Thanks," Sheryl whispered back. "I'll see you at one."

Pushing back the sting of tears in her own eyes, she turned and left the office. Keeping her head down to avoid interacting with anyone in the halls, she quickly made her way back to her office, where she shut the door behind her.

Sheryl placed the thick envelope on the desk and sat back in her chair, her emotions in turmoil. She felt her stomach clench as she thought of Carl and all he had been through. She longed to call him and ask for his advice. *I've depended on him for career guidance a lot during my fifteen years here, but, geez, it just feels like it would be rubbing salt in the wound.*

She considered calling Dave, but she already knew what his reaction would be. He would be all in with excitement and glee, but she was not at all sure that he would be as sympathetic about Carl. *And I still haven't heard from him.* She picked up her personal phone, suddenly anxious to see if her husband had called. She sighed, disappointed that there was no call, only a simple text that he was heading out to meetings for the day. She rubbed her temple, which suddenly pulsed with pain.

Scrolling through her notifications, she saw that there was one missed call. She frowned. It was from Carl. *Hmmm. Why did he call? Maybe it's okay to talk to him?* He hadn't left a message, but the call had come in a mere fifteen minutes ago.

She glanced at the plump, still unopened envelope. *Who else can I talk to? This is all still confidential.* She pressed the call button. Carl picked up right away. "Sheryl, did they talk to you yet?" he asked without preamble.

"Yes." Sheryl released a little puff of surprise. "I guess Todd wasn't lying when he said you had recommended me."

"Of course, I did. I know you will do a great job. Did you accept?" Carl's voice had an underlying urgency that seemed out of place to her.

"Todd didn't give me much choice," she answered wryly. "Or really *any* choice."

"You're going to have to learn to stand up to him if you're going to survive," Carl advised emphatically. "And quickly. He'll eat you alive if you don't. They all will."

"Like they did you?" she asked, her tone gentle.

"Yes, like they did me recently," Carl said with a long sigh. "Like they did me." His voice grew stronger and a little harsh. "But you can't let them, *any of them*, including the board members. I didn't let them for a long time, although the older members weren't nearly as tough as Hank and Anthony."

"By older members, you mean Gary and Duncan? I can't remember their last names." Sheryl had met the two men a few times in the last five years, when they had come in to meet with Carl about projects she was involved in. "They always seemed pleasant enough to me."

"Yes, yes. Gary and Duncan are pleasant enough," Carl continued roughly. "They're not the sharks that Turner and Russo are but don't underestimate them. They're not pushovers by any means. I just got myself into a bind. I'm not that good with people, you know that. The politics . . . you'll be much better at that. You can get along with just about anyone. Plus, you're younger, more 'hip,' and a woman. You'll make Todd–and the board–look progressive, something I didn't do."

"Great," Sheryl quipped sarcastically. "Any woman will do? Just to improve the optics?"

"No, no," Carl was quick to assure her. "Not *any* woman. You are very well qualified, and you know it."

"But I don't know anything about security or much about the hardware side of things," she protested, her voice sounding whiny even in her own ears.

"You know more than you think you do, and you'll learn," Carl shot back. "Look how much you've already learned on the job. Rick will help you. He's not the kind of guy who will resent your promotion. He genuinely respects you."

Sheryl released her breath in a long swoosh. "That's good to know. I like and respect Rick too." She paused, doubt creeping in. "Carl, can I really do this?"

"Yes, you really can," Carl insisted. "I would tell you if I thought you couldn't. But you're going to have to be stronger, more emphatic, and be *brave* about saying what you truly think. It won't always be popular, but you *have to.* Giving in or agreeing to something you know is impossible will create big problems for you."

Sheryl could hear the angst in Carl's words. Despite his protestations, she felt that he was devastated by what had happened.

She straightened unconsciously. "Okay. I can do it," Sheryl said, more to herself than to her old boss. She paused again, then continued in an anguished tone. "But, Carl, do I *want* to? That's probably the bigger question. Do I really *want* to have to stand up to them, to make the kind of decisions to lay people off and have guards walk them out? Do I really *want* all this responsibility and all the aggravation that comes with it? I'm sorry, Carl, but I don't care to work 24/7 like you did."

"And you're right not to. I was a fool," her former boss responded, his voice full of conviction. "The more I think about it, the more I recognize it. Don't make the same mistakes I did. And remember, there are benefits to taking the job too. Maybe you can prevent having guards walk people out. Maybe you can influence the way things are handled. You can build relationships with Todd and Jim and the others better than I ever did. You already have an ally in Janine. You need to look at this as your chance to make a difference—a real difference. You will, you know."

Sheryl tapped her fingers lightly on the desk, considering his words. "This may sound selfish," she said cautiously. "But may I call you when I get stuck? I feel like I'm just rubbing your loss in your face."

Now it was Carl's turn to sigh. "Yes, of course. Call me. I'll be happy to help you. Really. I wouldn't have chosen to retire now, but I did, however painful it is."

"Thank you for your vote of confidence. I was feeling really torn about this, but you've helped," she responded gratefully. "On one hand, I am excited."

"Hey, you just got a great promotion. Feel excited. Enjoy it," Carl assured her. "Don't worry about me."

Sheryl imagined that she could hear Carl's gritted teeth over the phone. *He's obviously trying to make things easier for me, and I'm super grateful for that.*

"Take it and make the most of it. Not everyone gets this kind of chance," he concluded.

"Very true." Sheryl felt her breath come a little easier. "Thank you, Carl."

"No problem. Seriously, call me any time. I mean it."

"Got it. But Carl, what are *you* going to do?"

Carl made a sound that seemed almost a growl. "I don't know yet," he admitted. "I guess I might as well take some time to figure that out. Don't you worry about me. You take care of Sheryl. You'll be fine. I'll be fine."

Smiling sadly to herself, Sheryl agreed, "Okay, boss, if you say so."

That did get a small chuckle out of the older man, just before he hung up. Sheryl felt marginally lighter, despite her conviction that Carl was putting on an act. She said a quick prayer of thanks for having her former boss's support. *That will make things much easier.*

Sighing deeply, she opened the envelope and began to read, skimming the opening letter quickly. Her eyes caught and held on the number in the middle of the page. Her new salary. She gasped. *Wow! Wait till Dave hears about this!* Then she glanced at her phone, deflating a bit. *Whenever he finally decides to call.*

She glanced back at the papers, the text blurring as she tried to absorb all that the letter said. Some of her excitement ebbed. Her emotions felt like they were attached to a yo-yo. Up and down. It was overwhelming.

She let the letter drop to the desk and dropped her head in her hands. The enormity of Carl's words crashed over her again. Suddenly, that salary number didn't seem quite enough for all she was facing. *Can I really stand up to them? Especially Todd and Jim? And Hank Turner.* The thought of the powerful board member, whom she had yet to meet, made her cringe.

Her head still lowered, she forced herself to take long, deep, calmer breaths. *Guide me,* she whispered, although she wasn't exactly sure who she was asking for help. *My higher self, perhaps?* But the thought soothed her. She continued her rhythmic breathing, purposely feeling her belly fill and empty with each inhale and exhale.

After several minutes, she sat up. Shaking her head, she straightened her shoulders, suddenly resolute. *You can do this,* she exhorted herself. *You have to do this. For your teams, if nothing else.*

Sheryl glanced again at the pink sticky note on her desk. Tina had rescheduled the meeting for four. Sheryl inhaled deeply. *I guess this meeting is going to be the first big test.*

Chapter Fifteen

A few minutes before 4:00 p.m., Sheryl stood in front of the largest training room in the building, watching as a hundred-and-twenty-six of her team members filed quietly in and took their seats. Another forty-five or so were connected virtually, their faces visible on the large screens on the side walls. Sheryl's direct reports were arrayed across the front row, interspersed by some of their staff. Tina, with a smiling, encouraging face, was also up front. Most people, as was typical, headed toward the back rows.

Three hours earlier, Sheryl had signed the offer letter and handed it over to Janine. She was committed now. Yes, she'd have her attorney friend do a quick read of the contracts before signing them, but after she glanced over them, they appeared to be straightforward and in good order.

Sheryl only hoped that the news about her promotion wouldn't detract from the intent of the meeting. *The last thing I want is for this meeting to be about me.* To her chagrin, the formal announcement had been released just fifteen minutes ago, and she was sure the company was already buzzing with the news. Stunned at how fast it had all happened, she felt an added pressure for this meeting to go well. She found it ironic that in a way, this was her first official act in her new role.

Taking a few deep centering breaths, Sheryl glanced down at her notes. She had added a few points about her new position and Carl, but she had already made a quick decision to save them to the very end. Turning her gaze back to the now full room, Sheryl fought back a sudden attack of nerves, silently gathering all of her energy to her and lifting her head.

"Welcome," she began. "Thank you f–"

The room erupted with applause, with most of the people on their feet. *What? What is going on?* Seeing nothing but a sea of smiling faces, she realized they were applauding for her, for her promotion! Tears formed in her eyes as she felt a rush of appreciation and gratitude. Thankfully, they didn't fall. She swallowed hard as she fought to control her feelings. That seemed to make the applause even louder.

After a minute, maybe two, she smiled broadly and gave a slight bow of thanks, although she was still blinking back tears. *Wow, I didn't expect this.* Surveying the room, she noticed a few faces that were more polite than happy, but only a few. *That's a good sign.*

Still smiling, she held up her hand for silence and attention. The clapping slowly dwindled and stopped, followed by the rustle of the crowd settling back in their chairs.

Sheryl took a deep breath, regaining her poise. "I see that you all have heard the news," she started again, and a ripple of laughter went through the room. "Thank you for that enthusiastic and gracious response. I am blessed to work with such a terrific group of people, and I am *very* grateful for your support. I had no idea that any of this was going to happen today, so I'm especially appreciative of your vote of confidence . . . or at least that's how I'm choosing to interpret your applause." She paused, seeing most heads nodding in agreement.

Her face sobered, and her voice deepened with an unexpected sense of grief as she continued. "But that's not why we're gathered today, and I don't want this announcement to distract us from the *real* reason for this meeting." Sheryl saw some puzzled looks. She had heard from Tina that at least a dozen people had asked the department assistant for more details about the meeting, which she had not been able to provide because Sheryl hadn't even shared the planned content with her aide.

"I know that the last few weeks have been challenging for all of us," she continued. "It's been difficult to see colleagues—and friends—leave us. I know that many of you, myself included, are still unhappy that these changes had to happen. We all know that it's part of business and that there are times when companies have to make difficult decisions to ensure the health and profitability of the organization as a whole. This was clearly one of those unfortunate times, and these decisions are never easy and never pleasant."

The atmosphere had become noticeably more tense as she spoke. Suddenly a male voice interrupted her from the back, although she couldn't see who spoke. "Are you announcing more layoffs already?" There was both fear and defiance in his words.

"No, categorically no," Sheryl responded firmly. "I promise there are no other layoffs being discussed right now." *I hope that is really true,* she thought with momentary panic, realizing that she didn't know for certain. "Nor am I here to announce any other organizational changes." She made sure her voice remained strong, and she felt some of the tension ease.

"So why *are* we here?" It was a woman's voice this time, but with a bit of laughter in it.

Sheryl allowed a brief smile to cross her face, then sobered again. "We are here because I want, we want . . ." She paused and motioned toward her direct reports before her. "We want to honor and acknowledge the people who were laid off."

Sheryl could hear the exclamation "what?" echo through the room and a renewed rustle as people shifted uncomfortably in their chairs.

"I know it's a bit unconventional," she went on, her voice steady and clear. "But I think it's important for all of us to remember that we are human, that we form connections with the people we work with, and those connections have meaning and value in our lives. Yes, we are 'only' work colleagues," she said as she made air quotes with her hands. "And many of our relationships are based in a specific time and place and reason. However, we are still connected, and there is a very normal sadness and sense of loss when colleagues are no longer here. When people leave individually on their own, we often have the chance to celebrate and say good-bye, but in situations like we've just been through, we don't."

Sheryl paused, taking a moment to assess the impact of her words, letting them sink in. The room was still. When she continued, her voice was tinged with a faint, emotional rasp. "Although the people that we are saying good-bye to aren't here to participate, that doesn't mean that we don't feel a sense of loss about their leaving, along with the desire to wish them well and say good-bye. That's normal, healthy human connection. It's what we're here to do today."

Pausing again, she allowed space for anyone to speak out. She deliberately made eye contact with as many people as she could, including looking directly at the video camera.

Another male voice came from the back of the room, but this speaker stood. She saw that it was Zach, a young programmer who had been with the company for just over a year. He had started right out of college. He was tall, red-headed, and, from what she had heard, generally very amiable. His face was anything but now. "This is bullshit," he said angrily. "You should have thought about all of this before you just fired people randomly." He turned and started to stomp out of the room. There were several gasps of shock as everyone watched him head toward the door.

"Zach, please stop," Sheryl said quickly and firmly, determined not to lose control of the situation. Thankfully, Zach did stop and slowly turn back to look at her, his face defiant. "First," she continued, "*no one* was fired randomly, and I think you know that."

"Well, it sure seemed like that," he grumbled sullenly. Standing in the aisle, his posture slightly slouched now, his brown eyes darted around the room before staring back at her. He crossed his arms across his chest.

"I can see how it might have seemed that way," Sheryl validated in an even tone. She leaned forward, her hands braced on the podium. She looked directly at Zach, but she could sense everyone else watching with rapt attention. "But it wasn't. Not even close. These decisions are always hard, agonizing even, to those of us who have to make them. But the company must be successful and profitable to survive. If not, *none* of us will have jobs."

She felt rather than heard a murmur go through the room. She took a deep breath.

"You don't have to stay in the meeting, Zach." She let her gaze slide across the upturned faces. "None of you do. But I'm asking for a few more minutes of your attention before you make the decision to leave."

Zach didn't respond, but he shuffled his feet, clearly becoming uncomfortable being so exposed. She could also see a few of his peers getting restless near him. *Are they embarrassed for him or ready to defend him?*

Sheryl shifted her focus back to the room at large. "What I'd like to do this afternoon is have a time of remembering and releasing, of wishing our departed colleagues well. Not that they are dead." She heard a few gasps and a couple of disconcerted chuckles. "I want to remember and *honor* them. They will obviously not be here to hear our words, but *you* will, and they will no doubt feel our words even if they are not consciously aware of them. I want all of us to remember that these are other human beings with whom we have connections, some of them deep, and to honor our own feelings of grief."

Zach's eyebrows drew together in confusion. Sheryl could see that he wasn't the only one. However, he did nod curtly and uncross his arms, sitting down again without uttering another word.

"Thank you for staying, Zach," she said gently. "Does anyone want to leave now?"

Sheryl carefully looked at every corner of the room, including the camera. No one moved. No one disconnected. The faces she saw showed a mixture of curiosity, concern, and perhaps a little resentment, but the heavy anger in the room, triggered by Zach's outburst, had dissipated. She glanced at her direct reports. They had encouraging looks on their faces as if willing her to continue. *Thank God!* She felt herself start to relax, then a sudden surge of power and energy moved through her. Her heart opened wider, and she smiled.

"Okay then," she said, her voice lighter and more upbeat. "Let's move on. This is how we'll do this." She explained the simple format in which a person who had been laid off would be named, followed by a few words highlighting their contribution and best characteristics. She would conclude with a statement of well wishes for their future.

Then, there would be a moment of silence so that others could wordlessly add their own thoughts. Because the list was fairly long, a total of twenty-five, and it was late in the day, there would be no time for any speakers other than Sheryl and her immediate team. However, she encouraged everyone to remember their friends and colleagues in their best light.

Sheryl began with the two managers who had reported directly to her, speaking in a warm, friendly tone. "I'd like to start with Wendy Campbell. Wendy was always optimistic and upbeat, bringing a smile or chuckle to everyone she worked with. Wendy is incredibly smart and her skill with Java was unsurpassed in the company." She went on to acknowledge two projects where Wendy's contributions had made a huge difference in the usefulness of the software being developed. "I wish Wendy all the best in finding a new job where her talents will be valued and rewarded."

Asking for a brief moment of silence, Sheryl glanced around the room, focusing on the members of Wendy's team she could find. She saw tears in a few eyes, gratitude and relief in a few others. Several people had their heads bowed as if in prayer. After a minute, she repeated the process for the second manager.

One by one, her direct reports stood and spoke about each of their team members who had been let go. Sheryl had been pleased that they all had decided to speak—an option that Sheryl had offered at yesterday's meeting. Jose had even volunteered to go first, surprising Sheryl and showing great leadership despite his initial anger and resentment. She focused on him with gratitude and saw others do the same.

After nearly an hour, Sheryl returned to the podium. Looking around the room, she saw tears. She saw smiles. She saw gratitude. Turning her gaze directly toward Zach, she was rewarded with a quick grin and bow of his head in a gesture of thanks. She noticed the tension was gone from his body and, for that matter, from everyone else's. As she stood there, standing tall, she felt a collective sigh of release and relief ripple through the audience. It was as if a burden had been lifted. Sheryl felt it herself.

Thanking her direct reports for the beautiful job they had done, she cleared her throat, pushing down a new rush of emotion. "I'd like to close with one final remembrance," she said, her voice breaking slightly. "Carl Schmidt was not laid off, but you all know that he retired this week. He said he didn't want the fanfare of a retirement party or gathering, but I want to honor him too." She took a breath, her voice stronger now. "Carl led our division for many years with great vision and energy. He is an amazingly smart man, who studied all things IT and knew more than most of us will ever know. I was *honored* to work with him and learn from him." Sheryl cracked a grin. "He had a great sense of humor, although I know many of you didn't see that, but I know you saw his dedication and his commitment to the company and to *all* of us. I'd like to send him our best wishes for a happy and fulfilling retirement. He deserves it. Let's take a moment to wish Carl well."

Sheryl closed her eyes and waited a full minute, sending her prayers and wishes for Carl silently as she had for all the others they had mentioned today.

Sheryl looked thoroughly around the room, including at the camera, before saying warmly, "That concludes our meeting. I apologize for keeping some of you here later than normal, but I warmly appreciate that everyone stayed. I want to say in closing that I value *all* of you who are here, all of you who continued to come to work during the last few weeks even though you were upset, and who have adapted, in some cases, to different teams and different bosses. I am truly grateful that you have continued to work on your projects, and I thank you for the contribution of your talents, skills, and personalities in making The Diamante successful and a good place to work. You are seen, heard, and deeply appreciated. Thank you. Thank you all."

Applause broke out after her words. Enthusiastic, generous applause. Sheryl smiled and indicated that her direct reports also rise and be acknowledged. She felt a wave of love for all of these people sweep through her as she added her applause for them. *We* are *all connected to one another, and I feel it in every fiber of my being.* She was relieved and joyful with the way things had gone.

Back in her office, after being congratulated on her promotion and thanked by her direct reports and quite a few members of her team, including Tina, Sheryl sank into her chair. She let the exhaustion of the day overtake her. The remnants of the adrenaline rush that had propelled her through the meeting were subsiding, but a faint buzz remained.

Having always experienced a sense of both energy and exhaustion after giving any presentation, today it was amplified by the emotional roller-coaster of her conversation with Todd, her promotion, and all that had been involved in planning and the execution of this pivotal meeting. She sighed, but it was a happy, relieved sound.

Staring into space for a moment, reliving the meeting, Sheryl heard a gentle knock on her door, and smiled when Keisha's head popped through the door frame. Sheryl waved her in, her eyes widening in admiration at the stunning aqua dress the younger woman wore.

"Well done," Keisha enthused, her head bobbing with her words. "*Very* well done. You brought the humanity back. I feel . . . I feel proud to work here again." Then she cocked her head, a slight smirk on her lips. "Maybe you've missed your calling, boss; maybe you should have been a preacher."

Sheryl chuckled. "Thanks, Keisha. I have you to thank for partially inspiring it," Sheryl admitted.

Keisha grinned widely now. "Then my work here is done," she said with a laugh.

"Oh no," Sheryl protested laughingly, sitting up straighter in her chair. "Please don't say that."

"No, no. I didn't mean I was leaving just yet," Keisha quickly assured her with a twinkle in her eye. "I *have to* give you a chance now after your big promotion and that very special meeting. Congratulations."

"Phew, that's a relief," Sheryl bantered back, pretending to wipe her brow. "And thank you for the congratulations. I'm pretty blown away by the promotion."

"I think you'll be great in that position," Keisha said, her voice suddenly serious and intense. "You have the chance to make a difference, like you did today."

"I hope so. I'm certainly going to try." Sheryl matched the young woman's seriousness, touched by her echoing Carl's words. "You'll have your chance, too, Keisha. I expect great things from you, no matter where you are."

Keisha blushed and tipped her eyes down, but then looked back up. "I plan to do great things," she said, her voice soft.

Sheryl smiled, waving her hand in a shooing motion. "Good. Now go home and enjoy your evening. I'll see you tomorrow."

"You got it, boss. Good night." Keisha gave her a cheeky salute.

Sheryl rolled her eyes at the younger women's antics as she watched her saunter out. *I hope I will be the one to mentor and guide you into a bigger role,* Sheryl thought. *You are a very special young woman.*

Turning off her computer, she prepared to go home herself. Once again this week, she knew she was one of the last to be leaving the building. She took one final glance at her personal cell phone, noting that there was another text from Dave saying that he was okay but busy. Nothing else. Frowning, she slipped the phone into her purse and gathered the rest of her things.

I'm sure I'll hear from him later, she thought as she walked through the empty workspace on the floor. A frisson of excitement slid down her spine, and her face lit up. *He's going to be so blown away by my news.*

She was still glowing as she reached the main office staircase, but her smile quickly vanished when she saw Jim Leaders leaning against the railing on the landing below. One long, khaki-encased leg was crossed over the other as he regarded Sheryl with a smug expression on his tanned face.

"Well, well, well. If it isn't our new C-I-O." He pronounced each letter of her title with exaggeration.

Sheryl's throat worked as she struggled to find her voice. "Jim."

"I guess you're feeling pretty good about yourself about now," he said, watching her descend the stairs toward him. "But you no longer have Carl to protect you." A chill cascaded down her spine as he paused, his features sharpening predatorily. "And you're going to have to deliver on the Portal Project or your tenure as CIO will be the shortest one ever."

Sheryl gulped and quickly pasted a confident look on her face. "Thank you, Jim," she replied sardonically. "I appreciate your well wishes."

His gray-blue eyes narrowed.

Sheryl met his gaze directly, ignoring her quivering stomach. "But we will have to talk about the Portal Project, as you know. We have plans to make it the most amazing customer interface on the market." *And by damn, we'll do it too.*

"By January?" Jim sneered, blond eyebrows raised in disbelief.

"Maybe not," Sheryl conceded, cocking her head to the side as she gauged his response.

"Ha! We'll see about that," the head of client services shot back. "We'll just see."

He turned on his heel and continued down the stairs, his mocking laugh trailing behind him.

Chapter Sixteen

Where the hell is he?

It was nearly ten o'clock in the evening, and Sheryl still hadn't been able to reach Dave. Sitting on the edge of the bed, their bed, she picked up her phone–again. *Okay, so now what?*

She had talked to nearly everyone else who was important in her life: her mother, Cindy, and other friends who shared Sheryl's excitement and a touch of her sadness about the reason for her promotion. Without fail, everyone had been supportive, enthusiastic, and totally happy for her. They also shared in her mixed emotions about what had happened with Carl because they knew about her close mentorship with him. She was the first among her corporate-focused friends to have cracked the C-Suite barrier, although a couple of them were anxiously anticipating potential opportunities.

Sheryl sighed loudly. She couldn't believe that there was still nothing from Dave, despite having left several voice messages and two texts, all asking him to call her.

Frustrated, she thought about calling Cindy again. They had had a terrific conversation earlier. In fact, what had pleased Sheryl most about the evening was sharing her triumph at the grief meeting with her friend.

"Cindy, it was so amazing," Sheryl had told her from the car, too excited to wait until she had reached home. "I felt so strong, so powerful, so . . . *right*, although I'm not sure that's the best word. Maybe the correct word is *aligned.* I felt so *aligned* with my higher self, with that positive energy. It wasn't just me; I could feel that there was something so much bigger in play. And . . ." Sheryl had paused, reliving the sensations. "I loved feeling so *connected* with the people in the room. I can't even describe what an incredible experience it was to support them."

"Wow! That sounds amazing! I'm so proud of you," Cindy had responded, her voice full of admiration. "I'm not sure I would have the nerve to do it." She paused. "Do you think anyone is going to complain? Will it cause problems?"

Sheryl had shrugged. "No idea. I don't think so. From what I saw, I think everyone was really moved by it, in a positive way, but the room was full of a lot of people. What is it we always say? 'Trying to please everyone is a recipe for stress and exhaustion.' I guess I'll find out tomorrow. Most people seemed pleased, even touched."

"Wow! That's so great. What an amazing idea. You took what I sent you and elevated it to a whole new level. That's just like you."

"I'm really glad I did it," Sheryl had affirmed, blushing at her friend's effusive praise. "A few people quietly took me aside and said they felt like they can get on with life and work now. I feel like a huge burden has been taken from their shoulders and mine. It really shifted the energy for me personally. A lot of my guilt and anguish about the layoffs has finally gone away."

And it had. The only remaining anguish was Carl, and that was because she knew how unhappy he really was about leaving. After hanging up with Cindy, the rest of her drive had been consumed with thoughts about Carl . . . and Dave's absence.

Back in the present moment, Sheryl glared at her phone. Grimacing, she finally sent another text to Dave.

Call me ASAP. Urgent news.

Maybe he would respond to *that*.

It was a full five minutes before her phone dinged in response.

At dinner. Can't call.

Can we talk tomorrow?

Sheryl read the text in disbelief, then texted back angrily:

Fine. Got promoted today.

Thought you might want to know.

The phone rang within seconds. "Wow! What happened to Carl?" Dave asked.

"Carl retired, or that's what he said," Sheryl ground out, rigid with anger. "I tried to tell you that this weekend. I don't believe him, but he swears that he and Todd agreed on it."

"Oh boy, I didn't expect that," Dave replied. "I'm sorry I couldn't talk more." He brushed past that quickly, adding, "That had to be rough."

"Hmph." She ignored his halfhearted apology. "Well, then, Todd and Janine met with me this morning and pretty much told me I was taking his job," Sheryl continued sharply.

She heard the sharp intake of Dave's breath.

"I'll be on the board now too," she added.

Dave gave a long, low whistle. "Wow. That's unbelievable! Congratulations, Sheryl." There was a brief silence. Sheryl waited. "Although I can see why you're upset about Carl," he conceded. "It's a tough way to get promoted but still . . . go you! I'm proud of you, sweetheart." Despite the clatter of the restaurant in the background, she could tell her husband's voice held genuine excitement and pride.

Sheryl blinked back a few tears. "Thanks, Dave . . . Damn it. I wish you were here! It would be so much better to share this in person," she said, suddenly angry with him for being so far away. *He should be here for this, not clear across the country.*

A woman's throaty laughter punctuated the brief pause before Dave answered. "Um, yeah, I know. It *would* be better to hear this from you in person. But we'll celebrate this weekend," he promised with what seemed to her like false heartiness. "Saturday."

"Yeah, that would be good," Sheryl replied slowly, sifting through his words to discern what he was really feeling.

"I'm so glad you texted me," Dave was saying now. "I should have called you back earlier. I'm sorry about that, but I'm *very* happy for you. You deserve this promotion. You really do. But, listen, babe, I gotta get back to this dinner. They're waiting. I'll try to call tomorrow evening so we can talk more. Okay?"

"Yeah, I guess, but . . ." Sheryl trailed off, realizing that Dave had disconnected. Abruptly and without saying 'good night.' Or I love you. *We've always said 'I love you' . . . When did that stop?*

Sheryl slowly lowered the phone, laying it on the bedside table. For a long moment, she sat staring at it, the excitement and pleasure from the day fading. She shook her head. *Maybe I'm being overly sensitive because of all the emotional highs and lows of the last few weeks, especially today.* She frowned. *But maybe not.*

Rick Sutton was waiting outside Sheryl's office door when she hurried in Wednesday morning. It was not even eight o'clock, and she was pleased to see him there so early. She was even more pleased when he held out his hand and offered very genuine congratulations on her promotion.

"I'm really happy that you got the CIO job," he continued as Sheryl hung her coat on the back of the door and stepped over to her desk. "And I'm really glad it wasn't me!"

Sheryl looked up in surprise. Rick had a big grin on his face. "Really? You're okay with this? I thought *you* were the best candidate," she said breathlessly.

Rick shook his head emphatically. "Oh no, I don't want that headache."

They were interrupted by Lauren, also there to congratulate her, and as soon as they left, another of her new direct reports came in with a smile on her face. The morning continued like that, with various colleagues, Sheryl's remaining three new direct reports, and many others, popping in or calling to congratulate her and wish her well.

Alex Thompson, head of the investment group and a new peer, was one of Sheryl's favorite visitors. She smiled when his boyish face appeared in her doorway.

"Sheryl," he said breathlessly. "I'm so happy for you! And for us! It's going to be great having you on the executive team."

Taken aback by his enthusiasm, Sheryl gave him a curious look. After all, she really didn't know Alex all that well. Her interactions with the investment group primarily had been with his subordinates, not him.

"Thanks, Alex," she replied uncertainly, watching him take a few steps into the room. Of average height, the Chief Investment Officer had sandy hair and light brown eyes. *He looks like the proverbial all-American boy, even though he must be in his late forties.*

"I also wanted to offer my support and assistance, if you need it," he said earnestly. "I know Carl left, well, in a hurry. So, if you ever have any questions, I'd be happy to help."

Sheryl blinked in surprise. *How nice!* Alex had always seemed very kind and pleasant to her, the few times they had met previously. She was pleased that her instincts about him had been correct.

"That's so nice, Alex," she said gratefully. "I'm sure I'll be taking you up on that."

"Great. I mean it. Call me anytime." He gave her another big grin and disappeared as quickly as he had come, leaving Sheryl with a warm smile on her own face.

There were many congratulatory emails as well, but the one from Layla Arch had Sheryl laughing out loud. How she had heard about Sheryl's promotion so quickly was a mystery, but the banker had sent a very charming note along with a request to "do lunch" some time. Sheryl rolled her eyes. *I guess I'm high enough on the food chain now to be courted rather than harangued.*

She had just sent Layla a polite, noncommittal response when Janine came in, closing the door behind her. The head of HR looked at Sheryl with deep concern before seating herself in front of Sheryl's desk. "What did you do?" she asked pointedly.

"What did I do when?" Sheryl parried.

"Yesterday? Meeting? Ceremony?" Janine cocked her head and raised her eyebrows.

Sheryl exhaled. "Ohh . . . that meeting, Well, I had a meeting with my whole department," she responded evenly. "I told you I had one scheduled."

"But you didn't tell me that you were holding a religious ceremony," Janine said, a tinge of real curiosity in her voice.

"A religious ceremony?" Sheryl was incredulous. "I didn't hold a religious ceremony!"

"That's not what we were told." Janine didn't smile, although Sheryl thought she detected a twinkle in her friend's eyes. "I got three formal complaints about the meeting. Three."

Sheryl looked at her in confusion. "From whom? As far as I could tell, everyone was happy about the meeting. I've gotten great feedback about it."

Janine nodded, one side of her mouth lifted. "Yes, truthfully, we've heard some good things about it too."

Sheryl stiffened. "What do you mean you've heard good things?" she demanded. "Who have you talked to?"

"I've talked to a few of your direct reports. Jose. Yvette," Janine replied matter-of-factly. "They all said you did a great job."

"What? Why would you talk to them instead of just coming to me?"

"Because I had to *investigate* the complaints, Sheryl," Janine retorted, her gray eyes sharp. "Especially because they were aimed at The. New. C.I.O."

Sheryl's forehead wrinkled. "I'd rather you would have talked to me first." She paused, looking hard at Janine, still trying to grasp that someone on her team had gone to HR. "You seriously had complaints?"

"Yeah, we did," she nodded, her voice and demeanor softening. "Three women apparently raced over to find me the minute the meeting ended. They found Kelly, our payroll coordinator, instead. So, she's the one that got an earful."

"Wow. I thought *everyone* felt a lot better after the meeting. What did they say?"

At that question, Janine rolled her eyes. "They said you had violated 'the separation of church and state.'" The petite HR leader made air quotes. "We all got a laugh over that."

Sheryl chuckled, feeling some of her tension ease. "Wow, that's a little over the top."

"It sure was." Janine's gaze sharpened again. "But seriously, Sheryl. That meeting was on the edge. You technically didn't violate any company policies, but you know we don't usually *honor* people who have left the company."

Sheryl cocked her head. "Come on, Janine. That's not true. We honor people when they retire. We often celebrate when people move on to a better job."

Janine gazed assessingly at Sheryl. She was silent for a long moment. "You're right," she finally said slowly.

"I'd do it again," Sheryl said emphatically. "I *will* do it again, if needed."

Janine's eyebrows rose again. She looked at Sheryl with . . . was that respect? "You would, wouldn't you?" she murmured, standing up. "Well, good for you. You'll need the courage of all your convictions."

Sheryl stood up too, unflinchingly meeting Janine's eyes.

"I'm actually impressed, Sheryl," the older woman admitted. "It was a brave thing to do, and–complaints aside–a smart one. Most of the people we talked to *did* say they felt better after your meeting. A lot better." She took a few steps toward the door, then paused and looked back. "But Sheryl?"

"Yes, Janine?"

"Give me a heads up the next time. *Please?*"

Sheryl laughed. "Yes, Janine," she said with exaggerated compliance.

Throwing a grin over her shoulder, Janine sashayed out, leaving Sheryl chuckling in her wake. *What a goof! But I'm glad to have my friend back.* Still, she wondered about the three women who had complained. *I won't hold it against them, but really, what will they do next?*

After lunch, Sheryl geared up for her two o'clock meeting with Todd. Guessing that the Portal Project would be his immediate concern, she carefully made two copies of the new Project plans, the shortcut one and the longer, more robust proposal. She went over them again in detail, wanting to have all the information on the tip of her tongue. She didn't know what else to prepare, so she included the last status report she had prepared for Carl in the folder for Todd.

Todd greeted her warmly when she arrived, meeting her at his office door, something she was sure he didn't normally do. He was in his shirtsleeves, his tie slightly loosened, as if he was ready to get down to work. His bright blue eyes actually seemed to be twinkling, she noted with surprise.

"Sheryl," he said, ushering her to his conference table. "How is your first day on the job?"

"It's been really good, Todd," Sheryl answered honestly, slipping into the chair Todd indicated. She unbuttoned her suit jacket as she sat, glad she was dressed more formally today, even if Todd was more relaxed. "Everyone has been so supportive and enthusiastic about my promotion. It's really been nice."

"I'm glad to hear that," Todd said, sitting in the chair at the head of the table, catty-corner to her. "You deserve to be congratulated."

Sheryl eyed him warily. "Thanks, Todd."

He chuckled. "Don't look at me like that. I am serious," he said, leaning forward. "I said that yesterday. But there is a lot of work to be done."

"I'm sure you want to start with the Portal Project," Sheryl answered, grateful that her voice didn't waver. Inside, her stomach was in knots. She had no idea how Todd was going to take the new plans.

Looking surprised that Sheryl had tackled the most difficult topic first, he nodded briskly.

Sheryl opened the folder she had prepared and laid it on the table in front of him. He glanced down at it, then back at her. "Just tell me, Sheryl. Carl already said that you're not going to make the January deadline. I want to know what you *are* going to do."

Pointing to the summary page on top of the file, Sheryl carefully explained the two options that she, Carl, and the team had prepared. She pointed out the pros and cons of both, putting extra emphasis on all the benefits of the longer plan. "It truly will be state-of-the-art, Todd," she said earnestly, wrapping up her pitch. "Better than any other client interface on the market."

Her new boss gave her a hard look, then picked up the executive summary page, perusing it thoroughly. "This is well done, well thought out," he acknowledged. "But it does put me in a bind. Jim has been insistent that we need the Portal updated by mid-January, as promised. He has said that we are at risk of losing more clients if we don't. That's something The Diamante cannot afford."

Sheryl winced but took a deep breath. "Yes, Jim has made that very clear," she said, tucking her hair behind her ear. "He, uh . . ."

"Has he threatened you?" Todd asked shrewdly.

"A little."

"Not surprised. What have you said?" he asked gruffly, his blue eyes laser-focused on her face.

Sheryl resisted the urge to shift back in her chair. "Not much," she admitted.

"Good," Todd approved, surprising her a bit. "It'll be better if I talk to him about this."

Sheryl momentarily sagged with relief, then sat up straight. She was going to have to face Jim someday soon, but she was glad it wasn't now. She saw a faint smile cross Todd's face as he observed her.

"Just this time," he clarified. "This isn't *all* your mess, so I'll handle it." He looked back down at the paper in his hand and studied it carefully once more. "I want the state-of-the-art version," he announced decisively. "Can you really deliver that by July?"

She paused, stomach churning, then looked him straight in the eye. "Yes, we can deliver that by July," she said firmly. She'd been over this with her team three times. Full transparency. She could back this decision, if that's what Todd wanted.

"Good. Then do it. No more excuses."

"Yes, I understand, Todd. Thank you. Truly. Thank you for picking that option. It's the one that the team and I prefer." Sheryl allowed her enthusiasm to surface. "We're actually quite excited about it and what it can mean for our clients–in the long run. And, thank you for talking to Jim. I'll admit, I wasn't looking forward to that."

Todd flashed a grin. "You're welcome, Sheryl. See? I'm not all bad."

Sheryl laughed. "No, Todd, you're not all bad."

He turned then to other topics, and she listened and took copious notes when he outlined his expectations and concerns on a variety of other projects. She was pleasantly surprised that he was so well informed. *Carl must have given him a lot of this information before he left.* She was grateful and relieved. It made the transition to working for Todd much easier, and she felt she could get her feet under her in her new position much faster this way.

It was after four by the time Sheryl left Todd's office, walking almost buoyantly down the stairs. She was energized by her conversation with Todd and over the moon that he had chosen the better Project plan. She couldn't wait to tell Patrick and Keisha.

She marveled at how comfortable she had been with Todd. *The man truly has a gift.* She had heard about times when he had been hard and unyielding, but it seemed that was not his normal style. *Thank God.* And the fact that he was talking to Jim Leaders. *Amazing!* She couldn't keep the smile off her face. Suddenly, everything seemed like it was going to be okay, maybe better than okay.

The high lasted until she got to her desk and checked her phone. The text from Dave read:

Have another important client dinner tonight and won't be able to talk. I'll call tomorrow. Promise.

Sheryl clutched the phone hard, itching to throw it across the room. She didn't.

Chapter Seventeen

Saturday, October 2

Sheryl waited until midway through the meal to drop the bomb.

It's time to tell Dave about the grief ceremony.

She and her husband were seated at a local restaurant, Casa Bianca. The place was small and cozy with good food and a pleasant atmosphere, but it was not fancy and not exactly what Sheryl would have chosen for a celebration. Not that she'd had a choice. Dave had made the arrangements, at the last minute she guessed, after he had finally returned from California yesterday afternoon.

She looked at her husband now, handsome in a dark blue, cable-knit sweater worn over a cream turtleneck. His thick light brown hair was long. *Too long*, she thought. *He's been away so much that he needs a haircut.*

Picking up her wine glass, she idly contemplated the rich, red liquid before raising her eyes again. "So, I had the grief ceremony on Tuesday," she said casually.

Dave's fork clattered onto his plate, his deep brown eyes widening in shock. "What?" he exclaimed. "The day you got your *promotion*? What in God's name did you do that for?"

Sheryl gasped at his reaction, then took a sip of wine, and slowly lowered the glass onto the bright red-and-white checkered tablecloth. "Because," she said quietly, looking squarely at her husband. "I felt it was important for everyone to get closure, to have an opportunity to acknowledge their feelings."

Dave snorted. "Feelings? Geez, I thought you had let that go," he said harshly. "You have a new role, an *important* role. You need to be focused on making a good impression, not going out on a limb talking about *feelings*."

Sheryl stiffened, her fingers clenching the wine glass stem. "What? Do you think people don't have feelings at work, Dave?" she challenged him fiercely.

Looking disgusted, Dave shook his head. "Of course, people have feelings," he said with disdain, "but it's not good leadership to stir people up and make them *more* emotional. You're supposed to be calming them down."

Every muscle in Sheryl's body tightened with rage. *I can't take this condemnation from him anymore. I'm tired of it.* She stared at her husband, wanting to scream, but she valiantly held it in.

"I'm not even going to justify that with an answer," she finally ground out, crumpling her napkin in her lap. Out of the corner of her eye, she noticed the people at the table next to them watching her curiously. She lowered her voice. "The meeting *did* help, Dave, but you don't seem to care about that."

Dave leaned back in his chair. "Well, that's a good thing," he conceded. "You lucked out. But you had no right to jeopardize your career like that."

Shocked, Sheryl put her hands on the table and pushed herself back in her chair. "What do you mean I had *no right?* It was my decision. I have every right to do what I think is best for my team."

She pushed her plate away and stood up, planting her brown leather boots firmly on the restaurant's tile floor.

"Where are you going?" Dave asked.

"To the ladies' room," she retorted sharply. "Why don't you get the check? I'm ready to leave."

"That's it? You're just going to walk away?"

Sheryl didn't think her body could get any more rigid. She struggled to take a deep breath. "Really, Dave? I can't even believe this is coming from you. *What is the* matter *with you?*"

"I could ask you the same question," Dave shot back.

Glancing to her right, Sheryl saw that the other couple was regarding them with obvious interest now, so were people at several other nearby tables. She shuddered. *We're making a scene.*

She looked back at Dave, who was glaring at her. "This is not the time or place," she said flatly. She spun on her heel and walked away with as much dignity as she could muster.

Dave was waiting in the restaurant lobby, holding her coat, when Sheryl stepped back out of the restroom. It had taken her several minutes to calm herself down, but she felt more in control.

"I'm sorry," he said, his cheeks tinged with pink as he held out her coat. "This was supposed to be a celebration, and I shouldn't have jumped on you like that," he continued in a conciliatory tone. "I want you to know that I *am* really proud of you. My wife, the CIO." His smile seemed forced.

Sheryl slipped her arms in the sleeves and wrapped the camel wool coat tightly around her. Turning back to her husband, she tipped her head slightly. "Thank you," she said quietly. *This whole argument is getting really tiresome. Why can't we talk this out like we've always done before? He hasn't even given me a* decent *explanation about why he's really so upset.*

They were quiet on the way home. Dave tried to start a more light-hearted conversation, but Sheryl couldn't force herself to join in. She couldn't shake the sense of Dave's deep disapproval. It was a feeling that she wasn't used to. *Is it just this issue or is something else going on?* Especially since Dave's response was in such stark contrast with the reaction she had gotten at the office, well, most of them.

By Monday, October 8, Sheryl was still disturbed by the ongoing distance between her and Dave. Following the disastrous dinner, they had both avoided the subject of the grief meeting, so this new disagreement just sat there between them, like the others, unresolved . . . and still festering. Sheryl couldn't even bring herself to raise the subject with him, largely because she had no idea what to say. Even the extra time she had been spending in meditation hadn't provided any insight, although the major side benefit was that it had shifted her to a more positive state for work and other areas of her life.

Now, starting another work week, she entered The Diamante's building and plodded up the stairs toward her office with a heavy heart. *I should be excited about my new job, not worrying about my marriage,* she thought glumly. Catching her escalating negativity–again–she forced her thoughts toward the day ahead. *It's going to be a good Monday,* she encouraged herself, thinking about the meetings she had planned.

Reaching her floor, she straightened and lifted her head, greeting the people she met in the corridor with a smile and a bright good morning. *Damn it. I am happy with my new job! I'm not going to let Dave bring me down.*

Buoyed by that new fire, she swung open her office door and prepared to work.

Another shock was waiting in her email. She gasped as she opened Todd's message, time-stamped very late Sunday evening.

October 7

To all The Diamante staff,

I regretfully announce the departure of our long-time CFO, Ed Barkham, effective immediately. Please join me in wishing...

Sheryl blinked. *What? Have they forced someone else out? Like they did Carl?* She picked up the phone to call Janine, wanting more information. She knew Ed, of course; he had been at The Diamante as long as Carl had, but she hadn't had much contact with him. He was the only one of her new peers who hadn't congratulated or reached out to schedule a meeting. Perhaps she now knew why.

Before she could dial Janine's number, the woman herself appeared.

"You saw it?" the HR executive asked in hushed tones, pushing the door gently closed, then taking a seat in front of Sheryl's desk. She was dressed in a dark gray suit and unconsciously smoothed her skirt as she sat, her eyes glued to Sheryl's.

"Yes, I was just reading it and was going to call you. What *happened?*"

Janine shook her head. "I don't really know. Todd called me yesterday afternoon at home and told me Ed had resigned."

"So, he just quit? Out of the blue?" Sheryl asked incredulously.

"Yeah, it looks that way," Janine answered, giving Sheryl a sympathetic look. "I had heard rumors that he was unhappy with the changes . . ."

"What changes?" Sheryl asked, then quickly grasped the look on her friend's face. "Oh no . . . Me? He was unhappy about my promotion?"

"Among other things," she confirmed. "You know how old school he was about everything."

Sheryl nodded thoughtfully. "Yeah, I kind of did. I didn't have much interaction with him, but well . . ."

The two women were silent, each thinking about the now former CFO. He was known for being a stickler, to the point of being ridiculous at times. One of Sheryl and Janine's private gripes was that, even though his second-in-command was a woman named Elise, he had given her little visible authority, respect, or support.

"Wow, I guess that means another change on the board," Sheryl verbalized her thoughts. "Will they promote Elise?"

Janine shook her head definitively. "No, she's not ready. Plus, I would guess that Hank and Anthony will want someone they choose for this role. Controlling the numbers and all that."

"Oh," breathed Sheryl. "That makes sense, but it's a little scary, isn't it?"

"Yes, very scary," Janine agreed quietly, concern wrinkling her brow. "And I'm probably going to be in the middle of it. I'll have to handle this recruitment myself."

Now it was Sheryl's turn to look sympathetic. "I don't envy you that."

"Gee thanks," Janine said as she rose. "Let me know if you hear anything on the grapevine."

"Will do," Sheryl replied, her mind still processing the implications of this development as she watched Janine leave. Her friend had more on her plate than she'd realized.

Sighing, Sheryl turned back to her computer. *I guess I'll just have to wait and see.* She thought of what Janine had said about Hank and Anthony and shuddered. She believed that a board could work together as a team, for the highest good of all, but the thought of that level of control—numbers or not—made her wince.

She was just opening the next email in her inbox when Tina came bustling in.

"Moving day!" she sang.

Sheryl frowned in confusion. "Moving? What? Who's moving?"

"You are," Tina enthused. "Moving down the hall, to your new CIO's corner office, that is. I'm here to help you pack up. Tech support will be here at ten to move your computer equipment."

Sheryl's heart skipped a beat. *Carl's office. No, I'm not ready.* "So soon?" she asked Tina. "Shouldn't I wait a bit? It seems, um, disrespectful to Carl."

Tina gave her an understanding look. "I know you miss Carl," she said gently. "But yeah, you *need* to move. It's been almost two weeks since your promotion. It's not disrespectful. It's time."

Swallowing hard, Sheryl nodded reluctantly. "I guess you're right," she said, sadly picturing Carl's lean face. *He would tell me to move.* She chuckled inwardly. *In fact, he would ask me why I hadn't done it long before.*

"Now, let me get started on your files," Tina said, moving purposely toward her desk.

By two o'clock, Sheryl was shocked to find herself ensconced at Carl's former desk, her computer up and running, her files nearly all in place. She didn't keep much paper, and Tina had been amazingly efficient in getting what she did have boxed up and moved. Even her photos of herself and Dave on the beach in Hawaii and skiing in Colorado and her most important women-in-tech awards were already on the walls. The only real problem was Carl's chair. Designed to fit her former boss's lanky frame, she felt dwarfed in it. Reluctantly, she asked Tina to find a smaller chair or order her a new one.

Jim Leaders bounded into her office just after three, a big smile on his face. "Hey, we landed another big fish today," he crowed, crossing the room in long strides. "They weren't even deterred by a demo of that crappy Portal."

Sheryl managed to suppress her flinch. Jim's sneering had all but disappeared, thanks to Todd, she was sure, but he continued to get in little digs like this one whenever she saw him. Her new boss had done an amazing job of smoothing things over with the Client Services executive, who had–to her surprise–accepted the change of plans for the

Portal Project with a reluctant grace.

"That's great, Jim!" she responded, genuinely happy to hear about new clients.

"So, how's my favorite CIO today? Got any good news for me?" he boomed. The cost of Jim's acceptance, she was discovering, was that he had begun stopping by nearly every day to check on progress.

"Still on target for July, Jim," Sheryl replied dutifully, repeating what she said every time he asked. She wondered how long he would keep this up.

"That's great." Jim eased himself into a chair in front of her desk, his bright yellow golf shirt almost blinding her. "Love to hear it. I can concentrate on my golf game tomorrow then."

"Yup, you sure can." Sheryl shot Jim an envious look. *I wish I could take an afternoon for something fun, although I know it's "business" for Jim too.* "How's the game these days?"

"Coming along. Can't seem to get my handicap below ten, but some day."

Jim was now sharing personal information and trying to draw her out. She wasn't quite sure whether he was truly being friendly or was looking for a chink in her armor. Despite Carl's warning, she was beginning to find Jim to be kind of likable in his own weird way. *But I can't let my guard too far down, at least not yet.*

Jim chattered about clients and golf for a few more minutes, needing little input from her. Sheryl's mind wandered to Dave, and all the golfing he seemed to be doing in California. *And he never even used to like golf all that much.*

"Well, Sheryl," Jim said jovially, interrupting her thoughts. "If you've got nothing else, I'll let you get back to it." He unfolded his well-muscled form from the chair.

"Good luck tomorrow," Sheryl said, watching Jim bound back out of the room, shaking her head at his energy.

Sitting back in her chair, she thought about how her work relationships were changing with her new role. In addition to Jim, Alex Thompson, the head of the investment unit, was another new peer.

Alex had been very helpful and kind so far, and she was enjoying getting to know him better. Her other new peer, well, was no longer an issue. She frowned as Ed Barkham's resignation crossed her mind. *Two of the five gone. That's a pretty big swing in the executive team.*

Pushing the thought away, Sheryl turned her attention to her department reorganization. She knew she needed to shift people around to better support the Portal Project and other key initiatives, but she wanted to assess the strengths of Carl's former staff first. She had worked with Lauren, Rick, Sheila Winters, the IT Strategist, Olaf Ahlquist, head of IT in the European operations, and three others as a peer, but she was being systematic about learning more about their abilities as their boss. In the meantime, she had simply kept her old team of Jose, Patrick, and the others reporting directly to her. For one thing, she felt that she needed more information before making a final decision. For another, she wanted to keep a close eye on the progress of the Portal Project.

Her biggest triumph was her inherited leadership team's response to the grief meeting. It hadn't taken long for the news of the ceremony to spread throughout the organization. Curious, Lauren and Rick had asked her about it at her very first meeting with her new department heads. After listening to her explanation, she was thrilled when the two of them, along with three others immediately asked her to help facilitate similar gatherings for their groups. Sheila, a bit more cautious, declined to participate, and the European offices hadn't seen the same cuts, so Olaf didn't see the need. Still, five out of seven was a great endorsement in her mind.

Interestingly, it was nearly three weeks later, on October 29, before Todd acknowledged her actions. Sheryl, anticipating *some* response from the company president, had been holding her breath, waiting for him to reprimand her or worse. She was starting to think he wouldn't mention it all. Then, they were having their scheduled Monday afternoon about the Portal Project when he abruptly broached the subject.

"I hear you have a potential new career as a preacher," he interjected abruptly.

Momentarily taken off guard, Sheryl drew a quick breath. "Uh, no," she replied carefully. "Not planning on that."

"You did a good thing," he said matter-of-factly. "But just be careful that you don't go too far."

She opened her mouth to ask what too far was, but a subtle shake of his head stopped her.

"I know the folks in your organization have recovered their productivity faster than any other in the company, and I appreciate that," he stated and, giving her one more semi-stern look, he shifted the conversation back to the business at hand.

Befuddled by the sudden change, Sheryl had to quickly refocus to catch up with the new topic. *Todd is an enigma,* she thought afterward. *He praised me, sort of, and warned me at the same time. What does that mean?*

The next day, during a conversation with Carl, she asked him about Todd's comments, but he was as baffled as Sheryl had been. As promised, her former boss had made himself available to her, answering her questions and filling in gaps in the reports and information she was trying to understand. Because of the abrupt transition, his input had been invaluable. At first, Sheryl felt a little guilty about intruding on his personal life, but most of the time, he was the one who called her.

Lately though, their conversations had gotten further and further apart. She was gaining confidence in her own abilities, and Carl, thankfully, had started to move on with his own life. She never mentioned her calls with her former boss to her new one, although she sensed that Todd suspected that she was getting insight from Carl from time to time. Her new boss, however, didn't mention it directly, so Sheryl took his silence as tacit consent.

The one thing Sheryl was truly grateful for was Carl's insight about the outside board members. The Diamante was required by law to have an equal number of non-executive and executive directors, at a minimum. Most companies in the industry had more of the former on their boards. However, The Diamante, smaller and more closely held, had traditionally populated its board with a large contingent of corporate officers, known as executive directors, hence Sheryl's appointment. But with Todd, Jim, Sheryl, Alex, and the as-yet unnamed CFO all on the board, that meant there were five non-executive directors. Sheryl knew little about any of them.

Carl had explained that Duncan and Gary, whom she had met a few times in the last five years, were long-standing board members and had been with the company for more than twenty years each. From what she understood, they were seasoned industry veterans who brought a lot of wisdom and influence to the table. Sean Rafferty, a complete unknown to Sheryl, had joined the board ten years ago. He was significantly younger than Duncan and Gary, and Carl told her that Sean was quiet, very serious, and typically went along with whatever Duncan and Gary supported.

It was Hank Turner and Anthony Russo, the newest members of the board, who were the wild cards.

"Hank's about the same age as Duncan and Gary," Carl advised her, during a call she had requested to prepare the board meeting. "But he's a much bigger player in the investment world. He's been on the board of some of the big guys, like Fidelity. We had a venture capital group buy a big chunk of shares at the end of last year, and they're the ones who got Hank and Anthony elected at the spring shareholder's meeting."

Sheryl nodded to herself, taking careful notes of what Carl shared. "What about Anthony?"

"He's an up and comer," Carl said. "Younger, about Todd's age, I guess. He's latched onto Hank's coattails and is riding them hard. My guess is that he wants to use Hank to increase his own credibility and influence."

"Makes sense," Sheryl murmured, feeling her stomach clench. She tried to keep an open mind about people, but she was frankly not looking forward to meeting these two.

"Hank and Anthony are being pushed by the VC group. Don't forget that. You never know where they're going to come down," Carl advised, his voice hard. By now, Carl had lost most of his bitterness and was enjoying his retirement. It was only the mention of Hank and Anthony that still triggered her former boss's anger.

"Okay, that all makes sense," Sheryl responded. "Doesn't make me feel much better, but it makes sense."

"You need to be informed," Carl said sagely. "That's your best defense."

"Yes and thank you. This is super helpful, Carl," Sheryl replied with heartfelt gratitude. *Forewarned and all that.*

They chatted for a while longer before Sheryl ended the call. Afterward, she sat at her desk with a wistful smile on her face. Her conversations with Carl were turning more personal and less about business, especially his burgeoning private life. *Carl was so enthusiastic about his wife today–again!* Apparently, once she got over her initial shock and anger, his spouse had been very happy to get more of Carl's time and attention. From what he said, they were taking daily walks together and had begun to plan some lengthy vacations in the near future. Their marriage seemed to be blossoming. Sheryl swallowed. That gave her hope for her own relationship, although she wanted to reconcile with Dave way before they reached retirement. *That's still way too far away.*

As if her thoughts conjured him up, Dave's number appeared on her personal cell phone.

"Hey," she said pleasantly, but with a hint of coolness. "I was just thinking about you!"

"Good things, I hope."

"Mostly," she said thoughtfully. "I was just talking to Carl, and he and his w—"

"Sheryl. Sorry to interrupt, but I only have a minute," Dave broke in. Sheryl slumped. *Not again.* "I wanted to let you know that my plans for the week have changed. I have to fly to San Jose. I should be back Thursday, maybe Friday."

"Again?" Sheryl asked plaintively, not trying to hide her disappointment and growing suspicion. "You've been going to San Jose a lot. That's not even your territory."

"I've got a big new client there. Groundbreaking work," he enthused. "I'm excited. It's a great opportunity to try something new that could mean bigger wins in the future."

Sheryl sighed. "That's great," she said, forcing herself to sound supportive. She couldn't ask him to celebrate her wins if she didn't celebrate his, she knew. "I just wish you didn't have to be gone so much."

"It's only temporary," he assured her.

"Dave, I don't want–"

"Hon, I gotta run. I need to hightail it to the airport. I'll touch base when I land," he cut in. The connection went dead.

Sheryl ground her teeth. *We'll never bridge this divide between us if we don't have time together . . . if he even wants to.* Spinning her chair around, she looked out the window. The bright sunlight reflecting off the long row of cars in the parking lot was blurred by the sheen of tears in her eyes.

She sat unseeing for a long moment as a wave of emotions swept through her. Anger, sadness, betrayal, hurt, fear.

Is there something in California besides this project? Her stomach clenched. *Or someone?*

Chapter Eighteen

Monday, November 18

Board Meeting Agenda, Sheryl read the email from Todd as soon as she arrived at the office. She grinned. *My first board meeting is only two days away!*

She was getting together with Todd that afternoon for one final review of her presentation, so she printed out the agenda, reviewing it carefully. Her first report to the board was scheduled almost last in the program. She felt the butterflies in her stomach again. *I hope I can do this,* she thought for the thousandth time in the last two weeks. Todd was confident, but this was a big deal. A really big deal.

First impressions are so important, she thought, fighting back the nerves. *I want Hank and the others to take me seriously. They'll have to if I want to have a voice and make an impact. If I mess this presentation up, if I'm not perfect, they will think I'm not ready.* Sheryl knew it would be an uphill battle to gain their respect if she flubbed this. *But if I hit a home run, then I'll have gone a long way to proving I do belong in the boardroom.*

Blowing out a long breath of air, she glanced back at the rest of the schedule, noting that the discussion about the CFO candidates followed her commentary. She frowned. She had not discussed this item with her boss, although he had told her to expect it. Putting down the agenda, she picked up a folder on her desk marked "candidates." Janine had sent it over on Friday. It contained the résumés and interview notes from the two primary candidates for the CFO role that needed to be filled.

The phone rang. Janine.

"Just checking that you got the folder for the board meeting," the HR head said brusquely.

"It's in my hand as we speak," Sheryl replied, flipping the file open.

"Great. Any questions?"

"I'm just looking at it now." Sheryl paused as she ruffled through the pages. "It seems thorough enough, but I'll let you know if I have any questions after I read it."

"Sounds good," Janine said. She hesitated for a beat. "There's a pretty strong recommendation from Todd and Hank Turner," she said carefully. "Pay attention to that."

Sheryl found the page. Her heart dropped. "Oh," she said flatly. "They want to hire Layla Arch."

"Yup. Didn't want you to miss that."

"Does that mean we have to vote for her?" Sheryl asked, chewing her lip nervously. *I've worked with Layla, and it hasn't been fun—at least not until my promotion.* Sheryl made a face, remembering the last smarmy email from Layla only a few days ago, pressing her for the lunch date that Sheryl continued to push off.

"No, but . . ." Janine let the "but" hang in the air.

"No, but we probably need to?" Sheryl guessed.

"I didn't say that," Janine prevaricated. "But."

"Yeah, I get the message," Sheryl said reluctantly. "I just . . . never mind. I'll let you know if I have questions."

"Sounds good. Talk to you later," Janine said before ending the call.

Sheryl flipped through the pages in the folder again. *Yikes. I don't know if I can really vote for Layla.*

She had been surprised that the company was far enough in the interview process for the board to vote on these candidates. After all, Ed had only retired or resigned about five weeks ago. She allowed herself a small sigh of relief, thinking about the rumor mill stories that had reached her ears. According to them, Ed's department had been very glad to see him go.

Just as Carl had warned her, it all came down to the new board members, Hank Turner and Anthony Russo. It seemed like so many changes had happened at The Diamante since they had joined the company last spring. She thought back over her conversations with Carl. Very, very aggressive, her mentor had informed her.

Plus, Todd, Carl, and Janine had *all* told Sheryl that Hank and

Anthony—and the investors they represented—felt that The Diamante's culture was too soft, too comfortable. They continued to push for more accountability, more focus on profit, and more aggressive approaches to projects and deadlines.

Reviewing the résumés, it was easy for Sheryl to see why Layla Arch would be their preferred candidate. Layla's CV was impressive and gave detailed examples about her fiscal acuity. *And I know firsthand how aggressive Layla is—and how abrasive. Plus,* she thought, remembering a few earlier and quite terse emails from the woman, *Yvette's team hates working with her.*

Sheryl sighed, pushing her bangs back. She carefully read the CV and notes about the other candidate, Blake Jones. He had worked for one of The Diamante's competitors. He and several other members of that leadership team had been ousted just over a year ago when a new board was elected and a new president appointed. The incoming president had wanted to bring in several of his people in top positions, and Blake had been one who had lost his job.

Sheryl frowned. *Blake's earlier situation sounds a lot like what's going on around here.* But looking at his credentials and experience, she was delighted to find that Blake was far more qualified than Layla. He certainly had much more relevant experience, but she wanted to be sure. Not liking one of the candidates wasn't enough. She had to make an educated decision in the best interest of the company—both short- and long-term, which meant she had to do more research.

Who would know more? Someone I can trust to give me the real scoop on Blake? She pondered for a moment, looking out her new window view as she mentally perused her rolodex of trusted associates outside The Diamante. Suddenly, she smacked her forehead. *Ah, Felix!*

She picked up the phone. She knew Felix from industry events she had attended over the years. He used to work for Blake's former company, but he had left financial services and was in Silicon Valley now. *No conflict of interest, and he'll have the real scoop on Blake,* Sheryl thought happily. *Plus, I know I can trust him.*

"Felix," she said briskly when he answered after one ring. "Sheryl Simmons. How are you?"

"Sheryl, nice to hear from you. I'm good," he responded warmly.

"Hey, do you have a minute? I want to pick your brain about someone you used to work with."

"Sure, shoot."

"Blake Jones. Tell me what you know."

"Ahh, is he a candidate for your opening?" Felix asked knowingly. At her surprised gasp, he laughed. "And you, I saw the press release a few weeks ago. Congratulations on your promotion. I was going to send you an email or call you, but . . . it's too bad we're not close enough for a celebratory lunch."

"Yeah, I know. You're busy. We're all busy," Sheryl said, chuckling with him. "But the lunch is a nice thought. Thank you. Not that I'd probably have the time for another six months! But I'm pretty excited about my new role."

"As you should be," Felix agreed. "But now you are involved in picking the executive team as a member of the board."

"Yup, so tell me about Blake, confidentially, of course. We're *not* having this conversation," she reminded him.

"Of course," Felix agreed before continuing bluntly. "Blake's a great guy. One of the good guys out there. He's smart, fair, and really cares about people. He's more than a numbers guy, although he's brilliant at that too. He could really see the fat in a budget, the real fat that could be trimmed, not just making himself look good. A lot of people mourned his loss after he left. I don't think most of them fully appreciated just how good he had been for the company."

"Hmmm . . . he sounds almost too good to be true," Sheryl murmured. "Any downsides?"

Felix laughed again. "I didn't work with him directly, but no one has complained about him in my hearing." He paused. "I do know he's a stickler for all the *I*s dotted and *T*s crossed, but that's not a bad thing in his role."

"You're right. That's a good thing, although I guess anything can be taken to an extreme," Sheryl observed, idly tapping her pen on the folder.

"You got it," Felix said. "Hey, I'd love to catch up some time, but I've got someone standing at my door."

"No problem, Felix. You've been a big help. Thanks!"

Hanging up, she looked at the file again. The notes on the pages only confirmed what Felix had said. *In my mind, this is a no brainer. But if Todd and Hank are behind Layla, it might not matter who I prefer.*

Monday and Tuesday passed in the usual flurry of activity, including Shery's final preparation. On Wednesday morning, she dressed carefully in a dark blue suit. Choosing a white blouse with an open collar and her Mikimoto pearls, she took extra time with her hair and makeup, wanting to look her best. She recognized that all her primping was more about giving herself confidence than her actual looks. Still, dressing well helped her feel professional and in control.

A quick workout had relieved some of her tension and still allowed her to arrive at the office early, even though the meeting wasn't until ten. She went through her email, had a short meeting with Patrick to make sure she had the latest info on the Portal Project, and updated her notes. Thankfully, everything on the project was going smoothly, so she had only good news to report—at least relative to the *revised* deadline.

By nine-thirty, she had reviewed her notes one more time and felt she was as prepared as she could be for the meeting. Sheryl smiled as she thought of the mockups she had included of Keisha's new interface, as she had come to think of it. *If the board isn't blown away by that, nothing will impress them!*

Wanting to center herself before the meeting, she let Tina know she didn't want to be disturbed and closed her door. Sitting straight in her chair, she turned the sound off on her computer and started the Insight Timer app on her phone. She closed her eyes, dropped her hands on her lap, palms upward, and took several deep, cleansing breaths. Then, she let her breathing settle into a steady rhythm.

Focusing on the rise and fall of her belly, Sheryl repeated her favorite meditation mantra: "I am part of the light." Almost immediately, she felt more at peace as the mantra reminded her that she was a representation of divine light in the world, that she was protected and loved, and that her higher self was pure and good. It also reminded her that she didn't have to have all the answers herself.

Feeling grounded, she envisioned the higher selves of all the board members, including hers, attending the upcoming meeting. *May any and all outcomes from the board meeting today be in the highest good for all.* After repeating the intention several times, she released it to the universe. She knew from experience that could mean different results from what she expected or thought she wanted, and she trusted that things would eventually work out. This newish philosophy and practice had come to serve her very well in the last two months.

A soft gong indicated that her meditation time was over. She gradually opened her eyes and brought herself back to the present. *I'm ready.*

An hour and fifteen minutes later, Todd introduced her segment of the meeting. Butterflies dancing lightly in her stomach, she stood and strode confidently up the length of the long conference room that served as the company's boardroom. Adjacent to Todd's office, it was impressive. That morning was the first time Sheryl had seen it. Reaching the small podium that others had used for their reports, she picked up the remote. She held onto her feeling of being centered and calm as she pulled up the first slide.

Before speaking, she paused, meticulously making eye contact with each of the eight dark-suited men arrayed around the long, black table. Todd had shifted to the side of the table to better see her slides, and his blue eyes met hers with encouragement. Alex Thompson, Jim Leaders, along with the non-executive members Sean and Duncan, sat in front of the windows behind Todd. Hank Turner, Anthony Russo, and Gary, the fifth outsider, were across from them.

Hank looked like a small mountain sitting there, with his broad shoulders, thick body, and a mop of gray hair that looked like dirty snow. His eyebrows were pinched together in a seemingly permanent glower. Anthony, beside him, looked slim and sophisticated, impeccably dressed, with piercing eyes and dark, almost black hair. They were clearly the two most intimidating men in the room.

Looking back at the friendlier faces—Alex, Todd, even Jim—she took a deep breath and began speaking. "Gentlemen, thank you. I'm going to break my presentation into three sections: security, hardware, and software development."

She and Todd had agreed to put the update on the Portal Project at the end of the presentation in case the discussion got heated.

In the zone, Sheryl breezed through the Power Point, making her points cleanly and clearly. She noticed Todd nodding approvingly, and she felt herself relax.

The blow up came when she brought up the slide with the revised release plan for the Customer Portal.

"What do you mean it won't be done until July?" Hank Turner growled, cutting off Sheryl mid-sentence. His full, square face was drawn into taut lines.

She swallowed hard but met the older man's glare. "After a thorough and careful review, we agreed that it was in the best interest of the company to postpone the implementation so that we could provide the best customer experience possible," she responded with only the slightest tremor in her voice.

"Did you agree to this?" Hank demanded, turning his steely, slate gray eyes on Jim Leaders. "You were the one who said this couldn't wait."

"Actually, Hank, I am okay with it," Jim said easily, although Sheryl saw him shift in his chair as if his unaccustomed suit was not comfortable. "It's not ideal of course, but my team and I recognize that we couldn't get a cutting-edge design in the original timeframe. A few of the big issues with the current design were fixed or improved, but I do feel that we are getting a much better product in the long run."

"Humph," Hank glared at him, then switched his focus to Todd. "We can't reach our profitability goals with stale software and missed deadlines. We can't allow this kind of slacking off in IT. Is that how it's going to be now?"

Sheryl smothered a gasp at his harsh words, and her cheeks flushed. She was just figuring out how to respond when Todd intervened.

"Hank, that's quite unnecessary," he said quietly. "Jim and I both reviewed the new plan and agreed it's the best option. IT is working hard to make something special for our portal. If you allow Sheryl to finish, you'll see that it's cutting edge and will blow away the competition. That's important."

Hank's eyes narrowed as he turned back to Sheryl. "As long as there aren't any more delays," he said pointedly, leaning his heavy torso forward, his elbows splayed on the table.

Sheryl swallowed and nodded, "Understood."

She took several more minutes to elaborate on the enhancements to the Portal, highlighting the innovation and creativity that Keisha was implementing. She watched Hank and Anthony pay close attention, both making occasional notes. Hank looked slightly mollified as she showed the mockups of the new design. But she was relieved when she concluded her presentation and went back to her seat near the far end of the table.

Thanking her politely, Todd called for a brief break while he called Janine to join them. Almost everyone stood up and headed either to the coffee station or out the door.

Sheryl followed those leaving the room, needing a few moments to compose herself. She had felt exposed and vulnerable under Hank's attack, but she was confident that she had handled herself pretty well. Although she was thankful for Todd and Jim's support, she knew that Hank had given her a warning that she needed to heed. *He is a powerful man who doesn't like to be crossed.*

Feeling composed again, she returned to the boardroom. Hank immediately caught her eye, and she noticed he was still staring at her with a menacing expression on his face. She returned his glare calmly, forcing herself not to flinch or blink. He was the first to look away, but he had obviously been trying to intimidate her. *But I'm not going to let him.*

Alex Thompson walked over and greeted her quietly. "That was tough," he encouraged her. "But you did good. Don't let him rattle you."

She smiled at the head of investments, grateful for his support. "It's all in a day's work," she said lightly.

They all returned to their seats as Janine walked in and Todd called the meeting back to order. Sheryl's shoulders slid into a more relaxed position now that her presentation was over. *No more run-ins with Hank or Anthony today,* she thought.

Resuming his role as Chairman of the Board, Todd reopened the conversation. "The final agenda item is selecting our new CFO," he began. "We are fortunate to have two excellent candidates. Janine provided you with their CVs and interview notes last week. I'll let her open the discussion with a quick overview."

Janine, seated next to Todd, began speaking. She presented a reasonably balanced case for both candidates, but Sheryl felt that she gave Layla Arch a more favorable outlook. Inwardly frowning, she listened carefully while keeping a neutral look on her face. *Janine's team knows Layla,* she thought, knowing that the payroll staff had worked with the candidate. *And they don't like her. Did Janine not ask them about their experience?*

Todd spoke next. "We all know how important the finance department and CFO role is to the company when it comes to achieving our profit objectives," he expounded, looking mostly at Hank and Anthony. They had satisfied looks on their faces, as Todd continued praising Layla. "She has demonstrated the ability to be ruthless and swift in making needed changes."

Appalled, Sheryl glanced around the table at the other faces arrayed there. She could see, but many of the other board members were nodding in agreement, including Alex. The knot in her gut tightened. She got that it was important, and Ed had left a bit of a mess with his outdated views and old-fashioned processes. *But still . . . Layla? For goodness' sake, she's likely to sweep out the whole department!*

"Not only that," Todd continued, "Layla has also shown that she's not afraid to recommend reductions in other departments. She helped improve the bottom line at the bank by recognizing areas that could be streamlined in IT and Client Services," Todd went on, basking in the approving gazes of Hank in Anthony. Sheryl shifted uncomfortably at the mention of IT and noticed Jim doing the same.

Todd paused dramatically, gazing around the room with a determined look. "While I respect Blake Jones and everything he has accomplished,

I'm not sure that he'll be as zealous as Layla in turning over every stone in the pursuit of profit."

Sheryl cringed. She observed that Jim and Alex did too, although they were quick to hide it, as was she. Todd was clearly playing to Hank and Anthony. *Carl told me that he sees them as keys to advancing his career. It sure seems like he's right about that!*

Todd opened the floor for the discussion period. Both Jim and Alex made halfhearted attempts to defend Blake, which she noted that Todd deflected neatly. Sheryl remained quiet. She wasn't sure what to say. Based on her boss's response to her colleagues, it would be taking a big risk to oppose the nearly unanimous opinion in the room. Plus, she had already been criticized once today for being too soft.

"For goodness' sake," Hank Turner broke in after Alex cautiously raised one more concern. "Why are we debating this? Layla Arch has the backbone to make the tough decisions. Blake is a good man, but that's the problem. He's too good, too nice for what we need."

When Anthony mentioned that it would be good "optics" to have another female on the board, Sheryl inwardly groaned. Although she supported women in higher level positions, she still felt strongly that they had to be qualified and the right fit. *While I'd welcome another woman on the board, I don't want it to be like this!*

Sheryl followed the brief debate about optics with growing dismay. She was close to speaking up when she realized that Todd was bringing the discussion period to a close. Before she knew it, she heard Anthony second the motion to end the debate and start the vote. *Oh boy, this is bad. I didn't speak up. Does that mean I have to vote for Layla now?*

Dipping her head to look down at her lap, Sheryl took a deep breath, gathering herself. For a moment, she pulled her focus inward, reaching for a place of peace inside herself, trying to calm her nerves and find an answer.

The voting began.

Vote one, vote two, vote three, vote four . . . all for Layla. With each vote, Sheryl's stomach ratcheted a notch tight.

It seemed as if everyone was voting for Layla Arch, although she noted some of her colleagues seemed hesitant. *Damn. Hesitant apparently means still going with the flow, even if it's against your instincts.*

Finally, it was Sheryl's turn. She knew she was expected to fall in line. She felt the expectant pressure in Todd's gaze. Glancing away from him and around the room, she thought about what it had taken to get here, to have this opportunity to influence the direction of the company she cared about deeply. Isn't this what she had worked a decade and a half for? Her husband Dave would certainly think so.

Knowing her vote was already counted in Todd's mind because of her silence, she looked back at him, and then away, her mind spinning.

Do I dare?

Still, she hesitated, stalling. Everyone was looking at her now, most with impatience on their faces. It was too late to do anything but say yea or nay. *Or is it?*

Time stood still. Her eyes closed, Sheryl could feel her heart pounding under the thin silk of her blouse. Images flashed through her mind. *The guards fanning out across the floor. Poor George, standing up for his rights. Keisha's distraught face. Carl's empty office.* She forced herself to breathe. *The women's empowerment meetings. The successful projects. Keisha's amazing Portal interface.* Her stomach roiled. *The fights with Dave. The grief ceremony: the applause, the release, the relief. Janine's admiration. Carl's warnings.* They all marched across her brain. *I've come too far to back down now,* she thought, the truth suddenly clear.

Sheryl drew in a deep breath, opening her eyes and sending up a brief prayer for support as she did. *I owe my teams more than just going along. It's too important to the company . . . and . . . I owe myself!* She focused her attention solely on Todd.

"I'm sorry," she said quietly, but with deep conviction. "As much as I'd like to have another female on the board, I just can't vote for Layla." Todd's gaze sharpened, and she heard Janine gasp, but she plowed on. "The employees have been through a lot of trauma in the last few months. Quite a few of them know Layla and how unpleasant she can be. Many also know she isn't well-liked by her staff because of the interactions they have with her team and others at the bank." She paused only long enough to draw a breath for her next statement. "I think she would be detrimental to employee morale and would cause more harm to the company and its profitability than good. I've also thoroughly researched Blake, and I think he would be a much better candidate."

Todd's face had turned to stone while she was speaking. Sheryl could almost feel the anger radiating from him. The room was completely silent for at least ten seconds as everyone absorbed her words. Daring a quick peek at her colleagues' faces, she saw Alex and Jim reflecting both awe and deep concern.

Suddenly, Hank leaned forward and started to rise from his chair, his face red. "I ca—"

"Motion passed," Todd said sharply, looking right at the irate board member. He turned to his assistant Mary, sitting quietly and unnoticed in the corner of the room taking the minutes. "Please note that there was one dissenting vote."

Sheryl watched Hank sit back down without speaking. The man exchanged a long look with Anthony. Sheryl shuddered. *That doesn't bode well for me.*

"Ladies and gentlemen," Todd said curtly, turning his attention back to the table, his jaw tight. "I think this concludes our meeting for today. Do I hear a motion to adjourn?"

Alex quickly answered, "So moved."

Jim Leaders immediately followed with "Second."

"All in favor?" Todd asked.

Sheryl dutifully responded "Aye" along with everyone else.

Todd stood up. "Meeting adjourned."

Chapter Nineteen

Sheryl sat frozen in her chair, afraid to move. Motion filled the room around her. Ignoring everyone else, Todd walked over to Hank and Anthony, who, Sheryl saw, were both now shooting murderous looks down the table at her.

"Thank you," she heard Todd say, extending his hand. Sheryl watched nervously as Hank ignored the hand and motioned the younger man into the corner of the room. An animated conversation followed, but the two men were quiet enough that she couldn't hear.

She did notice that Hank's gray, angry eyes slid to her once or twice. In spite of herself, she squirmed. The industry veteran towered over Todd's trim form. She sensed that he was using his size to intimidate. Leaning in, Hank's head full of gray-white hair was close to Todd's dark one.

Sheryl was impressed that Todd remained impassive. He didn't blink and seemed to respond in calm, low tones to whatever Hank was saying. Finally, after one more glare from Hank in her direction, the two men shook hands and Hank stomped out. Anthony followed close behind, his posture as stiff as his colleague's.

Becoming aware that the room had largely emptied while she observed Hank and Todd, Sheryl picked up her folder and started out herself. Jim and Alex waited politely at the door, but they merely smiled when she joined them.

They all hesitated when Todd marched toward the door, tacitly ceding the exit to him, but he motioned for them to precede him. When Sheryl tried to slip by, he caught her arm. "I'll see you in my office at 2:30 p.m.," he growled.

Releasing her arm as swiftly as he had grabbed it, he swept out of the room and down the hall.

Sheryl flushed. *Oh boy, I'm in trouble.* She pushed her hair behind her ear, glancing ahead to see if Jim or Alex had heard, but they were walking quickly away. She straightened her shoulders and followed them with her head held high. Her bravado lasted until she was back in her office.

Brushing past a curious Tina, she closed her door behind her, dropped her folder on her desk, and sank into her new, plush, and appropriately sized chair. *Well,* she thought, *so much for my first board meeting. It was probably my last. Should I have kept my mouth shut? Gone along?* Her opinion hadn't changed anything, except for making everyone angry. She could only imagine what Todd was going to say at 2:30 p.m. She cast her eyes upward. *How is this in my highest good?*

She dropped her head in her hands, her elbows propped on her desk, her spine slumped. She visualized the white light that had surrounded her that morning. *Was it only three hours ago?* But even as she thought that, she felt a sense of peace slowly washing over her.

You did the right thing, her inner voice whispered. *Right for you and for the company. Layla's not the right fit.* Sheryl knew in her heart that hiring Layla Arch would only mean more losses, more defections. *The talented people will leave. People like Keisha and Jose . . . and me.*

She straightened, rolling her head to stretch the tight muscles in her neck. *Todd might choose not to keep me on, but I maintained my integrity. That's what is most important,* she told herself, *my integrity.*

Looking around her office, she reflected on how far she had come in the last few months. *I'm proud of myself. Standing up for Keisha, getting the Portal Project on track, the grief meetings, and now this.* It didn't matter what happened next; she knew she could handle it. *Plus,* she thought wryly, *it's not like I'm going to starve if I lose my job.*

She turned resolutely to her computer. *I'll keep working until Todd tells me not to.* She had just opened her email when she heard a soft knock on the door.

Janine slipped in and closed it behind her before Sheryl could even answer. The HR executive's eyes were wide. "I don't know whether what you did was incredibly brave or incredibly stupid, but *it was incredible,*" she said in an awestruck voice.

Sheryl's eyes filled with tears. She stifled a sob with a quick laugh. "I don't know either," she replied. "But it had to be said. I *had* to say it."

Janine walked over and gave her a hug.

Sheryl stiffened at first, then hugged her friend back.

"I know you did. Sheryl, you were amazing. You *are* amazing. I'm so in awe of your integrity and your courage. I can't *believe* you had the nerve to do that!"

"It was probably foolish. Todd wants to see me at 2:30 p.m. I don't think he will be congratulating me," Sheryl told her drily.

A look of concern crossed the HR executive's face. "When did he say that?"

"As we were leaving the boardroom."

"Oh," Janine frowned. "That may not be good, *but* it might not be bad either. You never know with Todd."

"Yeah, right." Sheryl said in disgust. "That's wishful thinking."

Just then, a shaft of midday sun poured into the office. Glancing outside, Sheryl saw large swaths of blue in what had been an overcast sky. *Maybe it's a good omen.*

The sun caught Janine full in the face, and she squinted and put her hand up. "Wow, that's intense."

Sheryl closed the shades to reduce the intensity of the glare, but the room was still very bright. She turned back, giving her friend a long look. "You know, I'm not worried. What will be, will be," she said calmly, still standing behind her desk.

"It will be okay," Janine said. "You will be okay. You were awesome this morning."

"And yet, no one seemed to agree with me." Sheryl looked pointedly at Janine.

"It wasn't my place. I'm not on the board."

"You are the head of HR, for goodness' sake, Janine. If you don't have a say, who does? You're supposed to be supporting the *human* resources."

Janine took a step back, looking stunned by the anger in Sheryl's tone. Sheryl watched as her face suffused with red and took on a guilty expression. The older woman sighed.

"I couldn't go against Todd in public. We had agreed on the presentation beforehand," she argued.

"Why did you agree to that? You know it's going to be a disaster!"

"Well, I didn't know that people knew about her reputation or that her staff didn't like her."

"You didn't?" Sheryl asked, flipping her outstretched palms up. "How could you not? You know what she does. You work with people at the bank—or your staff does."

Janine cringed. "Well, Kelly, my payroll manager, did mention having reservations. But I didn't give her chance to explain," she admitted. "Todd was so set on hiring Layla from the very beginning."

"Because of Hank and Anthony?"

Janine shrugged. "Probably. They've been putting a lot of pressure on him. On everyone."

"They are only two votes. Would the rest of the board follow them?"

"They represent a lot of shares."

"But not the majority, not even close." Carl had made absolutely sure that Sheryl knew that fact.

"No, not the majority, but they have a lot of influence."

"That's obvious," Sheryl said sarcastically. She sighed. "It is what it is. You're right that I'll be okay no matter what happens."

"Yes, you will be," Janine assured her. "But I've gotta scoot. Call me after you talk to Todd?"

Sheryl nodded as her friend slipped back out, closing the door behind her.

Calling Janine proved to be unnecessary. She was already seated in Todd's office when Sheryl arrived. Mary had called Sheryl shortly after two o'clock to postpone her meeting with Todd until three. *And now I know why. Todd needed to consult with Janine.* Truly nervous now, she tucked her hair behind her ear with her free hand.

Todd looked at her impatiently. "Come in and sit down," he grumbled. He was visibly upset. Angry, frustrated, and something else that Sheryl couldn't quite define. She walked over and sat near Janine in the seating area. The arrangement was eerily similar to the way they had all sat less than two months ago when Todd had offered her the CIO job, but the vibe was definitely different.

For one, Todd didn't sit. He paced across the office, running his hands through his hair. Sheryl had never seen Todd so agitated.

"I want to fire you," he finally ground out. "Sheryl, there's a discussion period *before* the voting for a reason. Remember all the times I asked if anyone had issues or concerns? You didn't speak up and then you *grandstand* during the vote!" Todd's voice rose in both pitch and volume. "Oh, and by the way, you *had the final vote.*"

Sheryl blinked rapidly. "I'm sorry about that," Sheryl said honestly, her voice raspy. She *had* realized that she was breaking protocol with her comments at the time of her vote. "I was, well, surprised at the way the discussion went. It seemed like such a foregone conclusion that I was uncomfortable bringing up my point of view." She looked earnestly at her boss. "I know I should have. I thought that I was going to go along with the others, but when it came to my turn to vote, I just couldn't. I had to say what I said. I am *truly sorry* that I didn't speak up earlier."

"You should be," Todd shot back. "That isn't the way things work. I know it was your first meeting, but you know better than that."

Sheryl nodded contritely. "I do."

"Janine convinced me that I can't and shouldn't fire you. You should thank her," Todd went on. Sheryl snuck a quick glance at Janine, who gave her a quick, tense smile. "So, now I don't know what to do with you. You have caused me one *gigantic* headache."

Sheryl swallowed another apology, as Todd continued pacing. He looked like he was struggling with what to say next.

"Duncan and Gary told me during lunch that they have concerns about hiring Layla after hearing your little speech," he finally continued, utter frustration in his voice. "Then Sean, of course, followed suit." Sheryl and Janine shared a look of surprise, but neither said a word.

"Do you know what problems that causes?" He paused again. "And then . . . " Todd turned and looked right at her. "Then, your *peers* decided to change their minds too! So, now I have a recorded board vote that more than half the board doesn't agree with any longer." Todd's fingers threaded through his thick, nearly black hair again.

Sheryl gasped out loud. *That means Alex and Jim must have talked to*

Todd too. She hadn't seen that coming. Judging by Janine's shocked expression, she hadn't either.

Todd turned to Janine. "And what do you think?" he barked at her. "Do you have something different to say *now?*"

Sheryl watched Janine squirm in her chair; there was no other word for it. "Well, um, now that you mention it, um, I think Sheryl did have some really good points this morning."

"So, you're turning on me too," Todd said flatly, his eyes hard.

"No, I'm not *turning* on you," Janine defended herself. "It's just that, well, some of my team said the same things about Layla when I asked them this afternoon. She might be *too* disruptive, more than I originally thought."

"And you didn't think to ask your staff *before* we agreed what to present to the board?" Todd asked quietly. Sheryl thought it was amazing how she could feel he was yelling even though he didn't raise his voice.

Janine flinched but held her ground. "Honestly, Todd, Kelly had said something to me earlier about Layla being a barracuda, but you seemed to be so set on Layla that I, uh, didn't pursue it."

He shook his head. "You can't do this to me. Maybe I should fire you too."

"Todd, look, I'm sorry about that. I am. Even more than Sheryl, I should know better. You have every right to be angry with me," Janine said apologetically. Her face was flushed, and Sheryl thought she saw tiny drops of moisture on her friend's temple.

"What do I do about the board vote now?" he asked rhetorically.

He paced back and forth across the room again, coming to a stop in front of Sheryl. "I'm not going to fire you now, but if you ever pull a stunt like that again, I damn well will fire you. I don't care what Janine or anyone else says," he said flatly.

Still, Sheryl thought she heard an edge of respect in his voice. He didn't seem quite as angry when he continued.

"You speak up when you are asked to speak up, or you don't do it at all. Got it?"

Sheryl nodded vigorously. "Yes, Todd, I got it. I'm sorry that I didn't use the discussion period. It was my first major vote, and I wanted to support the whole company . . . and, well, I found myself between a rock and a hard place. It won't happen again. I promise."

Todd waved his hand toward the door. "Get out of here, both of you. I need to figure out what to do next." He looked darkly at Janine. "And you, don't send out an offer to Ms. Arch. *No offers.*"

"Got it. No offers," Janine agreed, rising. She and Sheryl hurried out of the office.

They were silent as they descended the stairs and headed together toward Janine's office. Once safely inside with the door closed, they turned to each other, disbelief mirrored on their faces.

"What just happened?" asked Sheryl.

Janine shook her head. "I have no idea, but wow, I've never seen Todd that rattled." She paused. "I can't believe it. I think you won."

"I won? Like he's really not going to hire Layla?" Sheryl laughed nervously.

"He did want to fire you, at least I think he did. But he hadn't told me about the others who changed their votes."

Sheryl's mind began to whirl with possibilities. "Do you think he agrees with me? With us? Is he relieved to not hire Layla? Was he just placating Hank and Anthony?"

"Those are all good questions," Janine answered. "I'm not sure we'll ever find out, but you might be right." She started laughing. "I just can't believe what happened. And thank God, I don't have to hire Layla. I was *not* looking forward to that!"

"Then why didn't you *say* something, Janine?" Sheryl asked with frustration.

Janine shrugged. "You know how intimidating Todd can be. He didn't really give me a chance to say much. He had picked Layla before we even started talking. I didn't feel like I had a choice. Kind of like you felt at the board meeting, I guess."

Sheryl raised her eyebrows. "Well?"

"Yeah, I should have said something," Janine admitted. "I'm not as brave as you are."

"You could be," Sheryl gave her friend an encouraging look.

Janine made a face. "Maybe."

Sheryl turned toward the door. "I've got to get back to work. But keep me posted. I'm proud of you for speaking up just now," she threw over her shoulder as she walked out.

Threading her way through the corridors toward her office, her mind turned back to Todd. *Is he really going to overturn the vote?* She allowed herself a small smile, and it stayed on her face the rest of the afternoon.

She was still hugging the memory of the conversation with Todd to herself when Dave called that evening from San Jose—again—to see how the meeting had gone. She had just gone upstairs to get ready for bed when his name popped up on her phone.

She answered hesitantly, unsure whether to even tell him what had happened at the meeting. Besides, at this point, she was getting more and more curious about what was keeping him in San Jose.

Dave preempted her. "How was the meeting?"

"It was, um, good. My presentation went well, I thought." Sheryl paced slowly through their spacious master bedroom, skirting the king-size bed as she did.

"Did they balk about the date change on the Portal Project?"

"Yeah, Hank did, but Todd and Jim shut him down," Sheryl replied, downplaying the drama, although she wasn't sure why. "It turned out okay."

"That's great," her husband enthused. "Another milestone. Your first successful board meeting. Congratulations!"

"Thank you," she murmured, feeling uneasy about leaving so much of the story out.

There was a pause, as if he were waiting for her to say more.

"So," she finally spoke into the silence, her pace momentarily quickened. "Tell me about *your* trip. You haven't told me much about this project or who you're working with."

"Well, it's a distributed network for a big tech company out here," he said excitedly. "I can't tell you the name because their Non-Disclosure Agreement was as tight as I've ever seen. But you've heard of them, and it's a really interesting challenge. Lots of nuances that we haven't dealt with before."

"That does sound exciting," Sheryl responded with forced interest. "Who's on the project with you?"

"Robert, you remember him?"

"Sure, how is he? We haven't seen him and his wife for a while now," Sheryl asked with genuine warmth and curiosity. She really liked Robert, who was a long-time colleague of her husband.

"He's good," her husband replied. "Doesn't like the traveling. He hates to miss his boys' basketball games."

"I'm sure," Sheryl chuckled, turning to take another lap around the room. "Isn't there anyone from the West Coast on the team?"

Dave hesitated a beat. "The sales people. Liam and Alisha. They're involved, of course," he answered casually.

Maybe too casually?

His statement was followed by a loud yawn.

"Hey, it's earlier there than here," she chided him. "Why are you yawning?"

"We've been putting in long days. I am kind of exhausted. Plus, all the back and forth. There's a little jet lag too, I think."

"Well, I guess I'll let you go," she said, not knowing what else to ask without sounding like a jealous wife.

"Sounds good," he replied. "Sleep well. I'll see you tomorrow. I should be home by six."

"Okay, good night."

Sheryl hung up, sinking down on the edge of their bed. She sat there for a long time after the call, feeling disconcerted by her own actions. *This is the first time I haven't shared something important with Dave. I've always been able to talk with him about anything. I couldn't tonight. I just can't bear another round of his criticism.*

Her mind shifted to his comments about his project and his coworkers. It sounded normal, but Alisha? *Had he hesitated a little before saying that name?*

Her thoughts spun, playing the conversation over and over, trying to interpret what he had said. Finally, she mentally shook herself. *Enough of this. I'll talk to him this weekend, when we're together.* But she wondered if she really would. *I'm not sure I trust him anymore to support me—at least not the way I want to be supported.*

Standing up, she padded to the bathroom to get ready for bed.

But when she lay down twenty minutes later, feeling tired and wanting to sleep, all she could think about was Dave and her secret that now lay between them. *I wonder if he has secrets too.*

Chapter Twenty

Thursday, November 18

"I need to see you right away," Todd barked, when he finally called her around eleven. She had been anxiously anticipating the call all morning. Pushing off a meeting with Rick, she headed directly to his office.

"You have sure caused me a heap of trouble," he growled from behind his desk as she walked through the double black doors. They had been open wide, as if welcoming her in—in sharp contrast to Todd's scowl.

She hesitated, not knowing quite how to respond. She was thankful she had chosen to wear her burgundy suit today. It gave her a little added confidence. She started toward him.

Suddenly, Todd shocked her by laughing. He pointed to the chair in front of his desk, and Sheryl hurried over and sat down. She noticed that Todd's yellow tie was slightly askew.

"I know you're proud of yourself for what you did yesterday, and you should be," he said gravely, surprising her further. She blinked rapidly, trying to digest his words. "I need people on the team who are willing to challenge me, to challenge Hank, even though it's not easy."

Sheryl's eyes widened. *He's happy I challenged him?* A warm glow started building in her belly.

Looking at her thoughtfully, Todd continued. "That doesn't mean that I want you to be reckless or to break protocol, though," he cautioned. "I respect and admire your integrity and your courage." He smiled ruefully. "I knew I was in trouble the moment I heard about your little meetings."

Sheryl couldn't hold back a full out grin. She sat up straighter in her chair but didn't speak. *This is not how I expected this discussion to go.*

"You have to be careful though, Sheryl," Todd advised her, his voice more serious now. "Choose your battles wisely. There are going to be times when tough decisions *do* have to be made, unpopular ones." Sheryl started to protest, but he held up his hand. "I know you've made tough decisions. You supported the layoffs because you knew they were necessary, and you were careful and consistent about who you chose to be laid off from your department. I know that. I talked it over with Carl."

"Thanks, Todd," Sheryl said, finally able to get a word in edgewise. "I really do always try to do what's best for the company."

"I appreciate that, but I've got to warn you. You have an enemy in Hank right now." Todd's blue eyes were full of intensity as he met her gaze. "I have to be bluntly honest about that. He's angry that we reversed that vote about Layla. She was his chosen candidate. You realize that?" His right eyebrow quirked up with the question until she nodded. "I know that Hank's used to getting his own way, especially when he teams up with Anthony. I know even the other board members find them intimidating at times. They make a formidable team, so I'm doubly impressed that you have the nerve to stand up to them. They have the power to make both our lives miserable."

"Yes, I know that," Sheryl said quietly, her hands in her lap nervously twisting her wedding band. "I don't want you to be miserable, Todd. I only spoke up because I feel that Layla would be such a detriment to the company and to you in the long run."

He sighed, leaning back in his chair. He tugged on his tie as if it was choking him.

"I found a way in the by-laws to negate that vote," he said frankly, catching her off guard. "There *is* a provision for second thoughts, it appears, but it's not something that can be used often." He wagged a finger in her direction.

Blushing, Sheryl couldn't prevent a small smile from curving her lips. "I know that. I don't plan to force you to use it again," Sheryl replied sincerely.

"I also can't move forward with Layla because of all the objections that have been raised after the fact, including mine, by the way. What you said made me rethink my position too, and I don't do that often." Sheryl was surprised that Todd admitted that. "I'll confess, I've seen how badly our productivity has suffered recently, and we can't afford more of that."

Sheryl nodded, wondering where Todd was going. It felt like praise and threats were being neatly interwoven in the conversation, keeping her off balance.

"*But* I'm going to have to call another vote to be fair to Hank and Anthony, who are the only ones not swayed by your passionate argument. They deserve a chance to be heard," Todd finished,

"That makes sense," Sheryl said, her stomach churning. *That means facing Hank.*

Todd seemed to hear her thoughts. "However, I'm willing to stand up with you, and so are Alex and Jim. I can't say what the other three will do."

Sheryl released the breath that she hadn't realized she was holding. Tears pricked her eyelids. *Wow, I never expected Todd to actually defend me—or Jim either!*

"Todd, thank you so much for your support," she said urgently. "I can't tell you how grateful I am. I know this is difficult for you, and I'm sorry I put you in such a complicated position. I promise to speak up appropriately the next time, not at the eleventh hour. I can't tell you, though, how very honored and grateful I am that you listened and took what I said into account."

Todd smiled wryly. "I'm not a monster, Sheryl, despite what the rumor mill might say. I know a valid argument when I hear one, and I must have had some of those doubts myself because what you said resonated with me." He gave a self-deprecating chuckle. "I'm calling another meeting at ten tomorrow morning. The non-executive directors will participate by video conference. I want you to be prepared for both Hank's anger, maybe Anthony's, *and* whatever outcome is voted for."

Sheryl blanched visibly.

"There's no guarantee that Blake will be chosen or that Layla won't win again. They will argue for her again today."

"I got it, Todd. Thank you. I'll be prepared for all of it. I'm grateful to have an opportunity for a do-over." She smiled nervously. *And I'll try not to let Hank get to me.*

"Okay. That's all then. I'll see you tomorrow."

"Thanks again, Todd," she said crisply, matching his tone. Giving him one last appreciative look, she rose and left, feeling her boss's eyes on her back as she went.

Alex was waiting for her when she got back from Todd's office. He shocked her by giving her a warm hug. "You go, girl!" he said, admiration shining in his light brown eyes. "You were awesome yesterday. I'm sorry I didn't get to tell you earlier. You said what the rest of us didn't have the guts to say."

"Thanks, Alex," Sheryl smiled brightly at him, grateful for his support. "But it's not over yet. Have you heard about the meeting tomorrow?"

"Yeah, I just heard about it. Hank's going to have a cow, but it won't be just you this time. You know that, right?"

"That's what Todd said. Apparently, even he has changed his mind," Sheryl answered. "But I'm going to be the one that Hank is going to kill." She shivered again at that thought.

"Hey, he's not going to kill you . . . exactly. We won't let him," Alex teased. "He can't do much if it's only him and Anthony opposed to the motion."

"He can't do anything now, but what happens in the future?" Todd's talk had made Sheryl uneasy.

Alex sobered. "You can't worry about that, Sheryl. You'll be fine no matter what. You're a smart, brave woman, exactly who this company needs."

Sheryl looked at him in surprise. She and Alex had become friendly, but she didn't expect this much support from him.

He looked a little sheepish. "Well, you are," he said. "You've inspired me in the last few months." His boyish face contorted in a grimace. "I think I might want to be a little more like you when I grow up."

Sheryl laughed softly, a pleasant warmth spreading through her at his words. "Thank you, Alex. That means a lot coming from you. I know I still have a lot to learn."

"Yeah, but you're off to a great start. We've got your back. Me, and Jim too, although he might not say it."

"Did Jim have Carl's back?"

"Geez, Sheryl. You don't pull your punches, do you?" He rubbed his chin. "I don't know. I doubt it. There was something between them, but it had nothing to do with you. You're building your own relationship with Jim, and he's respecting you. You can't worry about what happened with Carl."

Sheryl nodded. She knew that, although it still bothered her. She also knew that Carl was happy now, happier than he had expected to be. It seemed like things were working out for both of them, she and Carl. *I just have to trust that things will work out the way they're supposed to.* She was relieved to have Jim's support now, although she recognized that it might be temporary.

"Chin up," Alex said. "You did good. It'll be fine tomorrow. Just wait and see."

"Thanks again, Alex. I'm sure it will be fine."

"You got it . . . see you tomorrow." Alex loped out of her office with long easy strides. *It is good to know that he's on my side, unlike Dave,* she thought, unable to suppress a tinge of bitter emotion.

The next morning dawned clear and sunny, the sun creeping over the horizon as Sheryl drove to the office. She had woken early, feeling surprisingly refreshed. Deliberately replacing her cardio workout with yoga, she sought both movement and calm. She had a feeling she would need it.

Sheryl purposefully filled her time before the new board meeting by touching base with her staff. She helped Patrick solve some minor problems with the Portal and got an update on a potential security breach that had been stopped during the night from Rick. She gave Rick and his team the kudos they deserved, while learning a few more things on the hardware side. *IT is a lifelong game,* she though dryly. *Always something new.*

At quarter before the hour, she shut her door and opened the Insight Timer app again. She went through a similar practice as she had two days before. When the gong sounded, Sheryl felt grounded and uplifted at the same time. She strode up to the boardroom with a deeper sense of resolve and peace than she'd had for the first meeting. She was still nervous. How could she not be with the specter of an angry

Hank hanging over her head? But that was on the surface. Underneath was a calm that she was learning to rely on. *Another new skill I've acquired.*

When she opened the door to the large, elaborate conference room, Alex, Jim, and Janine were already present. A second look told her that Mary was in her usual spot in the corner, ready to take minutes. Todd's administrative assistant didn't look happy. The large television screen at the far end of the room was on. Gary, Duncan and Sean were already visible, but their heads were down, and they appeared to be working on other things.

She greeted Mary softly and sat down next to Alex on the near side of the table. Jim and Janine sat across from them.

"Ready?" Alex whispered.

She gave him a quick smile. "You bet."

He winked and started to say something else, but at that moment, Todd barreled in. "Let's get this started," he growled with no greeting or preamble. Seeing the scowl on her boss's face, Sheryl guessed he was not looking forward to the meeting. Todd knew what power Hank could have over his career, over *all* their careers. Bucking him like this was taking a big risk, but Sheryl had a feeling that Todd wanted to prove that he was his own man too. A force of his own to be reckoned with.

Two incoming call tones rang out, one right after the other. Hank and Anthony appeared almost simultaneously on the screen. Sheryl immediately noticed that Hank looked like a thundercloud, his ruddy complexion redder than normal. Anthony, his narrow face pale despite his olive-toned skin, didn't appear as if he was in good spirits either. She could tell that Hank was muttering to himself although she couldn't hear the words. Glancing at her colleagues, she saw them all nervously transfixed on Hank's dark glower.

"Yes, by all means, let's get this farce started," Hank sneered.

Sheryl's brow furrowed, and she saw that Gary and Duncan were looking at their cameras now, both frowning.

"I'm calling this meeting to order," Todd said, speaking with what Sheryl thought of as his presidential voice, very stern and deeper than usual. "This is a special supplemental meeting to discuss and vote on the proposed candidates for our new CFO. The previous vote has been set aside according to Section 15.3 of the by-laws because several members recanted their votes within twenty-four hours. I've ask—"

"I don't understand why some of you damn fools recanted your votes," Hank roared. Sheryl's eyes widened. She heard a rustling sound as everyone else in the room started at Hank's aggression.

"Hank," Todd said firmly. "That's not appropriate. You'll have time for your say, but you don't need to insult the people here."

Hank's glower deepened, it seemed to Sheryl, but he remained silent.

"Janine is going to present the candidates," Todd continued, "and our joint recommendation again. Please be courteous, even though I know some of this is repetitive."

Janine went through the background and qualifications of Blake Jones and Layla Arch again, as if the board had never heard them before. Everyone seemed to listen patiently, except Hank, who continued to glare at them. It was when she got to the recommendation that Sheryl felt the tension intensify.

The head of HR stated, for many of the reasons that Sheryl had brought up on Wednesday, that she and Todd supported Blake Jones as the preferred candidate. Janine also noted that because of his previous work at a direct competitor, he would be able to get up to speed and understand the business much more easily than Ms. Arch.

Sheryl listened intently, focusing on Janine and her words. Making sure that she kept her face calm and neutral, she nervously kept one eye on Hank. She didn't want to add fuel to Hank's already volatile fire by looking like she was gloating. But whatever her intentions, Hank grew more visibly agitated as Janine spoke. Sheryl could almost see his jaw tighten.

Todd thanked Janine and reiterated his support for hiring Blake Jones. He opened the floor for discussion.

At some seemingly predetermined signal, Anthony spoke first. He repeated many of his arguments about Layla from the previous day, although with more eloquence and passion. His dark eyes flashed as he stared straight into his camera while he made his plea. Sheryl saw

Hank relax as his cohort made another strong case for their preferred candidate.

Tensing, Sheryl glanced at Janine, who looked back with a skeptical face. In fact, no one seemed swayed by Anthony's speech.

"Thank you, Anthony," Todd said politely when he was finished. "I appreciate your points, but it doesn't change the fact that Layla's ruthlessness, as you put it, doesn't seem to be what is needed most at The Diamante right now."

She watched Anthony frown, and Hank's glower returned in full force. She could see Hank gathering himself.

"I agree, Todd," Alex interjected before anyone else could speak. "Blake has solid skills, exceptional ones, actually, from what I've been able to determine. He can help us cut costs without us bleeding to death."

Just then, Hank exploded. "You stupid fools!" he shouted, his face turning a deeper scarlet. "How dare you pull this crap? I told you that we wanted Layla Arch, and you're going to hire her!"

There was a collective gasp from everyone in the room. She leaned back in her chair, as if trying to avoid the heat emanating through the screen from Hank. Glancing around the room, she saw that she wasn't the only one. Even the other board members on video had their mouths open with shock.

"Hank," Todd said sharply. "If you don't calm down, I'll have to ask you to excuse yourself."

"Excuse myself?" Hank's face was now almost purple with rage. Sheryl thought he might be having a heart attack. "You're the one that's going to be excused. You and all the simpering clowns that are jumping in to placate that inexperienced and idiotic girl that you put on the board. We need a woman who knows how to do business and be a man!"

The room fell into a stunned silence. All the air left Sheryl's lungs in a whoosh, and she felt the eyes of the entire board on her. *What in the world? In all my years in the corporate world, I've never heard anyone say something so unprofessional – especially about* me*!* She stared at the screen in utter shock, her mouth gaping open.

Alex reached over and touched her hand lightly. She started to breathe again.

Anthony was the next one to recover. "Hank, that's enough," he said pointedly, grabbing everyone's surprised attention, including Sheryl's. "Todd is going to disconnect you, and I'll talk to you later." Hank started to object, but Anthony only nodded to Todd, who had the keyboard in front of him. He disconnected Hank's feed before the older man could say another word.

Anthony looked straight into his camera. Now, he looked less firm and a lot more shaken. "I'm truly sorry about that. Of course, I knew Hank was upset, but . . . well, even I've never seen him like that." He paused, shaking his head. "I'll take care of this on my end, although it's not going to be pretty . . . Oh boy," he added as the speaker sounded with an incoming call.

Todd hit the disconnect button again before Hank's face even appeared on the screen. He made a few more quick keystrokes to block Hank from the meeting, Sheryl guessed.

"We'd better continue," Todd said briskly. "Any discussion?"

Anthony spoke up immediately, although this time he looked weary. "Yes, while I don't agree with Hank's language or words, as I said earlier, I *am* concerned about the change in direction with this hire. I thought we had agreed on a more aggressive approach to internal changes and improving profits," he said diplomatically but firmly. "Hiring Blake doesn't seem to fit."

Todd nodded, his face somber as he responded. "Anthony, we did agree to that, and I feel that we've gone a long way already in addressing those goals. But we can't continue in a constant state of upheaval and expect to retain our strong staff members or even get much work done." Sheryl, her eyes still riveted on the screen, was relieved to see Duncan and Gary nodding at Todd's accurate summation of the situation. "We need to have some balance in our approach, or the change will be too disruptive. In that respect, I'm certain that Blake is the better candidate, and he understands our goals and will work toward them with us in a constructive way."

Duncan cleared his throat. "Anthony, you and Hank want to throw the proverbial baby out with the bath water. We need to keep what is good and what is working. This company was profitable before your investors took an equity position, and while I understand they want fast returns, I, for one, refuse to destroy the company to get them."

A few others nodded, including Gary and Sean from their remote locations.

Anthony frowned. "I don't think anyone said anything about destroying the company, Duncan."

"No, you didn't," Gary cut in, "but actions speak louder than words, as long as we're talking in clichés." Everyone but Anthony chuckled.

The room was quiet, waiting for Anthony to speak again. He looked down. At least thirty seconds ticked by. Finally, he nodded. "I can see that everyone's mind is made up. I don't agree, but let's go ahead with the vote and get this over with. I move to end the discussion period."

"Second," said Jim.

"All in favor?" Todd asked. He turned and looked directly at Sheryl, one eyebrow raised, as she nodded and clearly joined the chorus of "ayes."

Todd called for the vote. Anthony dissented this time. Sheryl thought he looked more defeated than angry when casting his vote, and she guessed he was worried about how he was going to handle the situation with Hank. *I know I would be.*

When the voting was finished, Blake had been selected as the new CFO, with Anthony the only opposing voice. While no offer would be made until the newly discovered twenty-four-hour wait time was over, she didn't think anyone would be changing their vote this time. Todd formally adjourned the meeting, but Anthony asked for one more minute.

"Look, I know what we want seems harsh at times, but we really don't want to hurt the company. I apologize again for Hank's words and actions today, especially to you, Sheryl. You didn't deserve that, and I can assure you that you won't be subjected to that again. Todd, I'll be in touch." He ended his connection before Sheryl or anyone could respond.

Gary, Duncan, and Sean all said a quick good-bye and disappeared.

Sheryl sat with the others at the table. She wasn't sure her legs would hold her if she stood up. She thought her shaking was only on the inside until Alex turned and asked her if she was okay. She nodded, unable to speak.

"That was unbelievable, even for Hank," Jim broke the silence.

"Yeah. He really stuck his foot into it. I'm sorry that you had to hear that, Sheryl," Alex said, looking sympathetically at her.

"I was pretty shocked," she replied, still shaken by Hank's words. "I've never had someone be so . . . well, so mean about women . . . or me."

"He should know better than that," Jim said. "Even if he thinks it. He should know better than to say it."

"Agreed," Todd interjected, also looking at her with compassion. "I'm so sorry about that, Sheryl. I expected Hank to give you a hard time, but . . ." He shook his head. "Nothing like that. I've never seen . . . Anthony is right, you didn't deserve that. Frankly, none of us did."

Sheryl swallowed and managed to find her voice. "Thank you, Todd. You don't owe me an apology. You didn't say those things." She took a deep breath, feeling the shock start to wear off. "I appreciate your support." She looked at the others. "And all of yours too." She meant it deeply, and she felt some of the shaking begin to subside. However, her adrenaline was still sky-high.

"So, what are we going to do about Hank?" Jim asked bluntly.

Todd tipped his chin toward the blank screen. "Hopefully, we don't have to do anything. Anthony said he would take care of it." The chairman of the board looked at Janine. "If he doesn't, well, we can't have Hank on the board anymore. Period."

"I'll make sure of it," Janine said quietly.

Sheryl felt a rush of gratitude toward her coworkers.

"Well, then, I vote we get out of here," Jim said, standing up as he spoke. He was already shrugging out of his expensive suit jacket.

"Good idea, Jim," Todd concurred, following his lead.

Everyone else stood, including Sheryl. She stayed still for a moment, checking her legs.

"We'll talk later, Sheryl," Todd said quietly as she passed him at the door.

"Thanks, Todd," Sheryl murmured. "I'm sorry ag—"

Her boss held up his hand. "No more apologies. Not after that." He motioned toward the screen and gave her a rueful smile.

Sheryl smiled back and followed the others out, glad that her legs were strong enough now to hold her. The walk back to her office felt like it took forever.

It wasn't until she sat down at her desk that she recalled that she had actually won, if that was the right thing to call it. *The company won,* she reflected. *I just happened to be the catalyst this time.* She felt that warm glow in her belly again. *This is why I took this job. To make a difference . . . and despite the fallout, now I've done that.*

Chapter Twenty-one

Sheryl felt a rush of relief when Todd called around four to confirm that Hank Turner had resigned from the board of directors.

"But I do have to warn you that Hank might call you himself to apologize," Todd told her. "Unless you tell me that you don't want to hear from him, which is what I suggest." As the company president, he had assured her that he was responsible for making sure that she wouldn't have to deal with Hank again.

"Thank you, Todd. I'll admit that I am thankful to never face him again at a board meeting," she said honestly. The more she thought about Hank's behavior, the angrier she had become. His words had been so infuriating, and they continued to repeat in her head even when she tried to stop them.

"Okay, I'll tell him not to call you then," her boss assured her.

"Wait, Todd, I didn't say that," Sheryl replied quickly. She took a deep breath as the image of Keisha's angry and distraught face swam before her eyes. "I don't want to, um, react the way Hank did. I don't want to be just angry and emotional." *Like Hank* or *Keisha.*

"I respect that, Sheryl, but what are you saying then?"

"Look, I'm still really pissed off right now, if you'll excuse the language," she said, gripping the receiver tightly. "But I also want to make sure that I'm acting in the best interest of the company."

"Okay, and?"

"*Is* Hank not being on the board really in the best interest of the company? To remove him? I know he has a big influence in the industry, you've made that clear."

"What are you asking, Sheryl?" Todd sounded confused.

Sheryl exhaled audibly. "Well, from what Alex and Jim said, this was the first time he had ever done anything like that. As much as I hate to say this . . . Shouldn't he have a chance to make amends and reform?" Sheryl asked cautiously, forcing the words out, all the while remembering how she had given Keisha a second chance. *I don't want to be a hypocrite.*

Todd snorted. "It doesn't work that way. With this type of thing, it's one strike and you're out. You know that. I'm surprised you even asked, especially after . . ."

"I do know that, but it hardly seems fair," Sheryl protested mildly. "We're all human. We all make mistakes. If everyone is tossed out at one mistake, we'll never have any workers *or* leaders. I made a mistake, and you gave me a break."

"I'm impressed with your generosity, Sheryl, but if this ever got out, and we hadn't forced his resignation, there would be a huge demand for our heads. At least mine."

"That's true," she conceded, knowing what happened when the media blew things out of proportion, and there was certainly enough fodder in the truth of what Hank had done . "I still don't think that's right." She paused, considering. "And if Hank wants to call, I'll talk to him, but tell him to give me a couple of days to calm down. He made a huge mistake, but . . . well, I've already told you what I think."

"You know, Sheryl, you're probably right, again," Todd said wryly, "but this time, it has to be this way. Hank has to go."

"I understand, and there is a part of me that's very happy about that, don't get me wrong."

He chuckled. "Thanks, Sheryl, and I'm sorry again that you had to be exposed to that."

After Todd hung up, she looked thoughtfully at the phone. *I'm not ready yet, but I will be gracious to Hank if he calls.*

"I hope Hank learns something from this," she told Cindy hours later, when she was finally home and relaxed on the long sofa in the great room. She had turned the gas fireplace on, and its soft glow, along with the candles she had lit, created a cozy ambiance in the open space.

"I doubt it," Cindy replied cynically. "Guys like that never learn. I'm surprised you even tried."

Sheryl lifted a shoulder. "You're probably right," she conceded, taking a sip of her favorite pinot noir.

"Still, my friend, it's completely amazing what happened. What you did. You're incredible. Look at all you've achieved, and it's been less than two months since your promotion!" Cindy reminded her, awe in her voice.

Sheryl smiled, feeling a renewed sense of pride sweep through her. "Yeah, it's been a pretty wild ride in a very short time," she agreed. "And I do feel good about it. Really good. Janine even told me today that she thought I had saved the company a lot of future headaches by speaking up about Layla."

"I'm sure you did, but what about Layla? I mean, you still have to work with her. Don't you?"

Shuddered, Sheryl groaned. "Don't remind me! But maybe this will stop her incessant lunch requests. I can't believe how two-faced she's been since my promotion. And I didn't even tell Todd about *that!*"

"You'll deal with her, I'm sure," Cindy encouraged her. "At least it'll be from a distance and not up close and personal."

Sheryl laughed. "Yeah, that's true."

"So, what next? You've got everyone working again, thanks to your grief meetings. You've got the Portal Project on track. Your courageous intervention saved the day with the board—and likely the whole company. What's your next miracle?" Cindy teased.

"Hey, no miracles here. I honestly feel like I'm still at the very beginning of this journey. That there are plenty of ladders still left to be climbed. The Portal Project is on track, but it's not out of the woods. We have absolutely no room for error, and you know how dangerous that is."

"That's true, but you've got a good team on it, don't you?"

"Yeah, I do, but I had to explain to Keisha today why I had chosen Blake over Layla. She was indignant about me supporting a man rather than a woman 'the first moment I had a chance to do something good.' Solidarity and all that." Sheryl rolled her eyes. "It took a while to explain. Fortunately, she now understands that we would only have had more of what ticked her off in the first place if Layla had been brought on." She loved Keisha's passion, but she was still a bit high maintenance.

"She'll learn," Cindy said wisely. "We can't support the wrong people just because they happen to be female."

"Exactly what I told her," Sheryl replied. She sighed.

"What about Dave?"

Sheryl pushed her bangs back, moaning softly. "What about him?"

"What's going on with him? Is he still in San Jose?"

"Yeah, until tomorrow . . . maybe. He was supposed to be home at six today, but he's not here. He called this afternoon to say he had to stay another day—again."

"Wow." Cindy whistled. "Again? What is he *doing* in San Jose?"

Sheryl took another sip of wine. "I asked him the other night," she told her friend. "What he said was plausible, but . . ."

"But you don't believe him?" Cindy asked derisively.

"No, I do believe him. I think the project is legit," Sheryl replied confidently.

"So, what's the hesitation? Do you think there's something beside the project?" her friend asked bluntly, getting right to the heart of the matter.

Sheryl swallowed more wine, her fingers gripping the stem of the glass tightly. She didn't answer. Didn't want to say the words out loud.

"Hello? Sheryl?"

"I'm here. I just don't . . ."

"Don't want to think about it? As in you think he might be cheating?" Cindy's voice was harsh. "I'll say the word even if you don't want to. I know all about that."

"Oh Cindy, I didn't say that. I know what you went through, but I don't think Dave would do that. I really don't," Sheryl protested.

"Denial ain't just a river in Egypt," her friend quipped.

Sheryl stiffened, unfolding her legs from beneath her. "Don't say that," she breathed, thinking of her own suspicions. It was one thing to think it, it was another to say it out loud—to someone else.

"Okay, I won't say it," Cindy said, her voice heavy with sarcasm. "But—"

"No buts," Sheryl cried. "None."

"Okay, okay. Got it. I just hope you're right."

"Me too," Sheryl whispered.

There was a long moment of silence. Sheryl actively focused on calming her breathing and racing heart.

"I'm sorry." She finally heard Cindy say. "I didn't mean to upset you. I should be celebrating your triumph, not trying to bring you down."

"Yes, you should!" Sheryl exclaimed, her breathing coming a little easier. She looked around the room, taking in the fire, the candles, the picture of her and Dave on the mantel. This was home. *Dave will be here tomorrow. We will talk then, really talk,* she promised herself.

"I am very proud of you, my friend," Cindy's voice broke into her thoughts. "You've come a long way in a very short period of time."

"Thank you," Sheryl answered with heartfelt gratitude. "I am proud of myself. You know, it's partially due to you."

"Me? How's that?"

"Well, I've been incorporating more of your centering work, you know. Breathing, meditation, visualization, accessing deep wisdom. It's actually working."

"Wow, I didn't realize all that. Look at you!"

"Yeah, look at me," Sheryl chuckled. "But it's helped, you know, working with my higher self and all. I don't think I would have accomplished all that I did without that."

Cindy hummed approvingly. "You've discovered your power, my friend. I mean it, and I can't wait to see what you do next."

Sheryl smiled, lifting her glass in a silent toast. "Me either."

Acknowledgments

First and foremost, thank you to my husband for his endless patience with my nights and weekends of writing this book and the subsequent books in the Ascending Ladders series. Without his forbearance, I would never have finished.

Much gratitude also goes to Bridget Cook-Burch and Hannah Lyons, whose critique, support, praise, and editing helped make this book much better than it ever would have been had I written it alone.

Thank you, also, to Rebecca Hall Gruyter and her team, who helped shepherd the book from my manuscript to the final copy and provided encouragement along the way.

Of course, no book is completed without a great deal of incidental help, and for that I thank Sally Anderson, Dara Myers, Tammy Warner, and my former boss, Paul Tinnirello, who is almost solely responsible for my own IT career. I'm sure there are others I've forgotten to name, but I'm grateful to you all.

Finally, thank you, readers, for purchasing and reading *Discovering Power*. I hope you found as much pleasure reading it as I did writing it.

Stay tuned for Book Two of *The Ascending Ladders* series, *Pursuing Truth*, in the fall of 2023, and Book Three in 2024.

About the Author

Karen Ann Bulluck is an engaging and inspiring speaker as well as a contributing author to three International Bestselling anthologies. Passionate about making a difference, Karen is also a Risk-taking Coach and the founder of DARING TO TRANSCEND. She partners with women leaders to push beyond the limits of their leadership, career, and life so that they can make a bigger impact in their work and beyond. Through her proprietary methodology, Karen works with leaders to EXPLORE what matters, INTEGRATE the Whole Self, and FLOURISH in new dimensions.

The first woman promoted to Executive Vice President at AM Best Company, Karen's career was marked by taking risks to make many cross-disciplinary changes and have an impact across a wide variety of people and processes.

An ardent traveler, she loves to explore new cultures, new ideas and new ways of doing things while learning from and valuing the wisdom of the past and present. She lives in New Jersey with her husband and very spoiled cat.

Karen can be reached at:
Email: karen@daringtotranscend.com
LinkedIn: www.linkedin.com/in/karenannbulluck
Website: www.dareingtotranscend.com
Facebook: www.facebook.com/karenannbulluck

Ascending Ladders Series Information: www.ascendingladders.com

Reviews

"From the moment I started reading this compelling story, I was hooked and couldn't put it down!! Karen Ann Bulluck made Sheryl, the heroine, come to life for me! Her inner dialogue was superb and I not only <u>wanted</u> to know how Sheryl would handle the situations presented to her, I <u>needed</u> to know she would handle them! A "page turner" beyond a shadow of a doubt!!!!"
-Misti Mazurik, Director of Operations, Your Purpose Driven Practice

*"You will be captured in suspense and pulled into the lesson-filled tapestry masterfully woven by Karen. Grab **Discovering Power** and immerse in the unfolding plots to inevitably seek your own power!"*
-Dr. Kasthuri Henry, Ph.D., CTP - Founder, Ennobled for Success Institute
International #1 Best Selling Author
www.kashenry.com

*"**Discovering Power** is a beautifully told story with great dialog and self-reflection as IT Executive Sheryl Simmons faces the trauma in business that many of us face day to day. Do I stay? Do I stand up for myself and others? These are questions she must answer for herself, keeping her team on track and looking to rise within the company. I especially enjoyed seeing relationships change and characters unfold differently as she engaged with them, exploring her strength to stand in her power. I look forward to the story unfolding more in the next book."*
-Susan K Younger, Relationship Architect
www.skyounger.com

"Beyond inspired by Karen Ann Bulluck's latest masterpiece, 'Discovering The Power' powerfully tackles what it takes to climb the corporate ladder as a woman. The way Karen writes really has you feeling like you are experiencing what the character in the book is feeling. I think the book will relate to both corporate women who will totally understand Sheryl's journey and also to corporate men. The more men in the corporate sector educate themselves on what challenges women face, the more we will truly embrace what TRUE Diversity, Equity and Inclusion really mean. The timing of this book is perfection; of all Fortune 500 companies, only 8.8% have women CEOs. This indicates that about 91% of Fortune 500 CEOs are male – this is just one statistic of many. I believe Karen's book is a fabulous contribution at this time to honoring the power & importance of women in leadership."

-Sally Anderson, Leadership Coach to the Influencers

"The material was so inspiring as to how to navigate towards resolution! I have been in similar scenarios in corporate meetings. The emotions that come up with what to do with being right vs going with the flow resonated with me. I have often chosen to not rock the boat and then rustled with my choices after the fact haunted me.
I look forward to reading more thought-provoking books by Karen. She speaks out with the words of truth and the right way of doing things in the corporate world!"

-Deborah Wiener

Author, Speaker, Entrepreneur, Healer, Coach

"This book perfectly lives up to its title. Discovering Power is a delight to read and a book I'd recommend to both women and men.
An absolute page-turner, the reader can't help but develop a personal attachment to the main female characters in the book, our heroine, Sheryl, and her protegee, Keisha.
The story touches on so many angles of the human experience, from dealing with bullies to trying to do what's right to inner personal growth as Sheryl struggles to trust her intuition and find the courage to act on it."

-Krista Mollion

Entrepreneur – Business Advisor – Digital Marketer, FROM ZERO 2 SIX ACADEMY
www.fromzero2six.com

"In "Discovering Power," IT Executive Sheryl Simmons faces a difficult decision when her company's culture takes a turn for the worse. As layoffs are implemented and her protégé challenges her leadership, Sheryl struggles to find her voice and maintain her integrity. This thought-provoking novel explores the intersection of career and personal values and asks important questions about responsibility, leadership, and the human experience. The book is a gripping and inspiring journey of self-discovery that will resonate with anyone facing ethical dilemmas in their professional life. Bulluck's writing is insightful and engaging, and her story will leave readers feeling empowered and inspired to find their own truth."

-Tamara Myles, Author, The Secret to Peak Productivity
www.tamaramyles.com

"Power and Drama in the Boardroom. In Discovering Power, Karen Ann Bulluck shares the story of a woman who seeks to find her courage to speak up and stand on the side of right."

-Maureen Ryan Blake, Maureen Ryan Blake Media Production

"This book captures the tough atmosphere of a woman named Sheryl, working in an executive position. I have been inspired by her drive and her determination to not back down, and it has helped me see how important it is to do the right thing."

-Brita Bigler Peterson, #1 International Best Selling Author
www.britapeterson.com